LIKE THE APPEARANCE OF HORSES

LIKE THE APPEARANCE OF HORSES

ANDREW KRIVAK

BELLEVUE LITERARY PRESS

NEW YORK

Originally published in the United States in 2023 by Bellevue Literary Press, New York

First paperback edition published in 2024 by Bellevue Literary Press, New York

For information, contact:
Bellevue Literary Press
90 Broad Street
Suite 2100
New York, NY 10004
www.blpress.org

The chapter "Moth and Rust" first appeared in *Image*, Issue 112.

This is a work of fiction. Characters, organizations, events, and places (even those that are actual) are either products of the author's imagination or are used fictitiously.

The Library of Congress has catalogued the Bellevue Literary Press hardcover edition as follows:
Names: Krivak, Andrew, author.
Title: Like the appearance of horses / Andrew Krivak.
Description: First Edition. | New York, NY : Bellevue Literary Press, 2023.
Identifiers: LCCN 2022007013 | ISBN 9781954276130 (hardcover) |
    ISBN 9781954276147 (ebook)
Classification: LCC PS3561.R569 L55 2023 | DDC 811/.54--dc23
LC record available at https://lccn.loc.gov/2022007013

Bellevue Literary Press would like to thank all its generous donors—individuals and foundations—for their support.

 This project is supported in part by an award from the National Endowment for the Arts.

 This publication is made possible by the New York State Council on the Arts with the support of the Office of the Governor and the New York State Legislature.

Book design and composition by Mulberry Tree Press, Inc.

Bellevue Literary Press is committed to ecological stewardship in our book production practices, working to reduce our impact on the natural environment.

∞ This book is printed on acid-free paper.

Manufactured in the United States of America.

First Paperback Edition

10 9 8 7 6 5 4 3 2 1

paperback ISBN: 978-1-954276-31-4

hardcover ISBN: 978-1-954276-13-0

ebook ISBN: 978-1-954276-14-7

In memory of
Irene Therese and Thomas Francis

Their appearance is like the appearance of horses,
and like war horses, so they run.

—JOEL 2:4

CONTENTS

LIKE THE APPEARANCE OF HORSES

UNTO THE LAND
(1933–1938)

1

She was eleven and she stood before the picture window of her father's house and watched the figure of the traveler as he came into view from the road. Watched him walk stooped from the pack on his back, then straighten when she knew he could see the house before he could see the treetops. Watched him quicken his step as though he had walked a long way for a long time and what he sought was now as close as walking through a gate, and this was his sole intention. He stopped for a moment and squared himself before the entrance of the property, his eyes moving, his head lifting slowly, slowly, all with a kind of wonder, from the orchard grounds to the stone foundation, the balcony and high framed windows, the slate tile roof. Then he lowered his head and stepped from the road to the dirt drive that skirted the long line of apple trees and pear trees and split off onto paving cobbles that bent like a silver river through the silver-rimmed grass and stopped at the foot of the stone front steps.

From a distance he looked like a man. Closer now she could see he was a boy in the clothes of a man. Clothes from a place where a man and the work he did were nothing like any man who worked and lived in Dardan. She remembered the photographs she had seen of people, to her eye, similarly dressed in the pages

of the *National Geographic* magazines her father brought to her
from Miss Cording's house (the woman who was one-third owner
of the Endless Roughing Mill handing Jozef Vinich a stack bound
by a lavender ribbon, and saying, *Take these for Hannah, poor
girl, all alone up there on that mountain of yours,* when Vinich
and Asa Pound met with her over brandy to discuss the finances of
the mill). The South American gauchos who rode their brown and
piebald horses along the lowland pampas grass, mountains snowcapped in the distance. The colorful Mongol riders of the steppes
who pressed forward mounts short and large-headed across land
some god had created for them alone to cross. And a people called
the Lovari Roma, outcasts wandering in great caravans of vardos
drawn by collared equine that followed paths among not mountains or grasslands but the hinterlands of the towns and cities of
Middle Europe. And yet for all of these riders her imagination
conjured, this boy, this young man, came alone and on foot and
looking as though the land he had left was land bereft of any
horse, rider, or path, and that was why he had come. His boots
were creased and scuffed and colorless from toe to shaft, the soles
themselves looking as though they were sewn tight to their uppers
by sinew known only to the cobbler who had fashioned them. The
trousers he wore appeared so faded and thin, the material of which
they were made seemed to carry as much dust as threads between
each woof and warp. On his back he had only a thin canvas coat,
not unlike the coat her father wore to pick out stalls and gather
firewood and looking no better, despite the shined medallions and
varicolored cords that hung from his arms and chest. And inside
the upturned collar of the coat, a bright white silk scarf hung in a
loose knot at the jugular notch, so that it appeared to be caressing
his neck as he walked.

She watched him bend before the porch from the weight of
what the pack held and climb those steps like one would climb the
steps of a church in which there waited sanctuary or reckoning,
or both. He removed the broad-rimmed hat he wore, pushed back
his black hair, studied the door. She could see his face through

the glass now, his eyes deep and round and strangely blue. His cheeks sunken from some hunger. A wisp of down beginning to trace a line of soot across his upper lip. He seemed to sense her and turned his head to where she watched from the window, but she didn't move. If he saw her through the glass, he didn't show it. He turned back, raised his hand for the hitching-post ring that had been fashioned into a knocker and polished and bolted to the oak-paneled front door, and drew it.

The knocks were loud and slow, and still she didn't move. Just stood behind the curtain close to the glass while the boom of the iron against the thick wood echoed inside the foyer and drawing room. When no one came, he drew back the ring and brought it down again. And once more there was silence in the wake of those echoes in the house. On the porch he looked down at his feet and toed the boards with his boots and looked in the window where she knew he knew she was. Then he reached for the knocker and brought it down a third time.

She heard the sound of footsteps then, coming through the hall in a quick and gentle counterpoint, and she turned and saw her mother standing in the foyer with her hands in the pockets of the kitchen apron she wore over a yellow housedress. She stepped out from behind the drapes and her mother started to speak as though to chide the girl for making her come all this way from her work in the kitchen because she would not answer the door, but she held one finger up to her lips. And there, in the foyer, Hannah Vinich whispered to her mother that there was a stranger outside, but not the kind of stranger she thought they ought to be afraid of. Rather (and she could not say why), he was someone she had been waiting for. With surety and in one breath Hannah described the boy and almost pleaded with her mother not just to let him in and feed him and send him on his way but to let him stay at their table at least until Papa came home. Because she knew he hadn't come from town like the others when they knew there was no other man around. He had come from someplace unlike any she or her mother could imagine, and she wondered if it was the place her father had spoken of, in a story told before she fell asleep one night, about a kingdom of people dressed like this boy, a kingdom so vast, its borders of mountains and rivers could not be crossed by foot in four phases of a moon. And if that was so, if that's where he'd come from, then they had to open their door, or this stranger, unlike the sheepish and shifty ones, would knock and knock until that knock was answered and the boots that looked as though they could go no farther came in through the door. She didn't just believe it. She knew it. Knew that whatever had begun in what was once his house, village, or kingdom even, would play itself out inside the walls her father had built not to withstand but to hold, his land not borderless but vast nevertheless. And the boy must know it, too. Had known it somehow since he was young and was told about the soldier who had carried him in a wrap to the camp on the river at the end of the war, as it was in her father's story. This same boy, who stood waiting in his colorful but worn grown-man's clothes on the porch, behind the glass by the door, because he had no other choice. He had no other place to go. Just as the story was told.

Helen Vinich looked at the door and back at her daughter, then walked to the door and opened it.

And there he stood, stooped and filthy and bareheaded. He pinched his hat in his fingers and looked up at the woman in front of him, over at the girl by her side fixed and mesmerized, then back at the woman, and asked if Mr. Vine was at home in English so accented and practiced, Hannah could tell without even knowing what language it was he spoke in his dreams that these were all the words he knew of the language she spoke in hers.

Helen Vinich stared at him and didn't answer, and he asked again.

Is Mr. Vine at home?

No, young man, Helen said with some hesitation in her voice. He's across town. But I expect him within the hour. Come inside and you can wait for him here.

The boy turned to the girl, and Hannah could see the slight

tremble on his lips and the question rising in the wrinkle of his brow. Helen reached out to take him by the hand, and he stepped back and hooked his thumbs in the shoulder straps of his rucksack and wouldn't move. His eyes swept from the chandelier on the ceiling to the oak newel at the foot of the stairs to the pier glass above a table on which sat a vase and a clutch of spring pussy willows and rested there, caught in the glass. As though the image in festooned coat and sinew-held boots had come to the end of its pilgrimage and another step would make the young man pilgrim no longer but orphan again, like the boy, beginning to end to beginning.

To je v poriadku, Helen said in Slovak, the tone softer now, and he looked at the woman with her long hair brushed and tied back, the eyes and face not yet etched with the lines of age (nor would they ever be), the kitchen apron so clean, it seemed she laundered it with the dress.

Si hladný? she asked.

Áno ďakujem, he said.

Of course you're hungry, she said in Slovak again. There's food on the kitchen table, but we can't eat it from here. Leave your coat and bag and come.

His shoulders dropped and he slipped off the rucksack so that it made a thud when it hit the floor, and she took his coat and hung it up on the one bare hook on the coatrack and left his pack in the corner by the door. Then she told Hannah to run ahead and put the kettle on.

They were drinking tea in the kitchen when the Ford AA pickup pulled into the driveway and parked near the barn and Jozef Vinich came in the house by the back door. The boy had risen to his feet at the sound of the truck, and when the door opened and he saw Vinich, he began to speak in Hungarian, a language Hannah heard spoken so rarely, it sounded to her like the harbinger of impending doom. Slovak was the language in which her father and mother spoke to their daughter and to each other, and with which they often addressed the priest. But the boy seemed to come alive as he tried to explain (Hannah supposed by the tone) why and how he had found the vine. And when he finished, he remained standing and staring wide-eyed next to the chair.

Vinich said nothing. He stood and looked at Helen and stroked his jaw with his hand, the scrape of calluses on that hand against a day's growth of whiskers and the ticking of the clock the only sounds that could be heard. The boy turned and walked from the kitchen down the hall to the front foyer.

Papa, please say something so that he'll come back, Hannah pleaded.

But still Vinich said nothing. And the boy returned shouldering his rucksack, out of which he produced an old rusted knife and a sling of coarse cotton, as gift or proof, Hannah couldn't tell.

Édesanyámat Aishenek hívták. Én Bexhet vagyok, he said to Vinich in Hungarian, the words sounding to Hannah like bees caught between a window and a screen. She glanced back and forth between her father and the boy.

What did he say, Papa? she asked.

He said his mother's name was Aishe, and his name is Bexhet. But I knew that already.

Where is his mother?

She's dead.

Jozef.

It's all right, Helen. She died just after the war, Hannah. Giving birth to this young man. I was there. I promised her I would deliver him to her family. And I did.

No one spoke. Vinich took off his coat and draped it over the back of the chair and sat down at the table, smoothed his hand along the weave of the wrap, and began to nod. Then he turned to look at the boy once more.

Fifteen years I've wondered about him, if he was alive even, Vinich said. Wondered if anyone in that camp along the river was alive. He sure must have loved this boy to have gotten him out.

Who is that, Jozef? Helen asked.

The old man. The grandfather. The one who hid me from the Honvéd when he didn't have to. His name was Samuel, but they called him Meska.

THE CALENDAR SAID IT WAS SPRING, BUT NOT THE COLD OR THE snow on the ground, and still the boy would sleep only in the hayloft when he found they kept a horse, a gelding Vinich called Pushkin. Each morning he was awake and sitting on the back steps of the house before even Helen had come down to fire the stove. When Vinich left for the mill in the Ford, and when he came home in the evening, he spoke to the boy in a hushed and direct voice, sometimes in Hungarian, sometimes in Slovak, so that even if Hannah could follow the initial questions about how he had conducted his day, the answers turned into clipped pronouncements or phrases so cryptic and oblique, she was lost again inside whatever language it was he spoke. She asked her father one morning before school what they talked about and Vinich shook his head.

There's no talk, Hannah. He asks me when the villagers are going to come for him, and I tell him we are the villagers and that he came to us. Then he asks if he can ride Pushkin out of here when they do come, and I tell him we don't ride the horse. Not anymore. Then he goes back into the barn.

She watched him like this each day. As though from a distance, separated still by the presence of window glass. And she wondered herself when he would leave, so beautiful and odd he looked to her as he moved about the house, the yard, the barn, and stuck out against what she had come to see as the ordinary portrait of the farm. The profile of porch, paddock, fruit trees terraced into the land, and forest and mountain rising up in the distance like an old painting she looked at differently now and saw other details that had always been there. Like the stained glass in the corners of the front window. The joinery of the wood as she moved from the foyer past the drawing room and into the kitchen. And the way the orchard received sunlight all day, because it was in each of these places he had stood and looked back at her with a wonder all his own.

Helen shortened the name he had given to them on the first day to Becks, but he would still only speak to Vinich.

Does he have a family name, Jozef? Helen asked at dinner one evening, the boy sitting out of earshot on a chair in the pantry because he refused to sit with them at meals.

Well, Vinich said. The surname on his passport is Konar, though that's likely counterfeit.

Supper was over and Hannah had begun to clear the table while her father stared down at his plate as though the pattern at the edge were runes he might study for the answer to an altogether different question puzzling him.

I can see why the old man would have taken the name and forged the documents, he said. But I can't figure out how after all these years he'd have faith enough to send him away, get him on a train that could take him to a port and tell him there would be someone waiting for him on the other side when he got off the ship. Someone who would take him in because he had saved his life once before and would do it again.

Vinich turned and looked into the pantry and watched the boy eat, searching there for the traces of the mother in the eyes and face, the woman Vinich had traveled with in the short span of a spring and a summer when she was with child and the land in which the two had found each other was no longer at war, though nor was it at peace, for all on the road seemed to be traveling back to or away from a home they once knew, and there was no telling in country, village, or bend of that road what manner of good or ill, peace or war, life or death one would find. And so Vinich made the promise to the girl, who never told him her name, only that it was a secret, the girl whose ashes he committed to the earth, believing he and the infant to whom she had given birth, the infant he took from her arms and swaddled and ran with after he had set fire to the woodsman's cottage in which they had sojourned, would be of that earth as well by end of day.

He turned back to his wife.

I can talk to Father Blok about getting him into one of those schools for orphans down in Hazelton, he said. If you think it's too much having him here.

Helen dried her hands on a towel.

Name or no name, Jozef, you made a promise, and he found us. *A father to the fatherless is God in his dwelling* is what Father Blok ought to say, if he's any kind of priest. Give him some chores to do. He looks capable enough. Tell him we're going clothes shopping for a decent pair of boots and trousers on the weekend. And if he wants to eat, tell him he'd better acknowledge the one doing the cooking.

A Saturday afternoon in May, rain having given way to a stretch of sun, so that a vast burgeoning of every flower and tree on the farm seemed to overtake the land (Hannah remembering to the end of her days the smell of honeysuckle and peony that came in through the kitchen window with the birdsong that morning and so always grew and loved the bloom of these flowers in the beds along the house), and Helen pulled the Ford into the cobblestone drive. Hannah and Becks climbed out of the cab with their parcels and went inside the house. Helen walked into the barn and told her husband they had returned, then went into the house herself to prepare their supper.

And when the soup and bread that made up their fare on weekends in the summer was on the table, the boy came into the kitchen and thanked Helen in Slovak for the new clothes and placed his Red Wing boots in the tray by the back door, washed his hands in the half bath, and sat at the table in the chair in which Helen had directed him to sit. Hannah came in, too, and washed, and sat, and watched Becks try to smooth the stiff denim trousers he wore, touching every now and then the arm of his new flannel shirt, bewildered, it seemed, by the contrasting feel of the two articles of clothing. Vinich came in from the barn finally, and they all waited

as he washed and changed his shirt and poured a glass of beer.
Then he sat and said grace over the meal, and for a long while
there was only the sound of the clack of spoons on the soup bowls
and the ticking of the clock. Then Helen began telling her husband
about the fine day out she and the children had had in Dardan,
and he told her he had spent the day bucking into rounds the apple
tree that had split in the heavy snow that winter. Hannah asked if
after Mass on Sunday they could drive out to Kravits's farm and
buy four new pullets so that there would be laying hens around
for eggs next fall. And Becks listened to the spare and easy conversation on the evening before the Sabbath, as it returned to the
pooling of the ordinary events that would make up the next week
on their own farm. And every now and then Hannah looked over
and watched Becks watching her, and she knew not just by the
new clothes her mother had bought him and he now wore but also
by the way he mirrored her posture and how she held her utensils
that he wanted nothing more than to sit at that table, wanted to
eat what they ate, and in time would speak the same language that
shaped the easiness of their conversation, so that words like *buck*
and *pullet* came just as readily from his mouth as from her father's
and hers, because these were the words he asked Vinich to trans-
late for him. Words that sounded no less miraculous to Hannah
than the prayer she had uttered on that cold day in early spring.
The prayer that had been answered.

Days of summer when time moved slow and she was
young, Hannah rose with the sun and bounded outside and
roamed amid the Rock Mountain world she knew at the gran-
ular level, and so each day redrew the maps she kept rolled out
and resting on a table that existed nowhere in the house, but in
her mind. She inhabited rock overhangs and built blown-down
tree hides as though she were alone in all the world. But when
the boy they called Becks arrived, and during the summer she

knew he would not leave, Hannah came down off the mountain and out of the forest and the world of the girl, and stepped into the world of the young woman.

One year later, Vinich built a back room onto the house with a separate entrance by the apple grove, and Becks took this as an acceptable arrangement. He did well the chores Vinich gave him, moving around the farm as though through a maze of things he recognized and things he did not, habits and work he embraced as though born to them (walking and grooming Pushkin), and others (feeding slop to pigs, or eating a fried egg) from which he turned away, as if they embodied some deadly taboo. Hannah saw what work Becks was given and asked her mother and father if she could have the same, or something close to the same. Asked to do anything that would place her in a curvature of proximity to him, the two never speaking more than a few words of greeting in Slovak to each other, but her eyes and ears never letting him out of range. And when her chores were done, not even remembering what she had done, so distracted was she by anticipation, she would crouch beneath the window of the barn and, unseen, listen to him as he worked. Mornings, slow afternoons, sometimes even when she should have been drying dishes in the evening, she could be found leaning against the stone fireplace in the orchard with the nighthawks and the bats, listening to the clank of metal, the thud of slamming doors in the barn, or the trod of boots and scrape of a shovel against the hard-packed floor in the stalls. And from this distance, when he thought he was alone, she could hear him sing in a voice old and mournful and slow with longing, though she knew nothing of what the singer and the words of the song longed for.

Vinich saw the boy was capable of more than wielding a broom, and so that fall gave him tools and directed him to make repairs on the tractor in the barn on his own. By the time another spring had come around, Becks was managing the early seedbeds, grafting fruit trees, and taking care of the tack for Pushkin. Another summer and Hannah watched him move among the animals and over the cultivated ground, longing for the young man, until her own longing sought to bridge the gap and she followed him one morning when he had gone to milk the cow, as he did every morning.

It was a warm Saturday in July, the light just turning from gray to dawn, when she slipped past her mother in the kitchen, went outside, and walked through the new-mown grass to the barn.

He looked surprised to see her and they greeted each other with a nod. He waited to see if there was some reason why she had come, some message to be delivered, but she leaned against a post and said nothing. When the cow lifted its head and lowed, he turned back to the milking, and she listened to the dull bell sound of the spray as it hit the pail.

Cow, she said out loud then.

He stopped and turned his entire body on the milking stool and said, Čo? in Slovak, the question in his voice and on his face.

She moved forward and patted the animal's spine.

This is a cow, she said again.

To je groóvni, he said, and she knew the word *groóvni* he attached to the Slovak was a word from a language all his own.

Yes, she said, but here it's called a milk cow.

A mil-cow, he repeated.

That's right, she said, and thrust her hands behind the bib of the overalls she wore. That's a pail for the milk. And that's a stool you're sitting on.

She pointed to each of these with a nod of her head and he repeated *pail* and *stool,* and they stood watching each other for a moment until the cow began to low again.

Finish up now, she said, or Mother will wonder what's taking you so long. I have to go help her with breakfast.

She turned and walked toward the barn door and looked over her shoulder to see if he was watching her. And he was.

By the end of another summer, Becks knew what to call every animal, every part of the tractor, every piece of fruit that began as a bud in spring and emerged on the stems of trees in the orchard and ripened in the fall. Hannah and her father and her mother didn't teach him English so much as leave nothing unsaid when they were with him, and he followed in the wake of this world to which the others gave voice and name and description, so that in the unseasonably warm early autumn of 1935, when he brought flowers of wild bergamot and aster in to Helen and placed them in a jar on the kitchen table, he could tell her what they were. She thanked him and she sat him down and told him about the time Mr. Vinich first brought her to this farm, when it was still a balloon frame of wood and foundation, and it was these same kinds of flowers he had picked and given to her, the same scent that rose to her then as it rose to her now, and she knew this was where her life would unfold, right here on this land, amid the scent of these flowers.

Becks listened as she spoke, until a deafening crack of thunder silenced them both, and a gravel-pouring cloudburst of rain came straight down outside, so loud that they sat in silence at the table while it pounded the roofs and ground of the farm, then let up as quickly as it had commenced, the birds singing in the apple trees again, and water trickling through the copper rain pipes.

Will I—unfold here, too? he asked in the wake of that rain.

Helen looked at the wild flowers in the jar on the table.

Isn't that why you came?

I came because he sent me.

He? Helen asked.

Puro dad, Becks said.

Your father?

No. Not my father. The older one.

Your grandfather, she said.

Yes. He was afraid if I didn't, I would be killed. Like the others.

By whom? she asked.

Fašistov. Everyone has become one.

They sat at the table in silence again, the scent of the ground rising up and into the open window on the breeze and mixing with the scent of the flowers. Then Helen nodded and told him to go on and finish what Mr. Vinich had asked him to do before he came home from the mill, because supper was going to be early that evening so they could get to the fairgrounds before dark and look into acquiring a goat. He pushed his chair out and rose and pushed it back into the table, and she touched his hand where it rested on the chair and thanked him again for the flowers.

2

Dardan, Pennsylvania, is named not for the oldest house and horse-men of Asia Minor who fought and died along the Scamander River, but after the second son of a Yorkshire landowner who chose the army and went to the colonies, survived the siege of Yorktown, and disappeared into the lowland swamps of Virginia and the Chesapeake of Maryland. He followed the Susquehanna River from its delta north for months, until he came to a creek that fed it west of the Luzerne settlement before anyone else thought to and claimed a crooked portion of the land along which that creek ran. Loggers came for the timber. Light-rail train tracks were laid after that. By the time the first supply store began selling boots and hats and leather chaps, all but the name of Matthew Dardan had been forgotten.

Hannah knows this is where the boy will find the villagers he feared, and that it is not hard to outride them. Only outlast them. What she does not know is that the boy recognizes what is different and what is the same about a place and a people in the work to which each is accustomed, work he had grown up watching and learning to lay his hands to or avoid in the place and people he had left in another land altogether. Pottery, leather, horse tack, tools for cutting and shaping, rough or fine. He knows what has been crafted well and what has not. It is as though he can sense the flaws, inherent and made, and finds them, for he knows the raw material. So, too, of the maker. He believes he can discern the honesty of a man behind a counter, or the dishonesty to which that man will go.

The day he arrived in Dardan (he told Hannah one afternoon in the orchard shade), unaware of the direction of the Vinich farm, he walked past shops along cobblestone sidewalks in some places, rough-hewn boards in others, watched cars pushing around the blinkered horses that trotted among them, and felt the eyes of the town were upon him, the stranger, unlike on the streets of Budapest, Kassa, Hamburg, or even Wilkes-Barre, for they were cities in which he ghosted, worlds in which he was at once invisible and known, a drop of mist in a sea. What she could not tell him, not until she was old and he alone was her companion as both memory and revenant, was that Dardan was settled not that long ago by others running away from war, or in the direction of fortune, and they wanted a place in which what remained known about them when the war was over or the fortune was not found mattered to no one but themselves. And yet, when it came to others, they wanted to know, as they'd been taught, who the father was and where he had come from. So, a young man raised to believe, and believing still, that the sojourner is nothing if not blessed and protected and given leave to remain in the country he has come to for rest discovers that those days of both suffering and wonder along the road and under the sky are, in this new land to which he has come, not recognized. Not counted. Because his father could not have fought at Trenton or Cold Harbor. Could not have felled timber for the railroads. Did not dream as in a fever of the Klondike. Did not wear the uniform of a doughboy. His face has erased nothing of the distance he has traveled, the distance as much of the generations of the faces he belongs to as of the dust and weariness of the road, and none of this matters because it is this they see and fear and believe they are right in fearing when they see Bexhet Konar's face, regardless of Jozef Vinich's standing in the town as a businessman and the owner of two thousand acres of land and forest, who came to his profession and his acreage through the blessing not of having been in the right place at the right time, but of knowing what to do at the right time and having the mind to do it. They fear him, too, Jozef Vinich, and have since he arrived in the town it is rumored he once lived in as a child before going back to the land of his father's birth. Land where he was raised in the corner of an empire in its last hour. Land for which he put on a foreign uniform and took the lives of many on a front they would never know. But Vinich is fired clay, hardened and set before anyone knew what it was he wanted to build in Dardan. Hannah, too, in what she will be given, passed down by the man in time, so that none may appropriate or divide the land, but keep it intact, even from the grave, and this is all the world she knows. What she doesn't yet know is that it's the boy they see, the stranger she watched come to the door and said to be everything from hustler to the man's son. Neither of which is true. And it is he they want to fire in a kiln of their own making, stoked with a fuel of spite and belief that he, too, is of a mind to know and do, and it is only a matter of time before he will do it.

ON A SUMMER AFTERNOON IN AUGUST OF 1936, HANNAH TOOK Becks to a matinee at the Rutherford, where he stood and stared up at the marquee as though the announcement for the picture was the feature itself, then stepped over the threshold and froze on the scarlet rug, shielded his eyes from the gaslights that burned in their crystal sconces, and saw the trained stares of the uniformed ushers bear down on him. He halted there.

What's wrong? Hannah asked.

I feel a strange desire to flee, he said, this last a word he had picked up reading a comic strip.

Hannah took his hand and walked him in and bought tickets for the animated shorts in the orchestra seats, but the usher, studying the tickets and glancing at Becks, would not let them pass the rope until the manager arrived and told them they had to sit in the balcony because of her age.

She told her father, and the next Saturday they went back to the theater to see the matinee of *City Lights*. Vinich purchased

seats once more in the orchestra and it was the manager who met
them this time at the rope and would not let them through. And
Hannah did not step foot in the Rutherford Theater in Dardan,
Pennsylvania, ever again.

On a Saturday in early October of that same year, Vinich,
Hannah, and Becks, returning from the mill in the morning,
where Becks had wanted to pick out a block of cherry from
which to carve a ring stand for Helen for Christmas, stopped
for lunch at a diner called the Junction on the old train tracks
that brought ice, timber, and feed for livestock from points west,
because Hannah had asked if they could. Vinich never liked the
owner of the place, but he couldn't see the harm in having lunch
in town. They sat down in a booth and waited as waitresses
walked past their table and ignored them. When Vinich cor-
ralled a woman he knew had been working at the diner longer
than he had lived in Dardan and inquired if they could get some
service, the owner, Mr. Carr, came over and stood with his arms
crossed before the table and asked Vinich why he was bringing
Gypsies into his restaurant.

Vinich looked up at the man and Carr loosened his arms,
shifted his feet, and stepped back from the table. Vinich stood,
too, and Carr tried to step back farther, but Vinich reached over
and put his arm around the man's shoulder and pulled him in
close, Carr seeming to shrink beneath the pressure of that arm.
And Vinich spoke in a whisper Becks and Hannah could hear.

This young man is like a son to me, Bob. His mother saved my
life in the war. Anyone ever save your life?

Carr writhed in Vinich's grasp, but the arm pulled him in
tighter.

Never mind, Vinich said. I know you didn't fight.

He let go of the man and Carr stumbled backward. Vinich
looked down at Hannah and Becks and they stood, and all three
walked to the door, where Vinich stopped and turned. The tables
and booths were full of lunch patrons and they had gone back to
eating, when Vinich said in a voice that carried above the din, You

ought to talk to a trapper or someone with a twenty-two about that rat's nest underneath your kitchen, Bob. There are so many down there, they don't even care it's daylight.

Carr seemed to rise on his toes.

That's a lie, Vinich, he yelled out. And you know damn right well it is!

The din dissolved into whispers.

See for yourself, Vinich said. I just know my boys at the mill and a lot of truckers hauling in from Mansfield are pretty picky about where they eat in town.

Carr began to move across the floor toward them and Vinich squared himself. Becks reached for Vinich's arm.

Je to v poriadku, Jozef. Prosím, pod'me.

What did he just say to you? Carr shouted as he approached, so mad that he was spitting. What did he just say?

Not a fork on a plate or a cup to a saucer broke that silence.

He said he's heard this all before, Vinich said, and Hannah took her father's hand in hers and squeezed it and they turned and pushed open the door.

THAT AUTUMN, VINICH SET UP A FIRING RANGE AT THE VERGE OF the woods and taught Hannah and Becks how to shoot the Remington .22. He began as his father had with him, showing them how to hold the rifle, how not to hold the rifle, how to load it and unload it, and how to breathe before they took aim and fired. Hannah seemed to know instinctively what to do, and, though she could not say why at the time, she grew closer to her father in those days, finding out there was yet something else he was master of, this man who could do anything he set his hands to. By November she and Becks had both learned to fire the Springfield .30-06, the Winchester 94, and a new Marlin 36 Vinich had purchased that summer. They took each of these rifles into the woods and over Rock Mountain, where they stood in the meadow above the fields that Walter Younger did not farm anymore, and listened to how each round sounded in the cold open air, how accurate it was in that air, and what a single breath of wind could do to that round on its way to the target.

Snow came early that year. More than a foot of it in the first week of December. On the morning of the last Sunday of Advent, Vinich took Becks and Hannah into the barn and showed them the skis he had gotten from a Norwegian cabinet-maker in Tunkhannock. There were three pair, two of which had once belonged to the man's daughter and his wife, neither one of whom was alive anymore, so he was happy to give the skis away to someone who might use them. Vinich took them down from the rafters and out to the orchard and demonstrated how to kick and glide like the Tyrolean guides had taught him in the Italian Alps on snow over which Vinich himself had trekked during a war fought more than a lifetime ago. Then they hiked with the skis up and over the mountain and out to the high meadow. There they spent the afternoon breaking tracks through the deep powder that had fallen and drifted at the mountaintop, then skied down the steep slope of the hill in long, carved turns to the edge of Walter Younger's barn.

On the way home, walking through the late-afternoon winter dusk, Hannah asked her father to tell them more about his time as a soldier in the Great War. He was quiet for a while as they moved over the snow, the sun low and weak on the horizon, and said finally it was a time and place where he traveled with two kinds of men—those loyal to the emperor and an empire, the borders of which were set in stone, and men loyal to the mountains alone. In the end, this seemed to be the real war. Entire armies hauled guns and ammunition on the backs of mules and themselves over those mountains so they could fire the matériel of war at other men who had done the same to defend their own borders. And yet all were at the mercy of the ice, and rock, and snow. He saw men die in the fire of artillery barrages. And he saw men die in the ice-cold blue of a crevasse. What did it matter? he asked, and let the question remain there unanswered. The only man whose death he ever mourned, he told them, was that of his brother, killed by a sharpshooter's bullet, and buried there still in that ice and snow. It was the winter of 1918, the last winter of the war, the year in which they had both somehow turned from village boys into young men, and the image of him as they set out that morning from a fort called Cherle was the image he held on to of that brother, winter the season in which he missed him most.

The day after Christmas all three rose before dawn and took the skis and rifles and went into the woods and up to the mountain again. The air was dry and still and so cold, their nostrils clung to the insides of their noses when they breathed. Another snow had covered the tracks they had made the week before, and they slung the rifles over their shoulders and skied until they came to the rocks of the summit, climbed with the skis cradled in their arms, then put them back on at the top and poled through the groves of white and slender birch out into the high meadow.

That day, Walter Younger and his son, Paul, a handsome and clear-eyed boy whom Hannah knew from town, came out of the house and climbed the hill in snowshoes to greet them. The two were dressed for hunting but had no rifles. Walter Younger complimented them on their skiing and pointed across the field in a direction away from the house. He spoke to Vinich then as though he were alone there with him, and said that a small herd of deer would be emerging soon from the woods, and, if they positioned themselves a little farther upslope, they could have their pick at two hundred yards of whatever buck was among them. All three looked in that direction, and when Vinich looked back to thank Younger, the man and his son were no more than the outsize tracks of snowshoes that led into the woods in the direction of the creek bend. And Vinich, Hannah, and Becks removed their skis, took up position there, watched, and waited until the herd appeared, just as Walter Younger had said it would.

A DAY IN EARLY APRIL SO CLOUDLESS AND WARM, THE DEPTHS
of winter seemed a sleep from which Hannah had woken and
shaken off. She alone remembered this was the day Becks had
walked into their home four years prior. She had heard him stirring in his room before it was light out and wondered now where
he could have gone. It was the afternoon when she saw him from
the kitchen window leading Pushkin by the bridle out of the
woods and through the orchard. He was singing to himself as
he walked with the horse toward the barn. She went outside and
into the barn and sat on a stall post and watched him as he
fed and watered the horse, then walked past her to gather the
grooming brushes, the smell of horse and earth in his wake. She
asked him where he'd been, and he told her he had gone with
Pushkin to see the bear.

He lives in a cave on your father's property near the border
with the game lands by the creek, he said to her. Last year, in
the fall, he called me, and I walked all that way and stood on the
rise, watching him forage for food. And I remembered the Ursari,
Roma who would pass by our camp in February on their way
to the fair. My grandfather revered them and called them heal-
ers, and for that reason they called my grandfather Meska. *The
bear.* He always had a meal prepared for them and they ate in our
company and traded stories of the places they had been the year
before. They loved my grandfather, and when I saw that bear, I
saw him. I've never stopped missing him or wanting to be with
him, Hannah. And so this morning I went back. With Pushkin. I
wanted to show my grandfather that I had come to a place where
there are good horses. And to see how Pushkin would do walking
along the path that leads over the mountain.

She had never seen a bear in those woods, though she had heard
her father and Walter Younger speak of one, and she wondered
how the horse himself would have fared staring into the muzzle of
a black bear in spring. She remained on the stall post and watched

him as he began to work the dandy brush down and back from the withers along the side of the horse, brushing in gentle strokes.

Come with me next time, he said.

Summer was hot and they never left the farm except on Sundays, when they went to Mass, then drove out to the lake and swam from a dock Asa Pound had on a stretch of shorefront, Helen and Jozef sitting on a pair of Adirondack chairs while Hannah and Becks dived into the cold water, the two of them never more than a few feet from each other. In late August the weather broke on a thunderstorm after a string of humid days, the air carrying on it the faintest hint of autumn, and they set out one morning before light for the far reach of the bend of the Upper Salamander. They brought no food and gathered ripened blackberries along the way and drank water from a spring that flowed over a mossy rock on the far side of the mountain.

Becks spoke to Hannah as they walked and told her he had seen the bear more than once. The first was a day when Becks was sitting on the bank of the creek while the horse drank, then stopped and snorted. Becks rose and took him by the bridle strap, and there across the creek stood the bear.

What could I do? Becks said, turning around every now and then to make sure Hannah was still following him. Pushkin didn't seem afraid. So I spoke to him. The bear. *You've come to see if I made it here, haven't you? Samuel sent you. Is he alive?* I asked, and the bear sat and swayed and poked its nose in the air with only the water between us, and I knew what the answer was. *Tell him it's better on the other side,* I said, and the bear rolled its head and walked up the mountain into the woods.

They saw nothing and no one that day. Three more times they made the walk together to the bend in the creek before the end of September, and each time there was no bear. When they came to the creek the last time, they sat down on a log by the shore. Hannah smelled the loam and dew of the forest in shade and listened to the babble of the slow and summer-shallowed water as it passed over stones. Becks stared at the bushes beyond the stream and began to sing. Not loud, but as though he were singing to himself, and Hannah listened to him as she had when she was younger and used to crouch at the window of the barn while he did his chores.

What is your song about? Hannah asked when he had finished and they were quiet and all she could hear now was the sound of the water.

He thought for a moment, then told her it was a song about love.

For whom? she asked.

His brow furrowed.

For anyone who is listening, he said. Isn't that why there are songs?

She didn't say any more. They sat close enough to touch but did not, until Hannah heard sticks snapping behind her, and she put her hand on Becks' shoulder and turned and saw a man with a rifle walking out of the woods behind them. It was Paul Younger. She and Becks both stood to face him and Becks nodded. Younger nodded back.

You scared us, Hannah said.

Didn't mean to. Why don't you have your rifles with you?

We're not hunting, Hannah said.

Younger spat a stream of tobacco juice into the leaves behind him.

I'm not, either, he said. Just out followin' a herd.

They stood looking at one another and listening to the creek. Then Younger bent his head in the direction of the woods.

You know, he said, one day you're goin' to have to accept the death of that bear.

I know, Becks said.

Younger turned and walked back into the grove of hemlock and seemed to Hannah to fade into those woods as quietly as if he'd never been there.

She should have known then, but she put no faith in the augury through which the same people in Brookside might have searched, had she grown up with them. By the time another

Thanksgiving came around (Hannah having shot the turkey
from which Helen made the stew that year), Hannah still knew
little of the place or the past from which Becks Konar had come.
She knew only what her father had told her, and that only of
the boy's first days. She knew nothing of the loneliness and grief
with which he had left his grandfather, the man who had sent
him beyond the water in search of the vine. What could a past
do or become or even matter if the present had become a place
of peace for her where nothing mattered, save his presence.
Years later, on an evening when the presence and voice of Bexhet Konar could not and would not ever be heard in the rooms
and hallways again of the great house, and Hannah sat in the
same chair in the living room, nursing an infant, the loneliness
and grief for what had been taken away from her so bitter and
raw she knew the child could taste it in her milk, it was her
father's presence and voice that reminded her of the day when
the young man came to the farm in Dardan, embraced their life,
embraced her, and never left the land that surrounded them,
except to go to war. She watched a meteor streak through the
sky across stars she could see from the window, then turned and
repeated to her father what the new priest (there only a month
when he was called to commit the body of her husband to the
grave) had told her, that a soul shaped by loss is a soul wherein
God surely dwells. She asked if God didn't dwell in every soul,
and Vinich told her in the same voice that had read stories to her
around the fire in the evening when she was a girl that it was not
a question of God dwelling, but the surety with which the soul
believed God dwelled. He had been there when the boy entered
the world, midwife who watched the baby's mother die, and he
set fire to the dwelling after her confinement and carried the boy
until he was near dead himself to the village of caravans in Eastern Hungary. The child was not Roma, and not Magyar, and for
that reason *gadjo*, a bastard whose forebear remained a secret to
all but his mother, unclean among the Lovari who traveled Hungary and Czechoslovakia and returned each spring to the same

stretch of ground along the Sajó, not believing river or ground could become a boundary between nations. And yet, he grew up as one among them and so dwelt nowhere and everywhere, neither lost nor found, as it is said God dwells. His grandfather Samuel loved the boy, raised him and defended him when the old ladies tried to shun him and belittle him because he was *gadjo*. The old man and the other men of the camp taught him what they believed he ought to know, until those who drew the boundaries in order to say who remained and who was left out came wearing uniforms and armbands nothing like any Rom or even half Rom had seen before, they who had been boundaryless since the Flood. It was the boy's luck to have Hungarian blood, a good man by his side, and blue eyes, if that can be called luck. The last words his grandfather said to him as the man shoved papers forged and falsified into his grandson's hands were, *You are Konar now, the branch. Stay on the long road until you find the vine.* On the tramp steamer to New York (Becks had told Vinich later), the sky at sea was so thick with those same stars, he lost the ones he knew. And when he arrived in New York, the network of Slovaks who cleaned Park Avenue apartments sent him to the Slovaks from the Brookside neighborhood in Wilkes-Barre, who had heard of the boy looking for the man named Vinich, suspicious at first of why this one sought out the one who had prospered, but who knew all of the places they knew in the old country, what to ask for, and whom to ask. It was not hard to work for a week to get the money for the bus ticket to Luzerne and walk twenty miles west through the pass and into the mountains to Dardan. In this way (her father told her), Bexhet knew loss and blessing and loss again, as much a child of the first two parents as those who gave life to him in the countless succession of children born of labor and a paradise within. And so, yes. God dwells in every soul, he said to her, but not every soul knows that a dwelling is not some hallowed still point of peace forever unto the land but a place where one rests after great loss, before having to pick up and move on again.

She could not see this yet, the heart of the girl searching for the heart of the boy, the place and time their hearts would entwine. The war. Their sons. The waiting. And finally, the questions of why the man who told her he loved her would risk his life and honor for a people who were not his family, who did not know he had a son in another country, and who had even driven him from their midst. Not yet.

3

It was hunger in the fall of 1937 that consumed the people of Wilkes-Barre and the Wyoming Valley who did not have land to cultivate or a skill that was in demand. In the towns of Pittston, Nanticoke, and Shenandoah, only the mines offered work. And when the mines were full and they cut the miners' wages, the men who worked had little to show, until there was only the hunger. When Helen and Hannah went down to Brookside to visit family, and they sat with the women in their empty kitchens smelling of mothballs from their sweaters and sulfur from the coal stove and drank pine-needle tea and coffee made from chicory, that's what they said when Helen, not thinking, just wanting to say something, asked them how they were.

We're hungry, Helen. We can get used to the cold. But who gets used to being hungry?

Vinich had no family or friends among the men who worked in the mines or drove trucks for the bakeries and felt that, even among the Posols, with whom he had spent more than one Christmas Eve *velija* feast with Helen when they were first married, he was considered a man in search of a place above his station, the resentment for what he had acquired palpable, if unspoken. Only Frances remained close to him, a woman now as aloof and prosperous in her way as Vinich was in his, except that she lived with her people. In the Slovak village of Pastvina, Frances was devoted to the motherless son what had been born in America and returned and whom she saw only in autumn and winter when he came down with his father from the mountains where they herded

sheep. Vinich was a boy of thirteen when he found the girl unconscious on the floor of the barn, her face twisted and bloodless
from the mule kick. He carried her two villages away to a horse
doctor, the path of her life taken when that man did his best to set
her broken jaw and left her looking as though the fractured sneer
the break healed to become was only a visible sign of the contempt
she held for the world that would for her entire life gaze upon her,
wonder at the beauty that had once been there, and turn away.

When Helen went home that day and told her husband how
bad things were in the city (as they called those towns along the
Susquehanna), Vinich and Becks loaded up the old Ford with
bushels of apples, beets, potatoes, and carrots from their winter
stores, crated two dozen eggs, milked both cows, and sealed up
the milk in jugs. Helen spent two days baking bread and put a
dozen loaves in brown paper bags. Then they drove to the valley,
crossed the river, and went into the city, bouncing down Chestnut
Street like the lost turnip truck they never were.

And the Posols, the Kussis, the Harčars, and the Hudáks
had their fill that day and all week. The sisters and the aunts,
the grandmothers and the mothers, all kissed Vinich and kissed
Becks, some having seen for the first time the boy (everyone knew)
who had come from the old country in search of Vinich. The men,
too, demurred and shook hands, offered up their šlivovica, and
said out loud how grateful they were to Vinich. And he accepted
their gratitude.

They visited Frances Posol last, Vinich having put aside the
best of those stores for her and adding a bag of his own ground
coffee to the food they brought. Her fourth-floor walk-up, which
overlooked the river, was spotless and empty of everything but the
sewing machine and copies of *Pravda* in Slovak on a reading table
next to a chair and a light. She wore a dark blue print dress she had
made herself and a black wool cardigan that smelled of lavender.
Hannah watched her mother and father change somehow as they
entered the apartment, and she wondered why it was she had never
visited this place. Aunt Frances came to Dardan for feast days and

in the summers when the city was too hot, but Hannah had never seen where the woman lived. Never imagined the spare yet elegant surroundings of the aunt who was no aunt and spoke to no one beyond a polite greeting except her father. With him she seemed to share an intimacy, and Hannah sensed a weakness in the man when he was around the woman, and a discomfort in her mother.

After they delivered the food, everyone was ready for the visit to be over. No coffee. No tea. Helen had to get back to prepare supper. Frances followed them down the stairs and out to the sidewalk, where Hannah slowed and watched her tug gently at her father's arm.

You saved me again, she said, and took his hand.

And the others.

Yes, the others.

Then, looking to see that Helen had gotten into the truck, Frances leaned forward and kissed Vinich on the cheek with her crooked mouth, and Hannah saw the man's eyes close for just that moment.

The following Sunday, they returned after Mass. The truck was packed with more bread, milk, root vegetables, and venison. The day was cold and Hannah and Becks sat in the truck bed with their collars up against the wind. Vinich parked on the street in Brookside again and all four of them lifted the bags and crates and canisters, and again returned the embraces and kisses from the widows wrapped in sweaters and shawls that smelled like they had been knitted not out of lavender but naphthalene and cabbage, the scent giving way as always to the sulfur of coal fires when they entered a kitchen to sit and sip brandy by the stove. They didn't visit Frances Posol again.

SPRING OF 1938, THE SATURDAY MORNING BEFORE HOLY WEEK, and Vinich and Helen drank coffee and made a list of what she and Hannah would need to get in Wilkes-Barre for their Easter

Triduum. When they were finished, Vinich dropped his wife and daughter off at the bus stop and drove to the mill.

He picked them up by the Miners Bank in Dardan after dark, and Helen could barely hold the parcels and bags she and Hannah carried. Two days later, she could eat nothing and went to bed and woke that night racked with fever and vomiting and a cough that robbed her of breath. In the morning the bed was soaked with sweat and her eyes were lost and empty of everything but what pain she managed to tell her husband she felt, pain that seemed to come from the marrow of her bones. The doctor drove up the long hill to the house at noon and gave Vinich, Becks, and Hannah each a cloth to tie around their mouths, then went upstairs to examine Helen. When he came back and walked into the kitchen, where the three sat quietly around the table, he placed his bag on the floor, went to the sink to wash and towel his hands, then turned to them and told them it was flu. The hospitals in the valley had begun to see a spike in cases, some severe, and he said that if Helen and Hannah had been shopping, she could have picked it up anywhere. She needed fluids—broth, tea with honey—and bed rest. What they needed to do was let her rest.

Vinich heard something in the man's voice, something between a quaver and resignation that could not be hidden by the voice of his trade.

Should she go to the hospital? Vinich asked.

The doctor was a small man with a full head of gray hair and a waxed mustache, and he stared down at the table, then looked up and caught Becks's eye.

She's better off here.

He lifted his bag onto the empty chair at the table, opened the clasps, and took out a bottle of Bayer aspirin tablets and told Vinich to give her two every four hours for the fever, then said he would be back the next day after he finished his rounds. He cast a parting glance at Hannah, as though he had missed something he was looking for, then turned and walked to the door. Vinich followed him.

Keep an eye on your daughter, the doctor said in a hushed voice when they reached the foyer. If Mrs. Vinich is this sick, everything tells me the girl will be, too.

What about the boy? Vinich asked.

I don't know, the doctor said, and shook his head. Call me if anyone else shows symptoms, including you.

It's already worse than you are telling me, I know, Vinich thought, *and yet we have to pretend there is more we can do than simply wait.* He pulled an envelope with ten dollars inside from his shirt pocket and gave it to the doctor, who took it without so much as a nod, placed his hat on his head, and wished Vinich a good day.

Afternoon, evening, and into the night he sat by the bed, next to his wife, dabbing sweat from her forehead and watching her chest rise and fall beneath the sheets. In the early morning he thought her fever had broken, though her breath was wheezy and rattling and she looked no better. She tried to drink some tea but could not keep it down, and after he wiped her face and emptied the basin, he let her sleep and went to the kitchen.

Becks was there with his head on the table and he looked up when Vinich came in. The two said nothing to each other while Vinich filled the percolator with coffee and water and placed it on the stovetop and sat down. Becks asked how she was doing and Vinich said he'd thought she might have been improving but didn't think so now. He would have to wait for the doctor, and Becks looked in the direction of the door through which that doctor had come and gone.

Have you been here all night? Vinich asked.

I kept the stove going.

Vinich nodded.

Pour yourself a coffee when it's done, he said. I want to check on Hannah.

He heard her say *Papa* when he opened the door and walked into the room, and this made him feel some relief, until she said it again, and he approached the bed and touched her forehead. She was burning with fever so hot, the pillow looked and felt as though it had been fished from a bathtub. Then she turned and vomited.

Bexhet! he hollered from the upstairs room, and Becks ran to him, taking the steps three at a time, and burst through the door and saw Vinich on the floor, cradling his daughter, who was soaked in sick and sweat and moaning, and he recognized fear in the man's eyes.

After they had cleaned up with water and ammonia and replaced the pillow and sheets, Vinich laid Hannah back down on the bed and took her arms out of her nightgown and dressed her in a clean one. Becks went to the kitchen and brought up a bowl of ice and placed it on the nightstand, and Vinich dipped a towel in the melted water and dabbed his daughter's wrists and forehead with it and spoke to her, telling her he would stay with her and watch over her, and that she and her mother would both soon be drinking tea together in a breeze on the front porch.

The doctor arrived after nine in the morning and went upstairs and into Hannah's room first, where he checked her temperature and listened to her heart and lungs and told Vinich she was very sick. The vomiting had stopped and she still had a fever of 104, but she had fallen back to sleep, and she tossed and turned in that sleep as though she were trying to catch up to someone or something she could not lay hands on, no matter how hard she tried. Slowly she settled, and without a word among them, Vinich and the doctor left the room to go to Helen, leaving Becks at Hannah's bedside.

FOR THE REST OF WHAT WOULD BE HER LONG LIFE, HANNAH told one person alone what had unfolded before her in the dreams of her illness, which lasted for the entire week but felt to her like the beginning and ending of a day. It was the young priest, and she spoke to him then not in confession but as one who might understand the balance of struggle and peace that had played out in the vision before the feverish girl, one that included her in a cast of characters made up of the living and the dead, although she and her mother were the only two she knew or at least believed were alive in the dream. It was midsummer, the house sweltering in the heat, so that everyone assembled in the living room moved slowly, if they moved at all. Her grandmother and grandfather Posol. The Hudák boy from Brookside who had drowned in the river. Mrs. Franklin, the piano teacher in Dardan from whom Hannah took only five lessons. And Mr. Cording, whose sepia photograph she had seen on the mantel of the fireplace in Miss Emma Cording's living room, and who looked just so. Hannah and her mother walked into the room and sat down across from the five, their faces fixed and white and expressionless, until one by one each rose and moved toward the open door and walked through it. Mr. Cording. The Hudák boy. Mrs. Franklin. Grandmother and Grandfather Posol the last. Helen rose to go with them and Hannah yelled out, *Mama!* Helen turned and told Hannah, the way she had always told her daughter the things she needed to hear when it was time, *We want you to stay, Hannah. They asked the Lord for you.* Hannah began to weep in her dream, but Helen pointed now to someone or something behind her daughter, and Hannah turned and saw the face of Becks staring out the window of her room, heard him singing in the voice and words in which he always sang. Words she never knew but which she seemed to understand in the dream. Separate lands separated by a river that was at times narrow, at times broad, but unnavigable regardless. Only love navigated the water, arm's length or ocean-wide, a love stronger somehow even than death, for death did come in the song, she knew now. *That's why there are songs.* And as she listened, the heat of the room lessened, the sound of the departing others abated, and she fell back to sleep just as the young man sang the final notes, drifting into a place of great cold, a place that was neither inside nor outside, but, rather, felt empty of all place and time and feeling. She looked for her mother and saw only the back of her walking off through this no place, and when she called out one more time, the woman did not turn and the back of her silhouette faded slowly in profile, like the outlines of a long memory she was too young yet to have had of people she was too young to have known.

SHE WOKE IN THE EVENING DARK TO AN EMPTY ROOM. THERE was a washbasin on the nightstand and a cup and saucer, but she couldn't tell if there was anything in it. She tried to rise and then lay back down, felt her forehead, and sat up again. One by one she lifted each leg and placed it over the side of the bed and steadied herself to stand. She made it across the room and found the cup full of cold tea and drank it, glad for the honey she could taste on the bottom as she swallowed. She was still in her nightgown and she walked slowly to the door, out and along the hallway, and down the stairs, her legs so weak, she had to hold on to the banister with both hands.

She stopped at the first landing and heard a faint whisper of voices and caught the scent of mothballs that seemed to have wafted all the way from Brookside, then behind it the clean paraffin smell of tallow, and the slightest scent of lavender. She descended farther and, just above the quarter landing, peered through the balusters and rubbed her eyes in the half-light at the specter of people dressed in black and sitting on chairs set out in the living room. They were facing a raised-lid casket placed along the length of the curtained front window, and her mother was lying motionless and propped on a pillow at the head. As though sleeping some sleep she never slept in her own bed, those attending waiting and wondering, too, if she would ever wake.

Becks heard the pitched and abandoned wail that filled the house from those steps and reached her first, then her father in his black suit coat, and he lifted her and carried her in his arms down the hall and back to her room, her cries the only sounds that echoed through the house now.

She wanted to see her mother before they buried her, and she told her father that was why she woke up, knowing somehow that the woman had died and disappeared while she, Hannah, slept on in the wake of the flu. Father Blok was the only one left in the house when Vinich came down the stairs and into the kitchen, and he told the priest they could not take the body to the cemetery in the morning until Hannah had seen Helen and sat with her, and said good-bye in whatever way she could.

Blok said it was unfortunate, but illness often meant believers missed the leave-taking of a loved one and that there were rubrics for burial to which the Church had to hold.

Vinich had a deep affection for the priest, who had been in the Great War, and Blok was fond of calling Vinich his *brat v zbrani*, then laughing and saying that he was glad, though, his brother had never had to raise those arms against him.

Yes, Vinich said to the priest. And while you might be in charge of what gets done for the house of God, my wife will remain in this house until my daughter has said her own farewell. Then and only then will I let that casket out the door.

But Jozef, Blok began. She's only a girl.

Vinich cut him off.

That woman out there's going to be with the Lord for a long time, Father. Longer than I believe is fair. We can let her daughter be with her for one more day.

Blok exhaled and looked down at the floor.

All right. Give her what time she needs, he said, then rose, took his black hat from the chair, and let himself out the back door.

THE GIRL BEFORE THE CASKET IS PALE AND UNWASHED AND dressed in her nightgown with nothing on her feet. She is hungry but will not eat. She has never seen a body before and wants to put her hand on her mother's shoulder and shake her and wake her up, but she knows, too, that neither this nor crying out in the middle of the room will rouse the woman. She knows she will never hear her mother's voice again. Never feel her touch. Never watch her walk through the house that will no longer hold the echoes of her footfalls, whisper, or laugh, and it is not a realization, not a coming to understand, but a vision she holds standing at the edge of an abyss.

Vinich carried her down to the living room in the morning, sat her up in a chair, then went into the barn and walked among the animals that did not know grief, or so he believed. At noon he returned and went back into the living room to offer the girl a glass of warm milk and to sit next to her. She drank the milk and never took her eyes off her mother, and her father remained at her side. When she slid her hand into his hand, he spoke finally, and told her that the emptiness she was feeling was the greatest pain for those separated by the pain of death. He did not know if those who had gone before them could feel it, too, but he wanted to believe that along with the great joy a man like Father Blok would say they know in the presence of God, there must be somewhere a sadness they feel for the loved ones they miss and have left behind.

Hannah asked him if he ever knew his mother, and he told her he did not, as he was an infant only a few months old when she died on a trestle over the Arkansas River out west.

I'm told I was with her, he said, and that she wrapped me tight in my blanket and threw me over the trestle into the water just before the train hit. It was a hot day and there were boys swimming in an eddy the river made. One of the boys saw me fall and swam out to save me. After that, my father took me back to the old country and raised me there in the mountains, just the two of us. Until Zlee, the boy I told you about, the one I called my brother, came and lived and worked with us there in the mountains. We went off to the war together.

She was quiet as she listened, then thought about the improbability of her father's story and the odd luck that he and she were both alive, and knew now that she, too, would be raised as he was, alone, by a father who could pass on everything but his grief.

So you don't feel what I feel, she said.

No one feels what you feel, Hannah. Nor you what I feel.

I mean, you never missed her? Your mother?

Vinich looked at the closed curtains across the large front window framed in stained glass.

My father had a photograph of her, he said. He kept it out on the table of the cabin in the mountains where we lived, and she was as real to me as anyone. I would see her in my dreams. Walk with her. Speak to her, even.

Hannah turned and stared at the side of her father's face.

Still? she asked.

Not for a long time, he said. Not since you were born. That was the last. I remember dreaming that I was walking along a road and saw her up ahead and I walked quickly to catch up. And when I did, she stopped and turned, and said, *Go back, Jozef. She needs you.* I looked behind me and your mother was walking up the same road with a baby in her arms, and I knew it was you. When I turned again to tell my mother that I had a daughter now, she was gone.

Hannah sat in the chair and stared at her lap, and her father put his arm around her shoulder.

So yes, I miss her, he said. Because the people I've loved in this world I can count on one hand.

He held out the calloused and misshapen hand with his palm up, the skin of the missing pinkie and ring finger scarred thick and whitened like stumps that might grow yet, and she wondered why he would tell her there were only three people in all the world whom he loved.

I can't feel what you feel, he said. But I feel empty and angry that she has been taken away from us. And I'm tired, too. So tired I want to stop and rest, but where would I rest? Anywhere I'd go, I'd be looking for her. Rooms. Orchards. Garden. The barn. Anywhere. And now she's nowhere. Nowhere.

He pulled her in close.

I thought I was going to lose you, too, he said in a voice that barely rose above a whisper. So sitting here and talking to you is some relief to all of this sadness. But then I look up and there she is. Or rather, there she isn't. And I'm empty and angry all over again. Just like you.

Though it was daylight outside, the house was curtained and dark and covered in a veil of silence punctuated by the ticking of the living room's fuseé clock, and they sat in that silence and stared at the motionless profile of Helen Vinich at rest in the bed in which she would rest for all eternity, until Vinich leaned over, kissed his daughter on the cheek, and stood.

I'll put the kettle on for tea and make some toast for you, he said. You need your strength.

In the waning light of the afternoon, it was Becks who brought tea and toast to her on a plate and placed it on the floor beneath the chair legs. She took a few bites of the toast, drank all of the tea, and asked him if he would sit with her. He nodded and sat down. And when the outer dark matched the dark of the living room, he stood only to light a small lamp on a lampstand someone had moved to the corner of the room by the window, and sat down again, the two of them abreast with their heads bowed and hands in their laps, silent still.

I understand the song now, Hannah said to him, eyes closed, voice raspy, as though she were speaking to the floor.

Becks turned his head to look at her.

The words, she said. The notes. The way you sing them. I know it's about a river, *pani*—I learned that much—but it's about a journey, too, isn't it? And in the middle of it, not at the end, but in the middle, there's a place of rest and love. It sounds like love to me, but the journey begins again. And then, not because the traveler wants to but because the traveler has to. There's a fear that once the journey begins again, everything in that place of peace will be changed. I can hear that. I can feel the change. It's like you're sewing a tear as you sing, so you have to hold the two pieces gently to sew them back together, until you realize you can't, not anymore, and the notes are what it feels like to sit and wonder what you will do now that you know the tear can never be mended.

He turned back to look at the casket in front of him and said nothing for a while, then told her that the song was a song his grandfather had taught him years ago, a song about two young women who grew up in two separate towns on two sides of one river, and who met one day on opposite sides of the banks while they knelt over the water and washed their clothes. They spoke across the divide as they worked each day and became friends, sometimes at a distance when the floods made the river wider, sometimes no farther apart than arm's reach when drought made all but a trickle of it dry up. One day they found that each was with child, and they marveled at what they shared together. And when the time came, each had her child at the same minute of the same hour of the same day. One a girl, the other a boy. And when they went back to their chores of washing, they brought their children to the riverside, and there the two grew up to be friends in the same way the women were friends. No bridge connected the towns. No ferry shuttled passengers from one bank of the river to the other. No one ever crossed over, not even when the river was just a trickle. But the times of drought were the days, the months, the season the girl and the boy waited for, because then they would exchange gifts with each other, handing them across the short distance like pieces of clothing to be washed, and allowing themselves in that moment to touch the other's hand. And the last time they gave each other a gift, the girl gave the boy a green woolen vest, and the boy gave the girl a brightly colored silk shawl. The last, because when spring came again after a long winter, and the river was very high, the girl and her mother went down to the banks and didn't find their friends on the other side. The next day they did the same, and still the others were nowhere to be found. Eight days later and still they had not returned, and the girl said to her mother, I want to cross and find out why. Why isn't he coming to the riverside? The mother tried to persuade her daughter not to go, but the girl tied her shawl around her head for the cold, stepped into the current, and disappeared beneath the water's standing waves.

But the girl was not drowned. The shawl kept pulling her down, so she untied it and let it go, then swam as hard as she could with the current toward the opposite shore, where she climbed, exhausted, onto the bank and walked upstream in the direction of the other town. When she reached the town, she found an old woman sitting on the steps of an old fountain in the center and asked the woman if she knew the washerwoman and her son. The old woman nodded and pointed to the church, and the girl walked up the steps, into the nave, and halfway down the aisle, where she saw a casket at the altar rail with the lid open, the boy in the green vest lying inside, and her mother's friend sitting and weeping in the front pew. She turned and walked from the church and continued walking out of the town. And all that was ever seen of her again was her shawl, many miles downriver, caught midstream in the branches of a tree that had uprooted and fallen across the water, so that it lay like a bridge from one side of the land to the other.

MOTH AND RUST

(Spring 1949)

1

Who will grieve for me like that? he thought, his cassock and stole rising and falling about him on the wind as he watched the woman—baby in one arm, young son holding on to the other—weep at the edge of the grave. A tear caught where her lower lip rose at the corner of her mouth, and he looked away. Looked at spring in the cemetery. The uncurling gray-green buds not yet leaves on the trees. The grass patchy where it had not filled in from winter. The brown mounds of other opened graves scattered across the now-thawed ground like round and name-less headstones of dirt. When he looked back again, it was his father's grave at which he stood and prayed, his mother a soli-tary figure in black flanked and held by her younger brother and sister, an autumn wind pushing against the stole he wore then stiff with the newness of his own faculties as a priest called upon to commit to the ground four months after Father Tomáš Rovná-vaha had said his first Mass the man who had raised him. Less than a week after the two of them had sat on the porch of the old house in the Hill Section of Scranton sipping whiskey and talking about where they might yet do some fishing before the winter. The man was everything to him. The classics professor who taught his only son Latin before the first grade. The pugilist

who taught the timid boy how to throw a punch. The outdoors-
man who taught the young man how to hunt and fish, and took
him to the Poconos for weeks in the summer because Mother
needed the rest. The father who embraced his son's decision to
enter the seminary after he had come home from Europe and
the war and taken a philosophy degree in two years on the G.I.
Bill instead of completing his studies in engineering at Lehigh
University, which he began in 1940 and left in '42 to enlist in the
army. Although Professor Rovnávaha had never known war, he
understood struggle, understood it the way the ancients understood it, and he was pleased with the reason his son had given,
the reason of no reason at all, and reminded Tomáš of what
Pascal had written, quoting it to him there on the porch. *C'est le
coeur qui sent Dieu, et non la raison.*

Then it was gone. The memory of the day. The memory of the
grave. The voice of his father. He was standing again in the cemetery in Dardan, Pennsylvania, before the wife of the man he was
burying, her sons, her father, the men from the roughing mill who
had come dressed in suits so rarely worn, they looked like blackened husks hanging from their shoulders, and a woman off to
the side dressed elegantly in a black wool overcoat and black hat,
beneath which he could just see the outlines of a misshapen jaw.
All that could be heard on the hillside now was the early spring
wind. He stood before them and said nothing, waiting between
the prayer of committal and final blessing with a silence that
might have seemed to those gathered like a respectful bow to the
dead, but was not. He was simply caught. He was too new at this.
Not to the grief but to the shepherding of it. He watched Hannah
Konar as she stared at the casket perched above ground that was
part dirt, part shoots of grass and crocuses, and wondered again
if anyone alive would mourn him one day as she mourned, and
he knew the answer. Then her father, Jozef Vinich, the man who
owned the mill and was the reason the others had come, not the
man being buried, turned his head in Rovnávaha's direction and
nodded, as if to say, *It's time to mourn him elsewhere, Father.*

The priest looked down at his book, turned the page, and asked out loud for the holy angel to watch over the grave, then gave the blessing and made the sign of the cross.

HE PULLED THE PLYMOUTH INTO THE PARKING LOT OF THE Church of St. Michael the Archangel and walked to the rectory with his stole draped over his arm. His left foot ached in the way it always ached in the wake of winter days, had ached in the cold ever since the night in France he slept in a foxhole and woke to snow and frostbite, and he tried not to let it drag. Twenty-eight years old and he was no faster or nimbler than the old ones tottering around the diocesan retreat house. He limped up the steps of the rectory, pushed the key in the lock, and called out for Esther, the housekeeper, then remembered it was her day off. Dishes sat in the sink, coffee from breakfast lukewarm in the percolator. He poured a cup and went into his office to finish paying the bills he had stacked on the desk and, if there was time before the 12:15 Mass, to look at the readings and jot down some notes for his homily on Sunday.

The bishop had kept the newly ordained Father Rovnávaha at the chancery in Scranton after the man's father passed away, so that he could check on his mother, and because the bishop saw his skill and was always on the lookout for men who had a heart for discernment and a mind for administration. But throughout the winter Rovnávaha, a late vocation they had rushed through to ordination, seemed lost, disengaged, and none of the priests he helped in Scranton told the bishop this one should be pushed up the ladder. Send him someplace as remote and aloof as he was, they said. So the bishop called Rovnávaha in at the beginning of Lent and told him the old priest at St. Michael's in Dardan was sound as a colonnade and would be a good man from whom Rovnávaha could learn how to run a parish, how to be a priest in what they called the sticks. And that was true for the first two weeks Rovnávaha spent in the beautiful stone church that sat on the side of a clear-cut hill like an erratic left from the ice age and reminded him of a church in which he once took cover with his platoon in France. Father Blok was magnanimous and kind when Rovnávaha moved in with the Plymouth his father had once owned and was his now, sitting down over coffee and telling the new assistant he wished more of the young priests these days had taken some time to see the world, as though Rovnávaha had just returned from a tour of Europe on the *Queen Mary*. Then Blok, seeing in his fellow priest the hardened patience and impatience of a man who knows other men have died in order for him to be standing there, realized his blunder.

Forgive me, Tomáš, he said. The bishop told me you had been in combat in the war.

I served with the Twenty-eighth, Rovnávaha said. Hürtgen Forest. Before the German push.

Blok looked down at the table and back at Rovnávaha.

Hard fighting there, he said.

Some of the worst.

You and the husband of a woman in town are the only two I know from the Twenty-eighth who came back. I was a chaplain with the Fifth Marines in 1918. Belleau Wood.

I know, Rovnávaha said. The bishop told me.

Well, Blok said, and stood and put fresh water and coffee in the percolator and told Rovnávaha over his shoulder it was the young ones he felt sorry for. Ordained priests who would meet men and women who had had to make harder choices in one day than those priests would have to make in their entire lives dressed up as monsignors in a rectory somewhere. Then he sat back down at the table.

And when they do, Blok said, they will believe that what they've chosen is somehow still a better choice, as though it were written in stone somewhere. When it's not. It's just a choice.

Blok introduced Rovnávaha to Jozef Vinich his first week in Dardan, when they went to Ruby's Diner for coffee after morning

Mass. Rovnávaha watched the Ford pickup with ENDLESS ROUGH-ING MILL painted on the side door pull into the parking lot, watched the man for whom they had come down off the hill into town move like any other man toward the front door, and yet Rovnávaha could tell the man had somewhere else moved with that same purpose through whatever battle had raged around him, too.

Our Cato, Blok said.

Vinich came into the diner and sat down in the empty seat between the two priests without looking for them, as though he knew where Blok would always be.

Dobré ráno, Padre, he said in Slovak, and Blok returned the good morning and introduced Rovnávaha, and they all three spoke in Slovak for the next hour like some backroom triumvirate discussing the handing off of affairs.

Rovnávaha did not understand all of it. Vinich's concern for the son-in-law returned from the war, his daughter, her hope that her husband would find a way back into their lives after having been cleared of the desertion charge, their son getting to know his father, and the baby who took up everyone's time. Blok listened and nodded and told Vinich that his conversations with the Cardinal Secretary of State at the Curia (an admission that surprised Rovnávaha) had given him a fuller picture of what had happened toward the end, the extent to which the Resistance was made up of those men who fought on when they found it was safer to fight with the French than to look for their units again. It was that or end up in a German prison.

Vinich sipped his coffee.

I had heard of men who did that, Rovnávaha said.

Did you? Vinich asked, and looked up at the priest.

When the push came in December, Rovnávaha said, everything fell apart. Supplies. Communications. Days I didn't know who was in my platoon, let alone which direction the Germans were coming from. There were men everywhere, and not always the ones you wanted to see.

Vinich stared at him, weighing something in his mind, it seemed to the priest.

Did it make you want to run? Vinich asked.

Rovnávaha shook his head.

Blok said how glad he was to have been sent Rovnávaha, and not some choirboy whose Latin was better than his own.

Tomáš was raised in the Poconos, Blok said.

Good fishing up there, Vinich said. Do you fish?

Still use the Heddon rod my father bought me when I was ten, Rovnávaha said.

I could tell, Vinich said. I've got a feeder stream to the Salamander on a corner of my property. Fast enough for brook trout, deep enough for browns. When this weather warms, you come up and we'll go fishing.

I'd like that.

Vinich rose and took five dollars from his money clip and placed it on the table.

Keep doing the Lord's work, gentlemen, he said, and walked outside to his truck.

WHEN ROVNÁVAHA WOKE BLOK ONE MORNING IN MARCH, THE side of the priest's face drooping and the words he tried to form slurred and scared-sounding, Rovnávaha drove him in the Plymouth to the General Hospital and knew he would never see Blok in the rectory again. Nor was the bishop going to transfer anyone to St. Michael's before the summer. Rovnávaha was on his own.

Then the rain and the cold. Weather he always hated for what it held off, what it reminded him of. Though winter was gone and the days were lengthening, the cold came in so fast and the rain in such torrents that everything seemed to follow it to a standstill. No baptisms. No spring weddings. No trips to the hospital or nursing home for Extreme Unction. And yet he welcomed it now. The chance to walk through the rectory and the church by himself, without having to tell Esther, or Jack, the sexton, or Rosemarie, who played the organ on Sundays, how this meal was cooked, that door was locked, or which songs were supposed to be sung. They knew better than he did. So that when the weather broke a week later, and spring and Lent and all of what those seasons held marched their way toward Easter, he was more comfortable in the church. More comfortable amid the silence of his own making.

When the phone rang in the late morning on a Monday in April, it was Jozef Vinich. He wasn't calling about fishing, but to ask Rovnávaha to come to the hospital, the request respectful and terse (*Our Cato*, he heard Blok say, and missed the old priest). Rovnávaha got into his car and drove to the General Hospital, where he was too late. He said the prayers for the dead and left the room to speak to Hannah Konar, the woman whose husband had just died from a bullet wound in his chest.

The doctors had already told her he could not be saved, and she had the look of someone who had gone past the shock and hope that what had happened to her husband was not as bad as it seemed, then moved to resignation and the acceptance of loss. A place Rovnávaha knew. Vinich was standing as he approached and the man didn't offer his hand, only motioned for him to sit next to his daughter, who had her head bowed, as though unaware of any and all around her. Rovnávaha took her hand, thin and strong, and felt her fingers lace into his, felt the warmth as it raced through him, so that he had to catch his breath before he could go on and say to the woman what he believed he should say, not knowing if she needed or even wanted to hear it. And, three days later, after he had come back from the graveside where he had buried the man and comforted the widow, Rovnávaha wondered again if the bishop hadn't put too much faith in his ability to be the kind of priest these people needed.

He heard the noon Angelus begin to peal from the church bell tower, and he rose from his seat at the desk, finished his coffee, and hoped as he walked down the stairs of the rectory and outside toward the church that Jozef Vinich was serious about inviting him onto his land to fish.

HE HAD NOTICED THE MAN IN THE BACK PEW DURING MASS, wondered why he was not at work, and here he was standing in the doorway of the sacristy, asking Rovnávaha if the older priest was around. When Rovnávaha told him Father Blok had gone on to his eternal reward, the man asked if they could speak privately. There was a nervousness about him, and not just from his lack of comfort about being in a church. Rovnávaha thought he had seen him somewhere before, a soul uneasy around others, like the scouts of the Twenty-eighth Rovnávaha had seen move past him in the cold and snow at broken intervals for the space of a week with only rifle, pack, and ammunition belt, then a long absence, until another slipped past, soundless, solitary, different and yet the same as the one who had walked that same way weeks before. Rovnávaha remembered then. Standing at the periphery of the mourners that morning, not even among them but closer to where the cars had parked, yet looking for some way to enter the grief. Rovnávaha nodded, hung up the last of his vestments, and asked the sacristan if he could have a moment alone.

Before Rovnávaha even moved to invite him to sit down, the man said he did not believe he was in need of mercy or forgiveness from God or Savior. If he had been wronged by or had a case against another, he took it up with that one himself, or left it, not just believing but knowing that nature had its own higher sense of right and wrong and acted accordingly in the balance. But now he had done something very wrong, and he needed to know that he was right in believing so.

You need to confess? Rovnávaha asked, and turned toward the drawer where he kept his stole.

And the man's voice rose there in the closed quarters of the sacristy.

I don't need to confess anything, Father. I need you to listen.

Rovnávaha closed the drawer. There was nowhere to sit in the sacristy and he needed to sit. He put his hand on the sink and stared into the drain, the drain plumbed into the earth where the wine turned to blood would mix with nothing but earth.

Why me? he asked.

Because there is no one you know in this town. Because you are not sure yet that you even want to stay in this town. Because, in this town, I have nowhere else to go.

Rovnávaha nodded.

Let's sit in one of the pews and discuss this.

No, the man said. In the box, or the booth, or whatever you call it. If anyone sees me, there will be talk of Younger's sorrow. Younger's need for forgiveness. But that's not what I need it for.

What do you need it for? Rovnávaha asked.

Do I need? said the man to no one, and walked into the church, paused to see that it was empty, then walked down the side aisle to the back and entered the confessional.

Rovnávaha was not long behind him. He entered the booth, opened the screen, and began.

No, Younger said. No blessings, no sins, no months or years or lifetimes it has been. Haven't you heard a word I said? I am here to tell you so that the record of the thing will live and be remembered at least by someone, even if you were to leave here as quietly and unnoticed as you arrived.

I see, Rovnávaha said. Go on.

And he told the priest about growing up on the land his father refused to call the Vinich land, the boundary between the forests and the field where their house stood and his father worked, at least when he had the desire to work. It was all he knew, all he had, and when his father died and he found out Vinich owned the house and field, too, his father no more than a sharecropper, if he could even call it that, he packed up and walked out. Left the house and moved into a saltbox on the Flats.

I've heard about the land, the priest said. The ownership and permission. Mr. Vinich's intentions seem right to me. Who cares about ownership, if care of the house and the land is all he wants. Care he must know you'll give it, as your father had.

Younger was quiet in the dark behind the screen.

When I was able to admit to myself that I was nothing when I was not on that land, he said finally, I went to him and asked if I could hunt there whenever I needed to hunt. For food. For myself. And he said yes. He said, *Paul, that house needs repair, too, if you'll do the same for it that you'll do for the land.*

And you said?

I said no. Not to the land but to the house. I wanted to be free of it because it only reminded me of what my father lost and how. His appetites. Then all those years of the war, when all those men were gone. They were like years of peace to me. The army wouldn't have me, so I just slipped back into the woods, and kept that house and my old man at a good distance. Then I married a woman who didn't mind the small house I bought for us on the poor side of town. That's what we were. And she let me go back to the woods when I needed to, sometimes staying for days up there, just waiting. Watching and waiting.

He told the priest he had seen them in the woods long before that, had seen them when his father was still alive, even met the man when he was nothing but a boy with Vinich and his daughter when she was a girl, in the field one day, and he wished they could walk those woods alone together because he had heard that the boy was good with horses, and he, for the first time in a long time, thought there was something someone might teach him about the woods that he didn't already know. But they never did. Walk those woods. Younger's father died, and the war came, and then one day, long after the war, he saw that boy, a man now, making his way up to the bend with Vinich's daughter, who had become his wife. After that, the man began coming to the same place alone. Younger followed him a few times before he made himself visible, and when he did come out of the thick hemlock and say, *You sure know how to make yourself scarce,* he realized Konar had been doing the same, following him, letting himself be seen by Younger when he wanted to, and Younger had never known it.

There was a kind of sameness to us, Father, he said to the priest. Knew right off. We used to sit by the creek there and talk and smoke, or rather, I talked and he listened, or asked questions about the game, where and how they moved, time of day, where I would lie in wait, and I knew he knew about more than horses.

The man was quiet then, and priest and confessor sat in the quiet of the booth in the dark (to which their eyes had adjusted long ago) so that each could see the other sitting back, relaxed almost, as though it were these two alone on the creek at the bend, waiting while what each knew about the other sank in amid the quiet of church or grove, the difference seeming unremarkable.

He came to you? the priest asked.

No. He came for the bear. On the edge of the game lands. I'd seen him before. And I'd seen the two of them at the creek, Konar talking to him like he was family or something. And I know he brought his wife up there to see the animal, too. I had come upon them once when I had watched the bear scamper before they got there. And I said to them, *One day you're going to have to accept the death of that old bear.*

And you think he was there, in the spring, to see the bear?

I know he was. There was no step that man took into a forest that was not a step he didn't know he was taking and why. I'll give him that. And I was both amazed and angry at what he was doing. A bear in spring. God Almighty. And he would not slow, would not back down, even when that bear turned and—I watched this through the scope I was sighting on my Weatherby—tried to walk away. And he, he called to the bear and kept moving after it, like a man in need, you know? And then that bear turned back finally, lean and hungry and confused as he was, and rose. I could see it in my sights. Konar looked up at him and I swear he smiled before he seemed to come to his senses and stopped smiling and looked pained. Then the bear raised a paw and struck him, and Konar went down. I swear he went down, Father. Went down right at the feet of that bear. I had the center of the animal's back in my cross-hairs, where I knew the round would pierce the heart. And I fired.

Rovnávaha listened to the breathing on the other side of the screen and waited.

I swear he'd fallen, Younger said. Swear he'd gone down from the swat that bear had given him.

But he hadn't, had he? Rovnávaha said, and he could see Younger shaking his head through the screen.

When I got to them, they were hugging. Konar on the ground and the bear on top of him. The two of them in an embrace like that. I was afraid the bear was still alive and the man was dead. But it was the opposite. I rolled the bear off of him and I could feel a pulse, but he was losing blood. The bullet had gone right through the bear and into Konar's chest. I fireman-carried him out of there as fast as I could to my truck on the old logging road and drove him to the police station in town.

He almost whispered this last bit of information and Rovná-vaha whispered back.

It was an accident, Paul. You thought you were saving him.

I know, Father.

An accident, Rovnávaha said again, as though he were saying it to convince himself. You're forgiven this, Paul. And Hannah Konar, too, will forgive you if you go to her and tell her what you told me. She will understand. She knew what her husband was going through. It was an accident.

Younger sat unmoving on the other side of the screen.

I won't go to her, he said. That's not why I'm here.

Why, then? Rovnávaha asked.

To tell you I know of his punishment.

His?

Your God.

For what, Paul?

For the vow I broke.

The vow? You mean your marriage vow? Is that what you mean?

Yes, Father.

I see, the priest said, and breathed as though he was tired now. Go on.

It was the hunting, he told Rovnávaha. In the beginning his wife found it romantic, the way in which he would disappear for days, then return with game they would salt or keep on ice as long as they could, the simple bounty, the dependence on no one, the raw hunger with which they ate. But in time, the days away and the work, the preparation to go on the hunt, the attention to the kill upon returning, the dressing, the preserving, the constant cleaning of everything—hands, house, knives, firearms, all but the unwashed and unshaven man—began to wear on her. And when he started looking out the windows of the house at the creek because there was no other task to occupy him, and she began making the long walk into the center of town for things like flour and fresh vegetables, he would be up the next day before the sun, the .30-30 and the .30-06 resting on the table in their cases, and he would say to her when she woke, I've got to go or else we'll be out of food. And for the first time that spring, she said, We wouldn't be if you'd get a job so that we could buy it regular. This is my job, he told her. His work. But he knew she would not see in him what he believed was a need. Would dismiss it, rather, as stupidity or stubbornness, and not change.

Younger looked down in the dark of the confessional and pushed out breath that Rovnávaha could hear, and smell, too.

I was at the bar in Luzerne during those days of rain, when it just wouldn't stop, he said, still looking down. I was drinking and not wanting to go home, and I knew who the woman at the end of the bar was. I knew how she hunted, too, what her needs were, and I had similar ones that evening. So, for the first time in my life, I paid for a license.

Rovnávaha did not move his head or his hands or any part of his body there in his priest's stall. Just sat as though frozen. He knew when Younger had directed him to the confessional that there would be some kind of reckoning.

Then I went home, Younger went on. Washed and shaved, and she treated me no better than when I hadn't. We ate and slept, and two days later, when the rains stopped, I went back up to the woods to sight my Weatherby for a hunting trip out to Western PA I'd always wanted to take. And that's when I found Becks Konar and the bear.

He finished and the priest was quiet, waiting, though for what he wasn't sure, until he heard the man's breath catch, and through the screen and muted light he saw him hunched with his head in his hands.

Paul, he said.

The man began to sob out loud, too loud for the close space of the confessional.

Paul, the priest said again.

And he began to wail now, so loud that Rovnávaha leaned back from the screen, where he had placed his head.

She pities me, Father. She pities me. Not for the whore. She doesn't know about that. But because she knows me enough to know that I didn't kill him on purpose. That it was him who was looking for the bear out of some madness, or the bullet out of some pain, and because of that I have to live in the shadow of his death. Because of that she has changed toward me. Last night she came to me in bed, told me that I didn't have to go to the funeral, that I didn't have to say to Hannah Konar, *I'm sorry*. I only had to know that she believed I am not a murderer, and the sooner I put this aside and get back into those woods, the better for us as a family. As a family, Father, and that was the first time since she had said *Yes, Paul Younger, I will marry you* that I believed my father's name might not stop with me.

He had composed himself by the end, Rovnávaha watching him as he wiped at his face with the back of his hand, and the priest moved close to the screen.

Will you tell her about your transgression? he asked in a voice that was low but not a whisper.

No. It's done enough to destroy one family. There might yet be a family to come in the wake of it.

She'll need to forgive you.

She'll never forgive me. Not for that. For killing a man, yes. But not for that.

Paul, the priest said.

Father, Younger said louder. Don't you see why I'm here? I aimed that rifle. I fired that bullet. And it found its way into the chest of a man because of my weakness and my need. I sent it the minute I drank off that whiskey and followed a whore back to her room and laid down with her, because I wanted to be wanted for what I had chosen to do, how I had chosen to live in this town, where they have no idea what the Younger name means anymore. And I swear I watched that man fall and rise again so that—that bullet would find him, even as it crashed through the shoulders of a beast. It took that man to make me see clear-eyed and harsh that I am to live with this guilt for the rest of my life.

Paul, Rovnávaha said in a voice he struggled to keep measured. What about the wife of that man? What has she done to deserve to become a widow with two sons? Can that be in the Lord's plan to punish you? To punish you both? The Lord does not punish with wrath. He heals with mercy.

Younger spoke in a flat tone now, as though answering an interrogation.

I don't know what's in her heart.

No, Rovnávaha said. You don't. But I have seen her grief. You have seen it, too.

And I did that.

Not by the hand of God.

That's all I've ever seen from God. The one who gives, and the one who takes away. Isn't that what you preach, Father? Because that's all I've ever seen.

All?

The priest was sitting up now and still trying to keep his voice even, trying to persuade this man that the balance he believed in was not the scale with which God measured. That there was no scale at all.

Paul, what if Bexhet Konar had gone in search of you out of his own sense of guilt and sin for what he had done? Believing so strongly that, though he was a father and husband, his children and his wife did not deserve to live in the shadow of that guilt? He was no murderer, either, though he killed men. In war. As I have. I see still the flash of the teeth of the man I shot when he stood to advance and I heard the stick snap and I aimed and fired. What of him? What of the men next to me with only the sound of their own breath pushing out of their mouths before they died? Was there the movement of some chess piece moments before that sealed their fates, because they had done something? Something sinful? And I hadn't? No. God does not act out of malice or retribution or spite. Only love.

Love, Younger said. Which God do you believe in, Father? The one who allows it to happen, or the one who does nothing to let it not happen?

That is not his way, Rovnávaha said. It is we who deliberate. We who have the will. We choose, even though all would be lost.

And we have been, Father. Lost. So where is your comfort in that now?

In the forgiveness, Paul!

He was almost shouting there in the close and dim-lit quarters of his stall, though both men still spoke nearly face-to-face.

That is the given. That is what is never taken away. He will forgive us no matter what.

Well, then your God is more of a fool than I thought, Younger said, and stood and walked from the booth, Rovnávaha listening to the sound of the man's steps as they echoed through the church toward the vestibule and ceased with a slam of the great doors.

2

One week later, after the 12:15 Mass, Father Tomáš Rovnávaha got into his Plymouth and drove up Rock Mountain Road to the Vinich farm. The sky had been changeable, but the sun came out as he pulled into the driveway and it lit up the budding apple trees in the orchard and the shoots of tulips and hostas emerging in green rows along the beds outlining the great house. The Ford pickup was not in the drive. He parked in the front and got out and walked to the steps and onto the porch and raised the hitching-post knocker on the door.

She answered with the baby in her arms, the child Blok had christened, the boy they called Samuel, his face red and his chin milk-streaked, and she pulled the muslin in which she had wrapped the baby across her chest in the same move she had made to open the door. She looked surprised to see the priest.

Hello, Father, she said, and blushed.

He looked down at the threshold, then back at her.

Good afternoon, Mrs. Konar. Is this a bad time?

Oh no, come in, she said. Please. Have you had lunch? There's soup on the stove, and I was just about to put the baby down for a nap. Come in. Please. I could use the company.

Well, I don't know what kind of company I'll be, but thank you, Rovnávaha said, and followed her in.

The house was warm and he could smell wood smoke and rising bread. A black retriever ran into the foyer and skittered about his legs. Hannah told him the dog's name was Duna, then took his coat and hung it up with one arm and held the baby in the other.

Excuse me for a minute, she said, and walked upstairs.

He had heard about but not seen the Vinich house. He knew only of the man's reputation in the town for being aloof and exacting, and, standing in the vaulted entryway with its grand staircase, crystal chandelier, and openness more suited to some robber baron's mansion in Scranton, he understood why. And yet there was a comfort to the vastness of the house, a warmth and purpose there in the wood and high windows and stone fireplace visible in the living room. And in spite of the fact that the foyer seemed a kind of dwelling in and of itself, he felt as though he could follow the smells of cooking coming from a kitchen somewhere down the well-lit hall and find a table on which food was served to any and all who sat down to eat. And that would be exactly what the woman and her father would want him to do. Would want anyone who crossed that threshold to do.

He petted the Lab's head and belly and spoke to it, and the dog rolled onto its back, until Hannah Konar came down the stairs again with a cardigan on over her dress. She had tied her long blond hair back and he could see her eyes were red and swollen around the pale and narrow-pupiled gray that made them so striking, so almost cold-looking, and she smiled at her visitor in spite of whom she had been weeping for not minutes before Rovnávaha came to the door. She stepped barefoot off the curtail and onto the foyer floor without making a sound, and he followed her down the hall to the kitchen, which was just as he imagined. Table and chairs and woodstove on which the pot of stock and vegetables was warming, two waxed paper–covered loaves rising on the counter a short distance from that stove. Rovnávaha sat, and Hannah ladled out two bowls of soup and set them down on the table.

They both ate quietly, Rovnávaha speaking only to tell her the soup was the best he had ever tasted, and he was not a man to exaggerate. She thanked him, and asked if there was a particular reason for his visit. He said he only wanted to come by to see how she was after the funeral.

To see if maybe there was anything you needed, he added. Anything more I could do.

Thank you, Father, she said, and stopped eating and looked down into her soup. I haven't had much time to think about more than the baby and Bo. And keeping the house in some semblance of order.

How is the boy? Rovnávaha asked.

Bo? He's fine. I asked him to stay home from school this week, but he said he wanted to go. Said they were catching frogs in science class for a terrarium, so that's where he is now. I'll walk down the hill in a little bit and meet him at the bus.

Rovnávaha nodded.

Does he understand what happened?

Yes, she said, and stirred her soup. He was shy around his father when Becks first came home. But in the past six months, the two of them had gotten close. So yes, he understands. And he's sad in the only way he knows how. I know, because he talks to Papa about it, and Papa tells me. They go on walks and do chores together, and I don't know exactly how they talk about it, but they do. I can tell Bo needs him. He's growing up so fast, that boy.

Rovnávaha finished his soup and touched the corner of his mouth with a napkin.

And you? he asked. Do you have anyone to talk to?

I don't know, Father. There's not much talking to do, is there? It can't help me now.

She stood and cleared the table and brought out cups and coffee.

I didn't know him, your husband, Rovnávaha said from his seat while she was standing at the counter pouring cream into a creamer. I found out later from your father that we fought in the same division, though I landed in Europe later. We probably even passed each other somewhere over there.

She sat down across from him again and feigned interest, but he could see she was already tired of their conversation and he had outworn his welcome. But it was why he had come, and so he went on.

I wanted to tell you, he said, because I'm not sure anyone else could, that it was hard there. The fighting was bad. The men who survived did so by some stroke of luck. Hand of God. I don't know. It wasn't until I was on my way to Berlin when I seemed to have woken up from the cocoon of survival I was in and began to wonder how it was I had not been left in the woods or on the roadside or in pieces in some village somewhere. We all broke in our own ways. Something inside. Something that died, though we didn't. I can't say. But you need to know that he was in no way a man or a soldier who lacked honor. Father Blok knew that. He showed me the cables from the Vatican. He was an honorable man, Hannah.

I know, Father, she said. I know what he did, and what he didn't do. And even if he wasn't an honorable man, even if he hid in a basement for the entire war, just to come home to me and our family, I would have forgiven him that. His not coming home was what I feared the most, and when he did, nothing else mattered. Nothing. That's why this is more painful than even that.

She wiped her eyes with the back of her hand.

I understand, he said, and sipped his coffee, and they were quiet again. He looked over at her staring down at the table, and she was crying, her mouth open and soundless, but he could see the tears dropping into her cup with short little splashes that rippled to the edge of the china. He stood and moved around the table and sat next to her and put his hand on her shoulder.

It's all right, he said. It's all right.

She heaved and burst into sobs and he pulled her in closer and let her cry, saying nothing now. Wanting to say nothing. Waiting for her to find a window into that grief on her own.

When she had finished and wiped her eyes, she touched his

hand and whispered *Thank you,* and he brought it back to his side and moved the chair out from the table so that he and the chair were facing her.

I wish I knew what to do, he said. What more to tell you. But I don't.

She pulled the cardigan closer around her shoulders and buttoned it in the middle.

I was thinking about a dream I had once when my mother died, she said. The two of us came down with the flu when I was just a girl, and my father told me later that she and I were both very sick. And on what turned out to be the night she died, I had a dream I'll never forget. It was midsummer and I was in a living room in a house that was sweltering from the heat, and I was surrounded by people I knew had already died. I was with my mother and we had just walked into that room and sat down, everyone's face fixed and white, until one by one each rose and moved toward the open door and walked through it. When my mother got up to go with them, I yelled out *Mama!* and she turned and told me, the way she had always told me the things I needed to hear, that I had to stay. Here. I hollered again, but she pointed to someone or something behind me, and I looked and must have been in some state between dreaming and waking up, because Becks was sitting in a chair in my room, and he was singing, like he always did. And when I turned back to my mother, she was walking through the door with the others. I called out again, but she didn't turn around.

Hannah looked up then from the table and her coffee cup and dabbed at her face with a napkin, so that the red that had once circled her eyes was now the color of her face.

Do you know how long I've been a priest? Rovnávaha asked.

Not long?

Nine months.

It shows, she said, and managed a weak laugh, so that he smiled, too.

They don't teach you in seminary what to tell grieving

widows, what you just told me yourself. But I know what loss he saw, Hannah. And I know it can change a man, so that he is both not himself and more himself. But your loss is real, too, I know. Where there was once the closeness of love, there is now a gulf between you. But a soul shaped by loss is a soul in which God surely dwells. So my hope, and this is all I feel I can tell you, is that something of that love for God and your husband will never be lost. That he will always be next to you, and that he, wherever he is, will need you to be next to him. That's my hope. And maybe you won't feel that for a long time. But maybe one day you will.

She turned the cup in its saucer with her thumb and took a deep breath to steady herself.

You're not as bad at this as you think, she said.

She stood and began to clear the cups and saucers, but he put his hand on hers and said, Let me clean up. I never get the chance to anymore.

She sat back down and smoothed her sweater and straightened her hair. He put the dishes in the sink and she told him to leave them there and he returned to the table.

How long will the baby sleep? he asked.

Not much longer now. I'll take him with me to get Bo.

And your father? He's at the mill?

No, she said. He drove out to Huntsville. He had to return the papers for a horse he bought. For Becks.

She took in another deep breath.

He seemed to miss Pushkin almost as much as he missed us when he came home, she said. And I suppose he would have. When he first got here—I mean, when he arrived here as a boy—that horse was the only thing that calmed him. I used to follow him to the barn, without him knowing, although I found out later he always knew, and I would hide beneath the window and listen to him speak to the horse in Romani. Sometimes he would sing. I loved when he sang. I didn't know what he was singing then. It sounded gentle and kind, and he told me one day it was a song about a lost love. I felt sorry for him in those days, all alone, no family, no way even to return to a family, and only my father could talk to him. So I didn't begrudge him the love he showed that horse. Papa wondered if perhaps a new one might bring that part of him back. Help him recover in some way.

She broke off and turned to look out the kitchen window that looked out onto the orchard, the apple trees a silver-green as their leaves started to uncurl. Looked out as though searching for someone she missed. As though this time she might see him there. Then she turned back to Rovnávaha at the table.

Papa bought a young mare named Irene just last week. She was supposed to be delivered today, but instead he's at the horse farm, negotiating the return.

I understand, Rovnávaha said.

I thought of keeping her anyway, Hannah said, as though she hadn't heard. Teaching Bo how to ride and care for her. But Papa said no. I don't think he has the heart for it anymore. He loved Becks like a son, and I know that the war and the disappearance and the charges against him hurt Papa as much as any of us. You ought to try those priest skills you've got on him, Father. Might do the man some good.

He promised me we'd go fishing one day.

That's a promise you should hold him to, she said.

They heard the waking cry of the baby then.

Go to him, Rovnávaha said. I'll let myself out.

She stood and they embraced and she kissed him on the cheek and stepped back again.

Will you come for lunch another time? she asked.

Yes, he said.

The baby's cries grew louder, and she turned and walked quickly down the hall. Rovnávaha listened to her light footsteps hurry up the stairs, her voice carrying as she climbed and spoke softly to the child, Oh Samuel, Samuel, don't cry. Then she began to sing a strange and mournful song in a language Rovnávaha had never heard before, the baby becoming quiet as soon as the first few notes reached him, until there was no other sound in the great house but the melody of that song, and Rovnávaha stood in the kitchen listening, his hands holding the back of the chair as if he would fall.

FROM A LONG WAY OFF

(1939–1949)

1

The Friday before Christmas at the Luzerne County courthouse on the Susquehanna River in Wilkes-Barre, Pennsylvania, Bexhet Konar raised his right hand and pledged allegiance
to the country he had come to as alien and walked down the steps
of that courthouse a sworn citizen, Jozef and Hannah walking
by his side.

That night, after the meal, Becks asked Vinich if he could
speak with him, and if they could go into his study to be alone.
Vinich looked at Hannah, who had just risen from the table and
taken the plates to the sink.

You mean you would like to retire to a room in which my
daughter is not present to discuss matters men have long discussed
in rooms such as my study, Vinich said to the young man in a
voice Hannah, at least, knew was a playful one. Even though, I
must confess, Bexhet, I have never discussed anything of importance out of earshot of her, let alone in a room with other men.
But there is something you need to speak of. Is that right?

Becks could see Hannah watching him in the reflection of the
evening-dark window glass.

Yes, Jozef, he said.

Hannah, if you'll excuse us, Vinich said, the men would like to discuss matters of business in a place where apparently these matters are best discussed.

The red embers of a fire laid in the afternoon still pulsed in the hearth, and Vinich took two crispated birch from the wood-box and placed them on the coals, which smoldered and smoked for a moment, then crackled back to life. He walked behind the desk and opened the door of a cabinet and took out a bottle of Old Forrester and two crystal tumblers, placed them on the desk, pulled the cork from the bottle and poured two fingers of the bourbon into each tumbler. Becks remained standing at the fireplace and watched the new blaze as though he had never seen fire before. Vinich came from behind the desk, handed him a glass, and raised his.

Na zdravie, he said.

They drank off the bourbon and exhaled, and Vinich poured two more fingers each and walked back behind his desk and sat down.

Tell me what's on your mind, son, he said.

Becks took the leather chair that faced the books on the varnish-darkened shelves behind the chair in which Vinich sat, stared at the whiskey he swirled in his glass, then looked up. He told the man before him that he was grateful for all he had given him over the years, from the day he walked into his house right up to the meal they had shared just now. He didn't believe in the ever-turning wheels of fate he had been raised among the Roma to believe, but there were days when he would walk down the hallway of the house from the room in which he had slept, or was going to sleep, or walk through the orchard, or into the barn, and he would stop and not know how he had come to this place without the hand or hands of some maker, or weaver, or God, if that were the case, benevolent or otherwise, having placed those hands on his shoulders and steered him onto this long road. And if so, then he was grateful for that being, as well. But what he had come to be thankful for most of all was the sight, the sound, the touch, when they held hands on their walks in the woods or simply grazed fingers when they washed dishes together, of Jozef's daughter, and he sat before the man that day to ask if, in the new year, when she turned eighteen, he might take Hannah's hand in marriage and be her husband. Raise her children, if God would allow. And grow old with her in the house to which he had traveled in search of the man who had brought him into the world, or in some other house entirely, one he, too, might build with his own hands.

Vinich gazed at the young man before him and Becks began to wonder if Vinich was not joking when he spoke to Hannah, and the look of contentment disappeared from his face as he stared down into his glass, drank off its contents, and placed the empty tumbler on the edge of the desk.

Jozef, he said.

Vinich didn't answer. He just stared forward, his face unreadable, his hands cupping the crystal, so that Becks could see the light from the flames behind him in the cut of the glass.

I see, Becks said quietly, and stood to go.

Wait, Vinich said.

Why? The answer is no. I see that now. Because of the blood, right? Because even to you I'll always be *gadjo*?

Vinich shook his head.

The answer is not no, son. I knew what you were going to ask.

Then what is it?

Vinich did not stand and Becks did not sit again. Vinich drank off his glass and wiped the corner of his eye all in one motion.

As little as six years ago, he said, I would not have guessed or even wagered that the swaddled infant I had delivered into the world twenty years ago would sit across from me and ask for nothing more than a blessing that his life might carry on as before, but with the companion now of the only other soul I had carried into this world, and on whom I can look and say in my heart that she is the greatest blessing of all. Only six years ago.

He turned and peered out of the window of the study into the December dark.

Did you ever dream of this? he asked. Not this moment or this room. This place. This land. My father told me I was born here, but I was young and so have no recollection of it. Still, I used to lie awake winters in the house where I grew up in Pastvina and imagine right down to the apple tree and the stone fire pit out there what kind of house I would live in when I was old enough to return to the country I never knew, but knew was mine.

Becks stood by the chair, silent, as in the days when he had to search for words he weighed before he said them.

It isn't possible to dream of this, he said. You, more than anyone, understand what it feels like to live with one heart in two worlds. I remember nights beneath the stars when I traveled in my grandfather's caravan, the only world I knew, the one he told me was all the world. Until he gave me those papers I came here with and kissed me and said there was another world across the water where the man who brought me into this world would welcome me because all good men make a vow to God to welcome the stranger, and I would be stranger and no stranger to him. So, no. I never dreamed of this. I dream of my grandfather. The wagons. The river. But this—this is all I know now.

Vinich turned from the window and reached across the desk for the Old Forrester bottle, unstoppered it, and poured another two fingers of whiskey into his tumbler. He didn't ask Becks if he wanted more. He sat back in the chair and cradled the glass in his hands on his lap.

It's not about what you are asking me to give, he said. She is not mine to give. I know she loves you. It's about what's yet to be asked of you both. There's going to be a war, Bexhet. And we're not going to get away with sitting this one out and sending supply ships across the Atlantic. You and I know better than anyone that what we hear on the radio is only half of what's been happening in Europe alone. And when the war does come, comes right here to these shores, will you leave your new land and new wife and go and fight? In the same place you were raised? The place you dream of? You who are of one heart?

Becks hooked an elbow on the mantel and stared down into the fire.

Because that's the promise you've already made, Vinich went on. When you raised your right hand. No land, no country, no nation will let us wander within its borders without exacting some price. I can't tell you what it will be. But you will pay. Something. The two of you.

Becks looked back at him.

We lose each other either way, he said. If it means I have to leave here and fight before I can return here and continue to live with her as my wife, then I will.

Vinich nodded and rose from his desk.

I can't speak for my daughter, but I know she would just as soon go with you to fight than let that be a reason not to marry you.

He walked to the fireplace and embraced Becks and held him close, then leaned out of the embrace and took him by the shoulders.

You have my blessing, son. You always have. Since the day I thought it would be the last thing I ever gave in this world.

The small jewelry box in which he carried the diamond ring felt like a talisman slipped into the pocket of his barn jacket, and for that reason he would not take the jacket off and made excuses for why he had work to do outside until supper. He carried it in that same pocket the day before, the twenty-third of December, after he had purchased if from James the jeweler in town, and he kept it with him as he and Hannah cut down the pine she had picked out among all the others in the grove and carried it into the living room of the house and trimmed it with ornaments made of crystal, glass, and wood until it resembled something of the Christmas trees they had decorated in the past. She wanted to sit with him for a moment before the tree. He shifted his feet back and forth and said it was beautiful and smelled liked the forest, but he needed to go back outside to the barn to feed Pushkin. She kissed him and let him go, then went into the kitchen to finish what she had started to prepare for the *velija* feast.

He gave her the ring on Christmas day, and they were married in May of 1940 on a warm Saturday afternoon at the Church of St. Michael the Archangel in Dardan. Vinich wore a morning suit and walked his daughter down the aisle, then stood at the groom's side as Bexhet's best man. And from the church, the small gathering of worshippers and witnesses drove up the hill to the house, where a reception was held under the full bloom of apple blossoms in the orchard.

By June, Hannah was pregnant, and in March of 1941 they had a son they called Bohumír, and Becks Konar held the next nine months as the happiest of his life. Until December of that year, when every man who was of fighting age and fit to do it put on a uniform and went to war.

HE WROTE TO HER WITHOUT FAIL ON THE MONDAY OF EVERY week from Louisiana, where they had sent him for basic training, then on to language school because of the Hungarian, Slovak, and German he knew. There he studied French, Italian, and Romanian, because, when he told the recruiters his native language was Romani, they put down Romanian, and so there was another language to learn. In late April of 1942, his company was given leave before their orders to ship out of Hampton Roads, and he wrote and told her he would be home in a week to celebrate their anniversary.

He took a Greyhound from Atlanta to Washington, D.C., then changed for the local to Scranton. He slept through Baltimore and Harrisburg and woke up in Sunbury, Pennsylvania, the morning sky pink as the bus twisted along Route 15 and the Susquehanna River, then followed Route 11 across the river north to the city of Wilkes-Barre. He was hungry and sore when the town bus dropped him off at the Miners Bank in Dardan, and he walked through the center of town along the Salamander south until he came to the bottom of the hill, where the water veered off into the pass that flowed down into the Susquehanna. He turned and walked the last two miles that led to the house, where he saw her standing in the road, the child swaddled in her arms. He dropped his bag and ran to her, and all three of them stood in that road locked and silent in their embrace.

HE CONTINUED TO WRITE TO HER EACH WEEK FROM THE BASE IN England, and in August he wondered why two of his letters had received no response. In his next, he asked her if everything was all right at home, and he read the reply that came on the first of September. She told him it was not easy to write about what had happened in the wake of his leaving, what had given her so much joy at first, and then the pain of loss that she would have had to have gone through on her own, if not for her father.

In May, she knew she was pregnant again, and this was enough to assuage her loneliness there on the farm without him. But she wanted to wait before she wrote to him with the news. She wanted to feel the baby in her belly when she sat down to put pen to paper and summoned his presence and spoke to him out loud as she wrote there in the emptiness of the house. After two weeks she could wait no longer, so overwhelming was her joy, and on a quiet July evening, every window in the house open to the breeze that rustled the leaves of the apple trees outside in the orchard, she sat at her desk and told him of the child they were expecting, then sealed the letter and walked downstairs and placed it on the table by the pier glass in the foyer to go out in the next day's mail. And then, just then, when she turned to go back to her room, she collapsed on the swell step in a wave of pain that doubled her over and brought her to her knees, and she cried out as she felt the blood that was the child leaving her. Her father ran in from the barn, where he was working late on the truck, carried her to the bath, and called the doctor, who came even at that hour, and he told her what she already knew. For the next two days she lay in bed, sitting up only to nurse Bohumír, who seemed to wonder why it was his mother did not speak to him or carry him around as she always had, but remained with her nevertheless in the bed in his own silence, his own grief, she wrote.

He didn't know how to respond at first, and so waited, carrying the letter around with him in his pocket. Not rereading it, only carrying it, believing that to return to its contents might conjure somehow even more pain and loss. He wondered if this was the beginning of how the war would come to them, but he knew the war had come to them already, and he dismissed the fear and superstition that rose to accompany him when he let it, dismissed it with the brush of silence he received from the old women in the *kumpania* where he grew up, those who made signs against the evil eye when he walked into their presence unannounced. He knew what it was she needed to hear, and so in the next letter he told her that he loved her, and that God's plans were not their plans, His ways not theirs, and he would pray for her peace as hard as he sought it for himself. Then he told her what he could about what he did, the typing he had learned to do, the translating, all so that she knew he was safe and would be safe and did not have to worry about him not coming home. He hoped this would bring her the peace she needed, though it brought nothing to him.

HE SPENT MOST OF HIS FIRST YEAR IN ENGLAND WITH A GROUP OF English and American personnel in the basement of an old building in a university town, interrogating captured German officers and getting little out of them. The captain in charge of the group, a man named Costantino, who had grown up in the Bronx and gone to the Jesuit high school and Fordham College, where he studied classics, liked him, liked his manner, liked that he knew

Europe better than the average GI with a map, and so Becks was kept in the intelligence pool, where he transcribed and translated the interviews, then typed them out and passed them along or filed them away according to their level of importance. In the evening he went to the pub and drank ale with the English soldiers, and at night listened to a Slovak radio station on the shortwave before he drifted off to sleep.

One early day in late winter of the next year, snow drifting and melting in the morning on the cobbled paths of the alleys along which he walked from his quarters to the old building, the British CMPs brought in a captured German major, and Captain Costantino wanted Becks in the room when they interrogated him. The team of four was already seated when they led the bound man into the spare room, which held a metal table, five chairs, and a single shaded lamp. The prisoner wore the uniform of his rank, though he was bareheaded, his boots showing only traces of the shine they no doubt had once maintained, and there was the mark of a blow to the left side of his face, which had already begun to purple and bruise about the eye. And yet as he walked, he still kept the bearing of his training and appeared not humbled for having been captured, but pleased to be surrounded by men who would be obeying his orders, if there were some natural law in which perpetual war held the fulcrum of the scales and all men obeyed one another according to their rank, regardless of the field of battle. The CMPs took off his hand shackles and he sat and rubbed his wrists and looked at his interrogators and studied them all, from Costantino on down. His gazed lingered last and longest on Becks, looking puzzled at first, as though he were on a stage in a theater where there were many stages and he had entered the right scene of the wrong stage and he needed to exit before it was too late, then realized he would spend the rest of the war in a prison, that these men would shoot him before they would obey him, and the fulcrum on which he placed his trust might just as well have been made of river sand. Becks watched the man's confident bearing sag, then lift with a sneer, and he began to shake his head and mutter *filthy bastards* over and over, as though reliving some mistake that had led to his capture. The captain said, That's enough, and that he wanted to begin the interrogation, but the major looked across the table at him and said in German he would tell them nothing with this one in the room. There was confusion in the delay of translation to Costantino, and the man repeated what he had said, his anger rising, but Becks understood even before the prisoner spoke. He rose from his seat to leave before Captain Costantino asked him to. And as he crossed the room and passed in front of the prisoner sitting at the table, the man whispered to Becks in Hungarian now that he could not hide behind the uniform of the Americans, and that the man himself had seen to the killing of many of his kind. Becks stopped before him and stood and wondered how quickly he could take the fountain pen from his uniform shirt pocket and push it like a tent peg into the beaten man's purple eye.

What did he say, Corporal Konar? Costantino asked, his voice rising. What did the prisoner say to you?

Becks turned and stood at attention before his commanding officer.

Sir, the prisoner uttered an old proverb. From the Bible. *Even from a long way off, the father could recognize the prodigal.*

What the hell is that supposed to mean? Costantino asked, and looked at Becks, who said nothing, then looked at the stenographer, who stared at the floor as though waiting for some prologue to conclude so that he might commence with his own part in the play, in which no word from a prisoner was left unsaid.

The captain cursed again, dismissed Corporal Konar, and ordered him to report to his office at 1400 hours.

HE REQUESTED TO BE REASSIGNED TO THE TWENTY-EIGHTH Infantry Division from Pennsylvania, training in Southampton, England, and in November of that year his request was granted.

Her letters had begun to arrive every week again, and she wrote of the war from a distance. As though he were separated from the loss by some luck or contract that kept him harbored in another town, in another country, one in which death and loss were not allowed to cross in or out. She wrote about the others in Dardan. The Hughes boy, who had gone to Canada to join the RCAF and was shot down in his Hawker Hurricane over the English Channel. Mary Flanagan's son, who died in the engine room of his ship at Pearl Harbor, something she had only found out these two years later. Families with boys being sent to Sicily and the South Pacific. Father Blok made house calls to these families when he received news of casualties by way of a wire transmission that came to the cardinal archbishop in New York from a channel operating out of the Vatican, and the archbishop's staff called the names in to the diocese in Scranton. Everyone rationed and listened to the radio. Her father went to the mill each day, where he had contracts to fill for a company that made shipping crates and another that framed army barracks. Her letters held within them so much of the war wrestled into the quotidian of the town that Becks read them as though from the increasing distance not of a continent or an ocean but of a past once lived and so irretrievable now, he could barely read beyond *My Dearest Bexhet* in her almost calligraphic scrawl. But he did, often over the space of days, knowing that was how long he had until there would be another one to open.

His letters to her said nothing about his transfer, his new life as a soldier, the barracks, the troop parade grounds, the rifle range, where he excelled, the men with whom he marched and trained and ate and slept, and who knew nothing of languages or interrogation, but who seemed the physical equivalent of some eternal hunter moving in search of prey all day, holding their lethality coiled within them like a spring, and it was in this observation that he touched for a moment the edge of his father-in-law's cloak, remembering the days on the mountain when the man taught him and Hannah how to shoot and in time how to hunt. Days he not only watched the man but felt the separateness of him as he moved across the ground, among the trees, through the air almost, he would say now, the man no man but a singular heightened sense that would either stop or be stopped once he had begun that journey. And so he wrote to her about the rain, the scent of alleyways that smelled nothing like the dirt and stones of the farm, but of some old world to which he'd returned, and the sights and sounds of a group of Welsh Romani with whom he had struck up a conversation and shared a drink in a local pub on the outskirts of town, after which, he wrote, *They greeted me as one of them by the language I spoke, nothing else, and I felt I was closer somehow to a part of myself from which I had hidden, or been cut off, knowing what I gained by the wielding of that knife, but wondering there as I walked back to my barracks for curfew in my uniform if what I had lost would come looking for me again one day, and what it might find.*

THE TWENTY-EIGHTH REMAINED IN ENGLAND LONG INTO THE new year and then for more than a month after the initial invasion at Normandy, going ashore in July of '44 and making their way east through the French bocage. They marched past overturned and burned-out trucks and Kübelwagens and abandoned locust-shell tanks. They met only the waft in the summer heat of corpses rotting inside buildings and behind hedgerows, and the blackened, bloated mounds of dead horses lying putrid and maggot-strewn in the dirt. There was no threat of attack, only mines placed in ditches where a man would stop to urinate, a doorway another might open in search of loot. It wasn't long before they learned to remain on the road in formation until the army sappers gave the all clear from the head of that road. Weeks of marching punctuated by nights of guard duty and a few hours' rest. He wondered if this was the end of the war and they were merely passing through the wake of souls who had fought the fight required of them and were waiting now to be assigned some place of peace.

In late August, they entered a liberated Paris and marched down the Champs-Élysées, and he did no more than take a turn at guard duty in the evening and assist engineers in the removal of barbed wire and barricades the occupying forces had left behind. On the evening before the entire division was to continue its march east, he was given a few hours' leave and slipped out of the makeshift barracks and walked the city alone. He collected a handful of holed zinc coins and bought a bottle of wine and a picture post-card of the Eiffel Tower, along with what he believed was a post-age stamp, at a shop on a corner in the Seventh with little more in it than those three items. He wrote, *I miss you* and *Kiss our boy for me* on the card with a pencil stub, addressed it to the farm, and slipped it in the pocket of his Parsons jacket. He crossed the river at the pont d'Iéna and walked into the jardins du Trocadéro, where he sat on the browned and rutted grass, the water in the fountain green and stagnant, pushed the cork into the bottle, and took a long swig of the wine. It was warm and tasted of earth and grape, and he let the flavor linger in his mouth and swallowed and took another pull. He pounded a dent in the grass with the edge of his hand, then put the bottle into it so that it wouldn't fall over. And he sat there and listened to the distant sirens, the intermittent crack of rifle fire, and the occasional rumble of a half-track rolling down the avenue along the river. He reached again for the bottle, drank deep, and put it back down on the grass.

He dozed off and slipped into a dream in which he was back among the *kumpania,* the caravan of vardos idle not along the river but in a place that looked much to him like the apple orchard in Dardan, and he searched for Jozef and Hannah, wanting them to see how he had lived before he came to them, but they were nowhere to be found. The house was there, too, but it began to recede into the distance as he gazed at it, wondering if they were inside, if he should go and look for them, but it continued to retreat farther and farther away in the dream, and a fear began to rise in him then, the fear that he would never bridge the distance to them again, even if he ran as fast as he could. And a voice behind him said, *Eh maintenant, monsieur soldat?*

He woke. A woman with a filthy-looking child at her side, the two of them dressed in rags, stood before him on the grass, holding out her hand like a beggar, and he knew who she was. Sleepy, and a little drunk still, he reached for the bottle and took a swig.

I spent all of my coins, he said to her in Romani, but I can give you the rest of this.

He held the bottle out to her, and she let go of the boy, put her hand to her mouth, and backed away as though she had seen a ghost. But he watched her, and he knew there was as much curiosity as there was hesitation in her step. She stopped and did not turn to go.

He sat up straight.

How desperate are you? he said, speaking in Romani still. He put the bottle back down in the divot on the grass, reached into his pocket, and took out a D ration. He palmed it, broke it in half against the heel of his boot, and tossed one half to the boy, who caught it in the air and began to gnaw on it. The woman put her hand down at her side again and stepped closer to Becks, as if to peer at something she had missed before.

Where did you learn to speak like that?

He took a step toward her.

Who did you think you'd find here in the dark? he said, too loud and too fast from the wine.

Not one of us.

I'm not one of you.

She held up her right hand so he could see the Hamsa Hand tattooed on the palm.

Then you are the devil, she said, and grabbed the boy by the arm and began to back away again.

You wouldn't have to look far to find him here, Becks said, louder for the distance she had put between them, then lowered his head and said in a voice as though speaking to himself, But I'm not the devil.

She stopped and walked a step toward him again.

How do I know?

Without looking, he took the postcard and his Zippo from his pocket, sparked the flame, and held it up to the card, then walked toward her until they were no more than a foot apart and she could see the message in English and the address he had written so neatly in a separate box to the right of it.

Because the devil doesn't write home to his wife.

The woman glanced at the message she could not read, then gazed at Becks in the flicker of that light, nodded, turned, and began to walk away, the boy's hand in hers. Becks snapped the lighter shut and watched in the dark as she tugged at the boy, who kept stopping and trying to eat the chocolate bar, against which he waged his own fight.

Sister, Becks called out.

She stopped and once more turned to face him.

He held up the Zippo and spun the striker.

Will you take it? Or is it unclean?

She made a sweeping motion with the hand that was not holding on to the boy.

Look around you, *gadjo*. Everything is *marime*.

He rubbed the black crackle of the Zippo, still warm from its lighting, and tossed it to her in the dark. She let go of the boy, caught it, and hid it beneath her wrap, all with the swiftness of a cat.

That should be worth something, he said, and thought he saw her nod.

How is it you left us? she asked.

I didn't leave. I was sent away. Like I said, I'm not one of you.

You are. I can tell.

He shook his head, and she left the boy and walked toward him yet again, until this time they were close enough to touch.

Give me your hands, she said. In exchange for the fire starter.

He held out both hands and she reached and took them, felt them, and bent them slowly, then pulled him closer to her, let his left hand fall by his side and held his right hand in hers, dorsal side against the palm on which the tattoo stared up at any and all evil that sought to trick its wearer. With her right hand she traced each one of his fingers and made circling motions in his palm, as though her finger had eyes on it, too, and, in spite of the dark, she could tell and would tell just what the story etched on this palm was. Her touch was soft, her hands strangely uncalloused, and he began to feel the pleasure of her skin searching the lines and crevices of his palm. When he looked at her, she seemed much younger, an age the rags she wore belied, and in spite of those rags, she had the faint smell of garden herbs about her. He began to feel the urge to lie down in the grass and sleep as her fingers touched and floated, touched and floated about his palm, no longer searching, it seemed, but wanting only to abide.

There is a line that fades in the early hours of your life, she said, but returns quickly. Strong but divisive. Deep. And then— then it is as though there is a new line. As though there is an entirely new hand.

She stopped suddenly and folded his fingers in and let go of the hand. When he looked at her, she had the look of neither the dissembler nor the survivor in her eyes.

What did you see? he asked.

She turned away from him.

The palm is not a place of visions, she said to the ground. It's a map of the soul and the body's journey along with it.

And the journey?

It's too dark. I mean here. Outside. Too dark to tell.

You can't? Or won't?

She didn't answer.

Tell me, sister, Becks said. Tell me if I'll go home after this war.

She looked up at him now, then stared back down at the ground and held her gaze on that ground. The boy in the shadows behind her gnawed on the chocolate. The city outside the park rumbled and cracked and seemed to wail softly, as though it were crying.

You'll go home, she said finally, and lifted her head. You'll go home. We all do in the end.

She turned and walked back to the boy, who had not spoken a word the entire time, indifferent or struck dumb by all that surrounded him as he wandered with the woman—mother, sister, companion of the road—through the city struggling once again to be the City of Light, day after day, night after night, he, too, perhaps knowing even at that age it was not hunger but hatred from which he would die. And Becks watched the two of them walk slowly across the grass and darkened park and out of sight.

2

They marched east into Belgium on a day of sun and high clouds, and the first resistance they met was a machine-gun nest in a bunker near a copse the scouts hadn't seen or didn't expect forward of the Westwall. As though in a moving picture, the sound for which was the small drum sound of boots on dirt pack, Becks saw men in the line of the column ahead of him wither, like they had fallen asleep in mid-stride, and then heard on the autumn air the rattle of guns no more sinister than stones hitting water at the bottom of a well. The captain of Alpha Company shouted to get down, and Becks dropped and pushed his hips and empty belly into the ground and listened to the groans of the wounded, until the captain ordered forward a mortar team and the squad to which Becks had been assigned, led by a sergeant from Pittston they called Big Rock. Under the cover of those mortars, the squad threaded its way toward the bunker and took position on its flank at a range of forty yards, Becks kneeling with his M1 Garand in position to fire. Two mortars found the roof of the bunker, and he watched as a German soldier stumbled into his line of sight and Big Rock whispered *Wait* in a voice that reminded him of Vinich. Another helmet and shoulders appeared and Big Rock said *Now*, and Becks fired twice and dropped both men in mid-stride. The captain ordered the sergeant to clear it, and Big Rock pushed his M1 to sling arms and leaped like a deer over the brush and past trees toward the bunker, where he pulled a grenade from his belt and slid it into the embrasure and ducked. A blast of light and smoke blew from the gun slits, and after a long moment of silence there at the edge of that copse the captain stood and told them to get the wounded back to the aid station and had the rest of the men move out.

They crossed the Our River in late September. A new private first class, who had come up along with another replacement for two men who were killed by a mine set off by a trip wire on a door frame when they were sent to check out a house in a village of nothing nowhere on that road eastward, told any man who would listen to him they were on German soil now, and he knew because he knew maps better than anyone, and according to his map, they were in Deutschland. The boy was from Edwardsville and seemed delighted with himself when he found out Becks was from Dardan and asked him as they advanced if he played any football, because his father had played for the Coaldale Big Green in the days when Blue Bonner and Honeyboy Evans played, and he'd be playing football now if he hadn't gotten drafted into a war, but it was all the same to him, because his father always said playing football in those days was a hell of a lot like going to war, and he knew because he had been in France in the Great War. Big Rock told the boy his mouth ran more than a sorry ass with the Hershey squirts, but Becks never told him to shut up, just listened and nodded, whether they were moving or at rest, the boy a constant monologue of autobiography and geographical facts. Becks thought there was something about this boy that made him seem like some messenger who had been given the job of finding them there in Deutschland, as he kept calling it, and reminding them of who they were, where they were from, and Becks didn't want him to stop talking about the corner store and the ball field at the intersection of Church and Pace, and so he let him. Then, the next day, marching since dawn, the boy telling Becks his stomach was growling like a black bear in springtime and he wished he could get some food like he got at a place he knew in Luzerne where the old lady cooked up chicken and dumplings and the old man poured the beer—You know the place I mean, Corporal, out there on 309 before you head into the Back

Mountain, the whaddya call it? Ah, I gotta piss, he said. And the boy, without permission, dropped out of formation where an old Panzer lay listing on half a track in a ditch. Becks marched on alone in the long line of men on that road, silent and waiting as he measured each step and cataloged each sound, believing the boy would catch up again. Until yards behind him he heard the hiss of the S-mine lift from the dirt, and he wondered as he dived for the cover of the opposite ditch how it was he had become so sharpened to sounds within sounds.

IN OCTOBER AND RAIN THEY CAME TO A FOREST EDGE THAT looked at once like some storybook paradise of mist and groves where there might be peace and rest for anyone who came to its edge, or a place of the lost, so thick and impenetrable it seemed, and no one who journeyed inside emerged whole, if they emerged at all. They called it Hürtgen, and they were there to relieve the Ninth Infantry, men who seemed to walk past them from out of that forest like they had left their souls in there. Anyone who could walk was carrying the wounded. No one asked where the dead were. And they passed by them in their weariness and retreat for the length of a day, two by two on that road, the only way out, until there were no more, and the men of the Twenty-eighth tightened their packs and shouldered their rifles and mortars and machine guns, and slipped in their own ragged line of twos into the same forest shade. As though passing from a clearing into a cave. Until it was night, and darkness covered every inch of moss and stony ground.

The enemy didn't need scouts to know that men had gone and other men had taken their place. They needed cloud cover to fire their 88s from positions near the town of Schmidt (the division's objective, passed down from Major General Cota) without fear of Allied air attacks, and just before dawn of the second day after the Twenty-eighth had arrived in Hürtgen, the light so slow in coming it seemed the world itself had settled into something no brighter than gray, artillery rounds began whistling and dropping onto the trees like rain. Men rose and died in a matter of steps, some from the rounds, some from the splintering trees that flew like javelins when they exploded. Captains shouted for companies to form up and take position, and those who could did, and they moved forward in those woods like fossorial animals pushed out from beneath the leaves by a predator determined to hunt them to the end. Pushed out in slow and peakless waves over every inch of that ground, day after day, week after week, month after month, advancing, digging in, advancing again through woods so desolate and racked by then, there was—in spite of the exploding and opening canopy of trees—an inherent darkness about the place.

The high command insisted Hürtgen was the way into a weakening German army beyond the Siegfried Line and the towns east of it, yet it was forest defended by men fighting on and for their own land, men who seemed able to anticipate every waking move of those gathered against them. When the infantry advanced beyond the mines and paths of the Tiger tanks they had disabled with pipe bombs made from metal tubes and jeep parts, they found bunkers with interlocking lines of sight from one nest of MG34s to another, and no chance for a soldier to discern from which direction came the round that would kill him. It was not the first man they took out but the second and third man in line, Becks realized one morning when he and Big Rock moved side by side in an attack meant to be a dawn surprise, and they heard the burst and could almost feel the wind from the rounds that traced behind them. Becks turned as he crouched and saw two replacements attached to their platoon drop as if they had stumbled and fallen. He and Big Rock split off and sat hunched down in their positions until the guns were silent. Big Rock tried to wave back the unit coming after him, but the guns opened up again and they were cut down, too, this time from the bunker to Becks's left. Then the woods were quiet. Big Rock motioned to Becks and pointed to the bunker, and Becks nodded and began to inch along the ground to his left, the 34s still pointed in the direction of the advance that had ceased. When he was right on top of it, he looked to see if Big Rock was in position, then took two grenades from his belt, pulled one pin with his hand and the other with his teeth, and pushed them both inside through an undefended embrasure. The blasts knocked him to his knees.

They were folded into a third company along with the only five men left from Bravo, and Big Rock was given command of a platoon, until it was no bigger than a squad, and they formed up with another platoon under a lieutenant brought in fresh from Belgium, and this one stayed alive. Men still arrived at their sides clean-uniformed and terrified, and by the end of the day these men were dead, and still the companies and regiments of the division advanced, one after the other, as though it were farmland or floodplain before them, not primeval pines rising out of tephrite-ridden ground, so that three hundred yards and three hundred men left dead in three hours of fighting from tree to tree, stone to stone, hole to hole, where there was a hole dug by some other who had died there hours or even minutes before, was the order of battle, the ground gained measured in yards alone, the lives lost measured not at all, until both armies huddled like the prey of owls that knew their movement over open ground was movement closer to the end that awaited them.

LATE NOVEMBER AND THE RAIN CAME MIXED WITH SNOW AND the division remained in place. Becks and Big Rock moved as one now, on patrol, in advance, or sitting back-to-back in their slit trench when they were dug in on clear nights after a day of bombing raids had pushed the German soldiers into hiding, and one slept while the other listened to wind, night birds, and the sliding snap of oiled metal in an M1 cleaned while there was time to clean it. They both knew what was never spoken. They weren't good, or blessed, or even destined. They were lucky. They kept their socks dry from the rain by tucking them under their helmets. They took new boots from the new men who would no longer need them. And when it didn't rain and the planes kept pounding away at the German positions, they took off their boots and wrapped their feet in their Parsons jackets to dry and warm them. When he did rest, Becks no longer dreamed of Dardan, the farm, or Hannah. The face and body he used to conjure in any place at any moment, in sleep or memory, as though a constant companion, he could not conjure anymore. Nor even an image of his son. Not out of fear these two things would distract him, but out of an inability to be distracted, and he found in this a comfort and told himself that what and whom he loved had no place in that forest, where there was little difference between sun and shade. This was the sacrifice being asked of him, as Vinich had said, and he would walk this long road, too, until he came to whatever door he was asked to open, in this life or the next.

A week later, in December, a priest arrived with a lieutenant colonel from divisional command one evening and said Mass for the men the next day. It was the first Sunday of Advent and the Twenty-eighth was preparing to fall back, south into Luxembourg, and they formed up and marched out of the Hürtgen Forest much like they had watched the Ninth Infantry do months earlier, passing by the 2nd, the 99th, and the 106th Infantry Divisions along the way. The second Sunday of Advent (the priest attached to them now) and they were east of Bastogne, on the line in the Ardennes, though it didn't seem to matter what another forest was called. Replacements arrived every day, and except for patrols along the line, they saw no action. Temperatures dropped and snow was general, and for a week they washed and rested and ate food warmed over a fire, traded K rations for extra socks with the new guys, and slept lying down most nights. Becks and Big Rock had evening guard duty on the fifteenth and, after they turned the perimeter over to the men on the next shift, they ate a bowl of ration stew the cook had saved for them and went to sleep in the foxhole they had dug well and deep and which they had covered with a poncho and pine boughs propped up on a stick to keep the snow out.

The morning hours still dark, they woke to the sounds they knew well from Hürtgen. Rounds from German 88s whistling and turning the forest into a battlefield again, the men who knew digging in, the men who didn't looking as though there was somewhere they could go to escape the shelling if they just ran in the right direction, and they could not. Becks and Big Rock hunkered down under cover, and the barrages worsened. This was not a softening before an area counterattack, but something bigger, the shelling concerted, focused, unrelenting. Their foxhole would do nothing against a direct hit, and if they survived until daylight, there would be mortar teams ahead of the SS troops that would come in behind the cover of tanks. They knew what their commanders would do. Get in front of the shelling and meet the attack head-on. There was no falling back. Becks and Big Rock didn't wait for the lull that never came. They bolted for the perimeter they had been guarding hours earlier.

The captain was alive and ordering men to form up and push forward in the dawn, the shelling behind them now, as though the guns were anticipating retreat and so followed them in that retreat, and for a moment they were not ducked and hunched, but standing like warriors, like they had always been, it seemed. They moved out and onto the forest road and could hear the diesels up ahead in the distance, the roar like the approach to a massive waterfall, and so they left the road, and that was when the mortars began. As though the enemy could see what they were doing, those who knew what to do. And they ducked and hunched again among the rain of fire pouring in like a deluge inescapable and complete, smoke and snow and dirt flying amid the shrapnel that came with the thud and exploding *poof* of each round. They moved so close together now that their strides were nearly in line, though Big Rock was taller, and because of this, Becks ran faster in the direction of the enemy and heard the falling arc of the round he knew was coming in closer than all the others, turned back to look at Big Rock, saw the struggle in the man's eyes and pumping legs to cover the two yards that lay between them, then felt the ground of the entire forest push against him in one blast and blackened moment from that round.

HE WAS COLD AND BENT WHEN HE CAME TO AND COULDN'T MOVE from a weight that pressed down on him. A pocket of air between his forehead and chest let him breathe and he sipped short breaths and then one long one and pushed up with his shoulders with what strength he had and crawled out from under the body of Big Rock onto the snow. He had fallen into the root hole of an old toppled pine and he sat and leaned against the root mass with his head down and listened for the sound of tanks or artillery, but he heard nothing. It was coming on evening, and while there was still light, he needed to find out where he was in that light. He stood and looked around at a forest emptied of war. Shell holes everywhere. Trees snapped off and charred. Ammunition belts and canisters strewn about the ground as if they had fallen from those trees. And the new snow splotched with copper, beneath which, he knew, lay all those who had been left with him and Big Rock. Only the sound of the wind remained. He ached and he smelled and he looked down to inspect his legs and belly, then ran a hand across his face and looked at that hand to see if it held any of his own blood. He turned and gazed at the body of his friend in the hole as though to study the man. The base of his head and shoulders was open and his Parsons was red with the frozen blood. Then he climbed back down to him and levered the body so that it faced the treetops and cloud-covered sky, crossed the arms at the chest, and pulled the eyelids shut. Big Rock's rifle, ammunition belt, K rations, and trench knife were all gone, but Becks could see the front sight of his own M1 sticking out from underneath the man, and he wondered who had stripped the dead GI and not noticed another body buried beneath him. He grabbed the upper handguard of the rifle and pulled it from the dirt, took the tags still attached to the chain around Big Rock's neck, then touched his fingers to his lips.

I'll be back for you when I find the others, he said, and began walking west.

HIS WATCH HAD STOPPED AT 6:05, SO HE HAD NO IDEA HOW LONG he had been walking, but it wasn't long before he heard German voices in the distance and took cover. There were tank tracks in the snow and the clear course of battle was west, so he knew the Germans had overrun Allied positions. He waited and the voices dissipated. Then he adjusted his route a few degrees south by his reckoning and walked on. Another several miles or ten and he heard vehicles approaching from what he thought was east. He took cover behind a clump of downed trees and could see he was close to a road on which a group of four German half-tracks powered along at full speed. When they were gone, he turned and opened up a wider arc and kept walking.

Night. The sky remained clouded over and a steady snow began to fall. He walked on, listening to the occasional rumble of explosions from what sounded like Bastogne. If that was where the fighting was, he had to continue walking in the direction he had decided was south, keeping to as much of a straight line as he was able in the night by doing what Vinich had taught him to do. From where he started, he picked a landmark in the direction he wanted to travel, and when he reached it (a split tree, an exposed rock), he turned and made sure the landmark he had left was right behind. The new landmark became the old, and he walked from one to another this way for miles. It took time, but he had to be certain he wasn't walking in circles.

The snow meant the night would not be pitch-black beneath the clouds, and so he stopped when he came to pine groves and dug for cones on the forest floor, searching them for nuts. He found little and ate handfuls of snow for his thirst, until he came to in the middle of the night on his knees and couldn't remember which landmark behind him was the last one he had seen. He was hungry and wished he had searched Big Rock for anything the scavengers might have missed. He rose again and kept walking, until he was crawling and found himself halted by a collapsed and enormous oak. He turned and sat and rested his back against it, tucked his rifle under his arm, and covered himself with as many leaves as he could reach. Then his head began to nod and he fell asleep there in the forest.

He woke in a barn, stood up fast, and reached for his rifle, but it was gone. His knife, too. An old man wearing a black beret and a threadbare wool sweater stood smoking in the light by the open door. He held the cigarette in his left hand and kept his right hand in his coat pocket. He waited for Becks to see him and asked in rough English if he was an American.

Becks walked toward him and the man stiffened and pulled out an FN 1910, a pistol Becks had seen a lot of in France and on the way to Hürtgen, men trading rations and chocolate for them with villagers when they came to a town, and he'd watched a soldier take his own life with one in a foxhole in the forest during a rare lull in the shelling. Becks stopped ten feet from the old man.

How'd you move me, and where's my rifle? he asked.

The man pointed with the pistol to an overturned milking pail near an empty stall, on which sat the heel of a loaf of bread and a tin cup filled with water. Becks looked at it and looked back at the man and held his hands up as though he were firing a rifle.

Où est mon fusil? he asked again.

The man shrugged.

Mangez, he said and put the pistol back in his pocket. He pinched out the cigarette with his fingers and put the fag end into the same pocket.

Becks ate and drank, and when he had finished, the man waved him outside.

Vous parlez Français, the man said as they walked.

Pas bien, Becks said.

Je ne pense pas, the man replied, and pointed toward a large unsprung cart and a mule in the shade of the barn and said to him in French that there were four barrels and a large swatch of canvas in the wagon and that he wanted Becks to climb into the back and hide under the canvas behind the barrels. He told him there were civilian clothes in there as well and that he should change into them and bury his uniform under the pile of manure in the stall. And quick. If he were caught, he'd be shot regardless of whether his clothes were those of a civilian or an American soldier.

Becks stood looking back and forth at the cart and the old man. He knew he could overpower him, take the pistol, and take his chances finding Americans somewhere before the Germans found him. The man seemed to know what he was thinking and walked toward Becks, took the pistol from his pocket again, and held it by the barrel with the grip out.

Prenez-le, he said. *Il contient sept tours.* He gave Becks the trench knife, too.

Twice they were stopped, each time by German soldiers. He could tell by the sounds of boots and the snapping of weapons that followed the questions and commands from one man. The soldier asked the old man where he was going and the old man said he was on his way to a small village called Uz, where he was delivering the barrels to the owner of a tavern there. The commander ordered him to throw back the tarp that covered the barrels and the old man did, leaving it heaped on top of the pile of canvas under which Becks hid with the pistol in his hand. Becks heard someone knock on the staves with the butt of a rifle, then the commander said to look inside. When they pried off the top, one of the soldiers said he was hoping there would be a pretty little French thing hiding in at least one of them, and the other men laughed. Then the commander told the old man to stay on the road or he'd be shot.

Long stretches of riding, the cart cramped, the path rutted and tortuous. He was cold beneath the canvas and hungry to the point of delirium when they stopped and someone lifted the edge of the tarp and canvas and Becks thought he was found. He hefted the pistol like a great weight in his hand and an old woman pushed a small block of moldy cheese and a gourd filled with water at him. He caught a glimpse of the sun setting through clouds in a field to the west. He ate and drank and drifted in and out of sleep—hours, days, he didn't know—until he heard the barrels being rolled from the cart and onto the ground. Then tarp and canvas were thrown off and he sat in daylight wide-eyed and exposed like a child.

In front of him was a man not old and not young, dressed for hunting, it seemed to Becks, in a red-and-black wool coat, wool trousers, and high boots, as though in costume for some Christmas pageant to which he was going from there. His face was expressionless and he didn't lift a finger to help. Becks stood, stiff and sore, put the pistol in the pocket of the coat he wore, and climbed down from the cart. They were at a crossroads. Two roads from the north and south. Two roads to the east and west. The four empty barrels were lined up neatly in a row on the north-south road in the snow.

Où suis-je? Becks asked.

The man didn't answer. He handed money to the old cart driver and pointed down the road to the west and told him that was the best way. Then he walked over to the mule at the front of the cart, took a carrot from his pocket, and gave it to the mule to eat. He patted the animal and rubbed its neck, checked the rig, and climbed up onto the cart and took the reins. He looked down from there at Becks.

I once knew a great horse trader of the Lovari Roma who would wait outside a village to see what kind of jackets the men wore, he said to Becks in English, accented and correct. When he wanted finally to enter the village and do business, he would take from a selection of coats with which he traveled one that looked best, like what the locals favored. And he sold a great deal of horses that way. *Attends ici.*

He shook the reigns and the mule stepped indifferently down the road to the east.

It was morning and cold, but as the sun rose, the day began to warm and all he wanted was food. He was about to set out in the same direction down which the man had driven the cart when he heard in a slow crescendo from the south the sound of horses, wagons creaking and rolling, and then voices speaking a language that was not French, or German, or English. A language he hadn't heard spoken in what felt like a lifetime, but every word of which he knew and understood and was drawn toward, like a man in the desert drawn toward a well, and all he could think was that they were too loud, that they'd all be captured if they traveled making that much noise, but the sound of the wagons and the voices kept rising.

They were a small *kumpania* of Belgian Roma in four vardos and they seemed unsurprised to see Becks standing in the middle of the road next to the four empty barrels. Two men in the front seat of the first wagon got down and rolled the barrels to the back of their wagon and loaded them inside. Then the one who had been driving went to Becks and extended his hand.

Good morning, my friend, he said in a Rom way. You are surprised to see us?

Becks didn't answer. He wondered if it might be a trap. If it was, it was played well, and he might just as well play the prisoner as the soldier now, but it was not.

The man's name was Jan, and he seemed no different in demeanor, clothes, hat, or mustache from Becks's grandfather, the man they called Meska, and he told Becks he would have to ride up front with him in the cold for now, because he was forbidden to ride with the women and children, and he smelled too awful for the men. Jan made room for him on the box and touched the horses forward.

They halted the caravan at dusk near a creek that rushed fast with the snow that had melted into it with the warmer days, but the temperature was dropping and he heard someone say it would be cold until Christmas now and more snow was on the way. From one wagon came the children, from another, the women though they avoided being seen by him and were like ghosts, the presence of whom he saw only in the shadows of their passing. In a third were the men, some older than Becks, some younger, all of them easy in their moves and brash and demanding when they spoke. The fourth wagon held supplies, and while the women lit the stoves and began to cook, the men took two of the empty barrels down from the first wagon and disassembled them, examining the inside of the hoops, where a message was scratched into the iron of one. They each had a turn reading and agreed on what it meant. Then the youngest of the group threw the hoops back into the wagon and split the staves for firewood.

Jan came to Becks and handed him a bar of lye soap and told him indeed the men said he smelled too bad to be around, and they were building the fire for him so that he could bathe in the creek. Becks nodded and took the soap, walked down to the bank of the creek, stripped naked, and waded into the icy water. He had not bathed his entire body since Paris, and he found the deepest part of the creek and went under, then came up and began to wash with the soap, which stung the sores and raw skin on his arms and legs and hips. He shouted and began to shiver from the cold and heard the men on the bank laughing, but he would not emerge until he had scrubbed off the stench that clung to him. He went under a second time, then walked out of the creek, stiff and still holding the soap, and collapsed on the bank in the snow. Two young boys ran to him and helped him up and wrapped him in blankets and walked him to the fireside, where Jan gave him coffee and new clothes and a hat. Becks dressed slowly and with great difficulty and sat as close to the fire as he could until he stopped shivering and began to feel warmth coming back.

That night they ate stew made from the meat and offal of

rabbits, which Jan said they'd had the good luck of taking from a large warren they had found, along with mushrooms, onions, and potatoes the women had stored. Becks ate in silence among the men, listening to their talk, until the one they called Pulika, the one who seemed the leader by sheer force of character, asked Becks if it was true that he could understand everything the men were saying. Becks nodded and said yes, and the men laughed again and told one another he was good luck and a good sign, now that he'd taken a bath. When the laughter died down and they finished their coffee and a bottle of šlivovica came out, Becks asked how they knew who he was and where to find him.

For better or for worse, my friend, Jan said, rumor is always one step ahead of your arrival.

He told Becks they were traveling from Switzerland later in the season than they had ever done because of the war. They had to keep moving, even in winter, when they would rather park their wagons and fire their stoves. If they stopped, the French would conscript them, or the Nazis imprison them. They had hopes of being back in Belgium for Christmas, but word had just come to them by way of the Resistance, the same way that brought word of the half Rom, that the Germans had pushed west beyond the Siegfried Line again, and the Allies were unable to stop them. Now they wondered how far they could go before they could go no farther.

Becks told them this was true about the Germans and that his friend had been killed and he had been separated from his company in the Ardennes when the push began, and all he knew was that the ground he had once fought on as a soldier with the Twenty-eighth Infantry was now German territory. He needed to find American or Allied forces to report to and get back into the fight before he was reported missing or killed to his family back home.

The men were quiet when he was done. Some of the younger ones whispered among themselves, but it was Pulika who spoke first.

There's no chance of that now, brother. The French Resistance is the only army you can report to and not be shot as a deserter.

But I haven't deserted, Becks said. I just need to find my unit again.

Pulika nodded.

Where is your uniform? Your rifle? How is it you have gotten so far from the fighting? That's what they're going to ask you.

My rifle was stolen and the clothes, these clothes, you gave me to avoid capture, Becks said.

There was silence around the fire.

You don't sound convincing, Pulika said finally into the silence. Did you really want to find your unit after they killed your friend? Don't worry, brother. There are others like you. And they are very good at what they do. Some of them speak French, some German. All of them soldiers still. But not one of those soldiers speaks Romani like you. And that has been what's kept us alive. Romani is the code no German spy can break. The secret messages that can hide in the hoop of a barrel, or even plain sight. They used to call us devils, robbers, filthy Gypsies. They used to drive us from towns. I know you know. And now.

His voice trailed off and he looked down into the fire.

Do you know how many Nazis my brothers in this caravan have killed between Switzerland and here?

Becks didn't answer.

As many as you have killed in your battles just to stay alive, I'll wager, Pulika said.

The fire crackled and someone unstoppered the šlivovica and passed it around. A light snow began to fall.

You'll get back to your army one way or the other, Pulika said, and took another drink from the bottle when it came to him. But why not help us along the way?

THE COLD AND MORE SNOW CAME AND THEY REMAINED THERE by the side of the creek. On a night when the women and children huddled inside their wagons for warmth, Pulika and Becks tended the campfire, which did nothing more now than serve as a place around which the men smoked and drank coffee, and he told Becks that the old man, Jan, had given him quite an account of where and how Becks had grown up on the Sajó River, along the border with the Slovaks and the Ruthenians. That he had heard about this half Rom who had fled to America, and Jan wondered in a sort of amazement when he was finished with the story if this was the one they were looking for, someone who could take what they'd done among the French and build it to the east, where the Fascists were stronger, and the Russians were not.

Pulika stood then and listened to the snow hiss as it fell onto the fire.

It's all true, isn't it? he asked.

Becks nodded, and Pulika shook his head.

Fate is stranger than we know, brother. Stranger than we know.

He slung the dregs from his cup into the snow and pulled a small bottle of brandy from his coat pocket and began to take long, hungry pulls on the bottle until it was empty, then asked Becks to tell him the story.

So Becks told him what Jozef Vinich had told about his birth in the spring following the Great War. How Vinich had saved him after his mother had died, then took him to her family among the Lovari, where he was raised. And how in '33, with the rise of the Arrow Cross, he left for Miskolc, made his way through Czechoslovakia and Germany with a false passport, boarded a ship in Hamburg bound for New York, and did not stop until he had come to the Vinich farm in the state of Pennsylvania. And he believed right up to the day he married the man's daughter that he would live on the land of that farm until the end of his days, far from the people and the caravans and the long roads of his birth. Then the war came.

Pulika tossed the empty bottle into the air and caught it again and put it in his coat pocket.

What was it you were trained to do when it was war, finally? he asked.

Becks told him about language school and the interrogations in England, and the German major who knew from the moment he walked into the room who Becks was. Pulika nodded, pulled a stick burning at one end from the fire, and lit a cigarette. Then Becks told him about joining the Twenty-eighth, the peace almost that he felt as he trained and drilled with the men who were no more than infantry.

They were disciplined and skilled with what weapons they held, he said. And still they died. Along the roads from France to Germany. Along the roads that led from village to village. Right up to the edge of the Hürtgen Forest. And they died in there, too.

He was quiet then, and Pulika didn't ask him any more questions. He smoked and stared at Becks, who was staring down into the fire.

The only thing we are destined to do is die, my friend, Pulika said. But you seem to have a thread attached to you the Fates have forgotten to snip. All you can do is what you will, where you are, with what you have.

And Becks did not look up from the fire.

AFTER THE EVENING MEAL THE NEXT DAY, PULIKA ASKED HIM IF he still had the pistol he had been given by the old Frenchman who drove the cart, and Becks said yes and wanted to know how Pulika knew.

We're good at what we do, Pulika said. Come. We're going to church tonight.

They walked for several miles through the dark until they came to a village where a church bell was ringing the quarter hour before midnight, and Becks could tell by the candle-lit crèche and the villagers filing in that it was Christmas Eve. He and Pulika and a young man from the caravan went up the steps and listened to the liturgy from the distance of the porch, the smell of gardenia from the priest's incense reaching him and almost lulling him to sleep in the warmth of the people gathered there to pray.

Two hours later, they walked around to the sacristy, where the old priest was taking off his vestments and drinking coffee from a pot the sexton had placed on a counter by the sink. They spoke in French and the priest told them the officer they were looking for had been at the service, sitting in the front row with his wife and child. He'd given him Communion, but he hadn't seen him after the recessional.

I don't want it to happen here, the priest said. Not in my church. Find him in the village. Before he goes back to the front.

His hands shook as he poured his coffee into the cup and drank, and Becks saw the man's eye widen then over the rim of that cup and heard the shot from behind him as the cup smashed and the priest's head snapped back. Becks spun, and in the doorway of the sacristy an SS officer in uniform had a P38 leveled at the young man they called Hanzi, who was standing next to Pulika, and fired again. Becks pulled the FN from his pocket, dropped to his knees, and from his position on the floor shot the officer through the chest. Pulika never flinched. He looked at Hanzi writhing from the bullet wound in his back and reached down, picked up the officer's own pistol, and shot the man point-blank in the head. Then he walked out into the church, where Becks could hear him banging the pistol butt slowly against the wooden pew backs aisle by aisle, until he seemed to find what, or whom, he was looking for, and fired all five rounds that were left. Then the church was quiet.

THEY CARRIED HANZI BACK TO THE CARAVAN AT THE CREEK, AND by morning he was dead. Becks and Pulika stood smoking by the fireside while the women wept and keened for the boy and dressed his body for burial out of sight of the men.

Jan came by and told Becks and Pulika to come and have some breakfast and coffee, and Pulika nodded and the old man walked back to his vardo.

You saved my life, Pulika said to Becks as he crouched down and stubbed out his cigarette and put the butt in his jacket pocket.

It was fully daylight now and Becks could smell the food cooking in Jan's vardo.

I wish you had told me what we were going there to do.

He killed one of my guides.

He seems good at what he does. Or did.

It's time for you to go, Pulika said. Word will get out about the priest, and the villagers will be angrier about him than that German piece of shit. They'll tell the SS everything just to protect themselves.

Becks pinched out his cigarette, gave what was left of the tobacco to Pulika, and said, I don't know where I am. How will I know where to go?

You can't go with us. You need to go east. Old Jan was right. They could use you. We have today to bury Hanzi and get back on the road. By first light tomorrow, these woods will be crawling with Germans looking for us. We'll be lucky not to be shot ourselves by sundown.

Hungary's a long way from here, Becks said. My chances are better with finding the Americans.

Pulika began kicking snow onto the fire, the flames dying as the embers hissed, and he looked up at Becks.

I would say your chances are about half, brother. Same as that blood you've got. And those are better chances than mine.

The men said good-bye to him in the evening, after they had all had their supper, and Jan gave him a good wool sweater and an overcoat for the cold and told him to stay off the roads and to walk in the creek whenever he could. Pulika had him repeat to him the names of places and contacts in Vesoul and Besançon, and told him they would get him to Chamonix.

Trust them, Pulika said, then pulled him into a close embrace. One day I'll repay you. Life for a life. Tonight, though, a kiss is all.

He walked through the woods until he had lost all sight and sound of the caravan and stood in the snow by the creek, listening to the water. If he backtracked and made his way north to Neufchatel or Verdun, he would find Allied units and commanders who might understand what had happened to him. He didn't know how far west the Germans had been able to advance. And he knew that after the Germans found and killed all those in the wagons he had just left, it wouldn't be long before they found him, too, and his dangling fate would finally become the same as the Roma who had raised him and taught him and cast him from them. And he knew why now. War. It had always been war, from the moment of his birth, life on the Vinich farm in Dardan merely a brief interlude of peace and a glimpse of a world those brothers around him would never know, and tomorrow would go to their deaths never knowing. He walked from the grove along the creek and the forest that somehow smelled so sweetly still of the campfire and the food from the cookstoves, and he moved south, listening for any sounds that might be out of the ordinary in the night—diesel engines, German commands, dogs—feeling the balance of fear and resignation he had come to welcome as a sign that he was alive, and so he kept to the creek, stopping only to sleep in the woods when he had put a full day and the *kumpania* of Jan, Pulika, the other young men, and the ghost women and children in their vardos behind him.

3

He waited until dark on a side street in Vesoul and watched for German SS officers before going into the Hôtel Pétremand, where he asked the man at the desk if he was Charles, and when the man said *Oui,* he asked if there was a room with a view of the mountain, just as Pulika had told him to.

Quelle montagne? the man asked.

Le Cervin, Becks said.

The man said it was not possible to see such a mountain from so far away, but he could show him a room that would suit his needs.

They passed through a door and went down a flight of stairs into a wine cellar and through another door, entering a room in which there was a small mattress on the dirt floor and a pitcher of water and a heel of bread on a table. The man told Becks he could sleep here for a few hours and that he would wake him just after midnight, when he should continue on his way as quickly as possible.

He ate and drank and slept a deep sleep in that basement, where he dreamed he was moving along a mountain pass, beneath which a river ran swollen and fast. Each time he took a corner, the pass narrowed and the river ran faster. And yet he felt not fear but expectation that the path should narrow, the current coursing faster still, and he moved at the same rate with each bend, until around the last he was awakened in the dark without a sound by a child, a girl no more than ten. She led him into the silent lobby of the hotel, out the door, and into the night, then handed him food wrapped in a rag.

Tenez, she said, then fished around in her pockets and took out a chocolate bar.

On m'a donné ça pour Noël.

Becks leaned down and kissed her on the cheek.

Merci beaucoup.

He walked five hours through that night until the sun came up, and he slipped into the woods and ate the bread and cheese and lay down to sleep among birch and pine that stood watch over him like thin sentries who hadn't known war and never would but swayed gently above the tired body of the man just the same, sleeper in a place of peace off the road. And when the sun went down, he rose and walked through the dark another five hours to the city of Besançon.

He arrived in full daylight and a heavy snow and hitched a ride on a cart loaded down with root vegetables from the outskirts through the Battant toward the city center. On the quay of the river Doubs he could see one of the arches of the bridge was partially destroyed and he turned left and walked until he came to a synagogue, where an old woman was sweeping snow from stone steps that led to a large and carved wooden door. He stood at the fence railing and asked her in French if Rabbi Nephesh was taking students. She stopped sweeping and, without straightening her back to see who was speaking to her, walked hunched over to the side of the synagogue along rue Mayence and disappeared.

The quay was empty and he felt conspicuous in spite of the covering snow, but this was all Pulika had given him about his connection in Besançon. He turned and walked down rue Mayence in the same direction the old woman had gone, and when he had come to the end of the iron railing that surrounded the synagogue, a man opened a side door.

The rabbi will see you for lessons now, he said to Becks.

He was a tall man with short-cropped hair and lines at the corners of his eyes. The backs of his hands were chapped and sunburned. Becks followed him through a narrow hallway that led to a bookshelf that opened like a door into a room in which there were stored packs and skis and harnesses and ropes. Becks kept his hand in the pocket where his pistol was. The man closed the door to the room and began to sort two small packs, placing in each of them a pair of wool socks and mitten covers, a flashlight, and something that looked like sealskin with loops of webbing sewn to the front and back. On top of the contents he placed a block of cheese, a small round loaf of bread, and a canteen that sloshed with water inside. Then he cinched up the packs and handed Becks a pair of boots and socks, better than the ones he wore, and told him to put them on and that he could keep them, because the one to whom they once belonged didn't need them anymore.

Becks watched the man as he worked, as though brought to a standstill by all of the movement, until the man looked up and asked Becks if he was going to change or not.

Becks put on the new boots and socks and the man told him that a truck would stop outside the side door on rue Mayence at 1700 hours that evening and take them to the Haut Jura, where they would go overland on skis to Léaz. From there, an acquaintance of his would take him to Chamonix, and the guides who stood guard in the Alps and were part of the Resistance would get him over the mountains into Italy.

Becks looked up from his bootlaces.

You don't look like a rabbi, he said.

The man smiled and seemed to study Becks for the first time, his face unshaven, his coat oversized and worn, yet something about the eyes and the way he moved suggested a man still fit for a fight.

You don't look like an escaped prisoner of war. What's your name?

Bexhet Konar. Corporal. Twenty-eighth Pennsylvania Infantry.

The man nodded.

What are you running from, Corporal Konar?

I'm not. Not anymore.

The man turned and walked over to inspect two pairs of skis leaning against the wall. He picked up one and ran his fingers down the effective edge and placed it back against the wall.

Pulika told me my contacts would take me to Chamonix, Becks said. Why there? Switzerland is still neutral, isn't it?

The man paired the skis and tied them together and grouped them with a set of poles and walked back to where the packs lay on the floor.

The Resistance liberated Chamonix last August, he said. So there are no Germans there. At least not ones in uniform. But you don't know what guards you'll find at the border. Swiss, perhaps, but paid by whom? The Swiss have stayed neutral by being welcoming to both sides in this war. They harbor escaped Allied prisoners, and they buy Nazi gold. If Switzerland is not your destination, my friend, then you'll want to spend the least amount of time there as possible. How many rounds are in that FN?

It's empty.

He walked over to a canvas duffel on the floor and took out a small box.

Then you will need these, he said, and tossed the clip to Becks.

His name was Jérôme, and at 17:00 a truck that had carried fish to the market that day was waiting outside. They threw their packs and skis with poles into the back of it without speaking to the driver and he drove them out of the city along the Doubs, south through Champagnole to the commune of Syam, where the truck stopped and they unloaded their gear, accepted two salted fish from the driver to eat, and waved as he disappeared. Then they hiked to a trailhead in the forest.

The snow was deep there and Jérôme said he was glad for the early storms they had had, as it would make their way faster, depending on how well Becks could ski. They ate the fish the driver had given them and washed it down with fresh snow and sips from their canteens. Then they shouldered their packs and attached the sealskins to the length of their skis, stepped into the bindings, and set off along the trail, Jérôme in the lead with an electric miner's lamp lighting the way.

They skied hard and without stopping long into the night, the first several hours a steady climb to a ridge they followed, the snow falling still, so that all around the forest was blanketed in white. When the battery in the pack Jérôme carried went dark, they stopped and he reckoned by the length of charge and their pace that they were forty kilometers into the Jura and it was a hundred from Syam to Léaz on the other side. He told Becks he could sleep for a few hours, but no more. They had another five hours to go, but the trail would begin to turn downhill, and with luck they could make the next sixty kilometers in the same time it had taken to go forty. Becks said he couldn't sleep now and wanted to keep moving. He reached into his pocket and took out the chocolate bar the girl had given him in Vesoul, snapped it in two, and handed half to Jérôme, who looked surprised and put it slowly into his mouth and let it rest there. Then they removed the skins from their skis and stepped back into their bindings. Jérôme took a flashlight from his pocket and tucked it into a loop of webbing on the shoulder strap of his pack, and they set off across and down the ridge by the light of the torch for as long as the small battery lasted. When it dimmed to nothing, they skied in the dark, Jérôme seeming to know every tree and rock in the Jura, until they began their descent from the ridge and Becks could feel nothing but the wind as he sped down the trail, with only the shadowy outline of this man he had no reason to trust in front of him.

THEY EMERGED BENT AND EXHAUSTED OUT OF THE FOREST AND into the fields of Léaz as the morning sun rose from behind clouds that skittered fast above the tips of the forest pines, the world around glinting in the morning light. Cocks began to crow through the wind as though late in their announcing of the day, and a dog barked farther off. The snow led right to the door of a barn at the edge of the commune, and they leaned their skis against the side of the barn, pushed open the door, and went inside.

A lone man in a knit sweater that sagged at the arms looked up at them from the stool where he sat milking a single cow.

Qu'est-ce qui t'a pris autant de temps? he said to Jérôme.

Tu sais, Michel. La guerre.

He finished his milking and stood and patted the cow's spine. He looked at Becks. *C'est l'Américain?*

Oui, Jérôme said. *Un gitan aussi.*

Bon, Michel said. *Viens. Vous devez avoir faim.*

They hid the skis behind hay and went into the house and Jérôme greeted Michel's wife with a kiss. She put hot coffee and bread with butter on the table and Becks and Jérôme ate and drank without speaking. When they were finished, Michel told them both that, though the ride to Chamonix would only take a few hours, they had to go on the back roads to get there, as France was still occupied and there were Germans everywhere, and there was even talk that the Nazis were going to attempt to take Mont Blanc by way of Italy, where they remained strong.

Becks was quiet as he ate, then asked in French how it was each man he met along the way since he'd been lost seemed to be expecting his arrival. Roma, too.

Michel looked at Jérôme and back at Becks and told him it was not a question of who or what would arrive along the way, but who or what would not. Some men journeyed. Some stayed put. Regardless, each one played out the role given to him in the place where he was found. The place where fate had found him long ago.

This war we are fighting now, *monsieur le gitan,* is not a matter of anticipation, but acceptance, he said. The men who come to us are the men we fight with, the battle waged on whatever field onto which we step. If another man were to arrive tomorrow, we would do the same as we are doing for you.

What if the man who arrived were the enemy, and you didn't know it? Becks asked.

We would know, if only in that last moment before death. You see, it is like a chain. Each link is connected to the one next to it. Not the third, or the fourth. Only the one before and the one after. And so, we let the others be, trusting their link until the chain is broken by the one who comes to tell you, me, or some other that this day is the day of our departure.

ON THE MORNING OF NEW YEAR'S EVE, MICHEL DROVE HIS truck slowly past an abandoned German guard post outside of Chamonix-Mont-Blanc and lumbered up rue du Docteur Paccard and parked at Place Balmat. He took a small jug of milk and two loaves of bread into the post office and returned with two bottles of wine and a bottle of armagnac. They continued up the main street and parked in front of an outfitters store. A short gray-haired old man came out of the store and shook hands with Michel, who gave him the bottle of armagnac, and all three went in.

Midday, they emerged at the back of the store, Becks and a guide, who introduced himself only as Bruno, a small man no older than Becks who spoke little and moved with a fluid motion that seemed not to know fast or slow but modulated between continuous and steady, regardless of purpose. He had approved of the boots and clothes Jérôme had given Becks and added to their packs a white ski suit for the weather at altitude, a pair of mittens, glacier glasses, and a canteen of fresh water. From town, they hiked through Les Pélerins to the Gare des Glaciers and took the open work tram to the col du Midi. There they put on their skis and skied the Vallée Blanche into Séracs du Géant and down the Glacier du Tacul. It was nearly evening when they climbed to a small wooden refuge that Bruno called Charpoua, and they ate a dinner of dried sausage and cheese and did not light a fire. The day had been overcast and, in the alpenglow of the winter sun emerging in the west, the Aiguilles des Gran Charmoz stood before them like a shrouded guard. Becks said out loud that the war in France seemed far away out here.

Not so far away, Bruno said. We were watched by Germans as we skied the *vallée*. He pointed south in the direction of Italy. They have taken the Refugio Torino. My father died there.

And he told Becks then of the fight in the summer by the Chamoniards to break the Nazi occupation, a fight they won, with the help of the mountain guides, Swiss and French, who seemed to fight as one. But Chamonix was a loss for Hitler because it was the loss of Mont Blanc, and he was determined to put the flag of the Reich on that peak.

Then last fall, in October, Bruno said, in a snowstorm, so that no one guarding these mountains from anywhere in France or Switzerland believed they were in danger, the German mountain unit came from Entrèves at night across the Toula Glacier with the help of a man in the Jäger named Heckmair. He knew every crevasse on the glacier. My father and the others stationed in that hut had no chance. They fought until their ammunition ran out. A few escaped. The man who greeted you with Michel in town. The rest were killed. Now the Germans have a view of the entire Vallée Blanche.

He took a bite from the heel of bread he was eating, chewed it slowly, then sipped from his canteen, his breath rising in puffs of vapor as he breathed.

Yes, we were watched, he said again. But if we're only two, they might wonder if we're worth the chase.

They woke to cold and a bright sun, the sky a blue Becks had never seen before, a blue that looked as though it had descended like some master's painted backdrop to the mountains' own play of peaks outreaching one after the other toward what heavens may have released that blue, and would release more if their heights could convince them their majesty was deserving. They ate a cold breakfast of cheese and water and put on their white ski suits and glacier glasses and skied down the Mer de Glace, then up the pas de Chèvre to the Grand Montets and into the Glacier d'Argentière. Then they began their ascent to the col de Chardonnet.

For hours they skinned up the long and immutable slope of

snow, the sun rising, the wind rising with it, the glacial surface of the world they traversed a world of light and rock alone. Neither one of them spoke. They rested only to sip water before rising again and climbing on across a landscape that could consume them in a moment were it not for their skis, and they passed through the small gap in which there was little room to stand. When they were on the other side, Bruno took harnesses and rope from his pack, and they removed their skis and strapped them to their backs and rappelled forty meters down the opposite side of the *col*. They were in Switzerland now.

It was past noon when they came to the plateau du Trient and skied along the fine and trackless snow toward what looked to Becks like an unlikely hotel that high in the Alps. They stayed out of range of it, though, and skied to the south, where there was another small refuge of piled stones and a pine-log roof perched on a cliff overlooking the Aiguille Dorées. The hotel was the Cabane du Trient, Bruno told him, and there would be German officers inside, still sleeping off their New Year's celebration. It was best if they left them to their rest.

Snow fell all night and by morning the front was gone. They skied down to the col des Ecandies, then removed their skis and strapped them to their packs and took out ice axes and boot-packed up the slope for several hundred meters. When they came through the gap, the sun had broken the white and granite horizon of the mountains to the east, and they looked out across the vast Val d'Arpette, put their skis back on, and skied on deep snow another two hours through the wide-open bowl into an alpine meadow and the village of Champex-Lac, where they walked among winter guests who seemed not to know or care that there was a war on, and never once looked or even glanced at the two climbers filthy and sunburned and carrying skis and ropes and ice axes on their backs.

Bruno entered a ski shop and nodded to a man at a desk and this man led them into the store and out a back door and into the alley, where a small truck was idling. They placed their packs and skis in the truck bed and got into the cab with the driver and drove to Bourg-Saint-Pierre, where they slept in a barn next to the house where the driver of the truck lived. There were neither names, nor greetings, nor food exchanged. Only shelter. The driver woke them before dawn and took them to the edge of town, where they got out and began to hike along a path thin with snow and sprinkled with larch needles. When the snow was deep enough, they put on their skis and skins and began their ascent along the trail that led out of Bourg-Saint-Pierre.

They came to the Cabane de Valsorey just after noon. Bruno stopped at a distance from the door of the hut. He expected there to be a set of tracks laid by the guide who manned the hut, and there was, along with the imprint of a single pair of poles. But when he looked closer, he could see there were tracks inside the single track. He followed these along his line of sight and saw by the door the place where one of the other skiers had put his poles, too, into the snow. Bruno thanked him for his mistake, held a finger to his lips, and pointed to the tracks for Becks, and they skied away from the hut in tracks of their own making.

They bivouacked beneath a shelter of rocks that could not be seen from Valsorey and put on every article of clothing they had, then their white ski suits, and huddled in the snow against the ledge. Bruno told him there were Germans in the hut, he was certain. Jäger forces who had likely come up from the Italian side and did not want to be seen by the way they had approached. There was no telling if the Swiss guide in the hut was dead or alive. They would get what sleep they could and rise early to climb the plateau, then continue on to the col du Sonadon, and make their way to the Cabane de Chanrion, if the Jäger hadn't seen them by then.

In the morning they rose without speaking, so cold was it, and they packed up and put crampons on their boots and began the ascent to the plateau du Couloir, the sun low and south in the winter sky. At the traverse, Bruno looked back and told Becks they were being followed. Six armed Jäger beginning their ascent. At the plateau, they removed their crampons and put on their skis, and Bruno bemoaned the good weather and the tracks they would leave. Then he clasped Becks on the shoulder.

We have a descent, a short climb, and then another long ski down the glacier, he said. Stay right behind me. These men are fast, but if we can make it to Chanrion, there are others there who can help us. If not, then we'll be frozen together for a long time, my friend. *Es-tu prêt?*

Becks nodded and they took off in single file down the glacier.

The skiing was not easy, and as much as Bruno seemed to want to drop as fast as he could in a straight line down the snowfield, he would pick one line of descent, abandon it, and begin another. Becks knew in his exhaustion he was slowing his guide down, but Bruno stayed with him and told him, when they came within earshot, that the crevasses were large and everywhere on this glacier, and the new snow made them difficult to detect. He looked over his shoulder even as he spoke.

Allons-y, he said in a resigned tone.

And they skied on.

At the col du Sonadon, Bruno and Becks both could see that the Jäger had topped the plateau and begun their own descent. Bruno looked at Becks and nodded and they skied through the pass and Bruno halted below it and told Becks there was only one way to stop them now. He riffled through his pack and took out a grenade.

You have to keep going, he said. Fast, if you are going to get out ahead of the avalanche.

But the crevasses? Becks asked.

One way or the other, Bruno said, and seemed to smile.

Then he told Becks not to worry, that he'd be right behind once the slide settled, and he reached into a side pocket on his pack and took out a compass and handed it to him.

Take this. Follow the glacier and ski southeast. You won't see Chanrion until you're right on top of it. God be with you, my friend.

Then Bruno began to climb up the rocky side of a convex slope that led out and onto a ridge, at the top of which a massive cornice of snow overhung, and Becks watched his guide scramble across the ridge like a goat born to it. Becks turned and poled down the mountain as fast as he could.

He looked back only once before the ridge and snow were out of sight, and he saw the figure of Bruno on the slope above, the six Jäger skiing in short turns down the snowfield that checked and crossed the tracks he and Bruno had laid so meticulously there. Then he watched as the guide who had brought him through these mountains leaned back to throw the grenade like a bowler on a cricket pitch, and the Jäger in the lead stopped at the face and raised his rifle. Bruno, arm out still, tumbled off the ridge, the sound of the rifle crack whipping across the glacier in the space of a breath. Then there came the low, muffled thump of the grenade blast Becks could feel in the ice beneath his feet. And he watched as the massive cornice of snow began to break and slide with the growing roar of something that sounded as though the mountain itself were separating from the earth, those men of the Jäger helpless and scrambling now in its path. And Becks turned and kicked hard in his skis and the new snow and descended fast.

HE FOUND THE HUT AT CHANRION FLYING THE SWISS FLAG, BUT empty of anyone who might have raised that flag on the pole visible as he came up and over the rise toward it. Inside, there were still bags and ski suits on the floor and maps and some food on a table, but whoever had left them had done so quickly. He looked for blood, but there was none. He packed what he could use, went back outside, and continued in a straight line by his compass until he came to La Sengla. He made his way along a route that wove itself in and out of the invisible border between Switzerland and Italy in that final year of the war. Some nights, he slept in a *refugio* that was no more than piled stone topped with a slanted tin roof. Other nights, he bivouacked, shivering inside two ski suits, in what shelter of a ledge he could find, the ground bereft of anything that would burn above the tree line, until the Matterhorn rose before him like a crooked prehistoric tooth.

Days later, he came to a wooden hut built along the approaching ridge and found a blind old man inside who sat alone at the door, unfazed by the arrival of the climber. He stared blankly at some spot above the window where light shone and patted a Luger tucked into a belt outside his knickerbockers.

I won't hurt you, Becks said in German, and the old man nodded and told Becks to come in and close the door, then motioned to a chair at a table on which there stood a glass of goat's milk, as though waiting for the traveler. Becks drank and the two sat in the quiet of the hut for a long time, the old man's eyes opaled and cataractous and flitting in the light as though in constant search of it.

Are you alone? Becks asked finally, and the man said he was and that all of the guides and the guided who had come through were traveling west now across the Haute Route, back to the Vallée Blanche, where they knew there would be a fight for Mont Blanc against Hitler before the spring. Becks asked why they had left him here, and the man smiled into the light, waning now in the shortened day, and said he could not guide anyone anymore because he couldn't see, and only came up to the hut when his son roped him in and brought him here, and this is where he would stay until his son came back from France and the fight for the mountain. If his son did not come back, he would die here, too, and happily, because he knew no life other than these mountains. He said his name was Bernhard, and he spoke of the men he had known in the war, guides who had fought and died, Allied prisoners who had escaped and come to Switzerland and found themselves fighting with the Resistance, too, not because they could not go back to their army but because they did not want to. Did not want to leave the mountains once they'd come. Could not leave the mountains, even if the borders themselves opened up and asked them to leave, let alone armies ordering them. He spoke of the Great War before this one, how he had served in the Tiroler

Landesschützen of the Austrian Landwehr, when the Dolomiten did not belong to Italy, and he led men and machines and matériel high into those peaks where men died then just as they died now, and still the mountains changed not at all.

He stood and lit a candle and sat down again and stared at the flame.

You are welcome to stay and wait for the others, he said.

Becks thanked him and said that he would be grateful for a warm night's rest, but he had to leave at first light.

So you're going to fight?

Yes, Becks said. But not for the mountain.

And he told the old man of his journey in the American army and the battles he had seen against the Germans, the ferocity with which that enemy fought on its own soil, and the battle that finally broke the lines of the Allies in the Ardennes. He told the man about the death of his friend and being lost in the forest after the battle, like a blindness, too, he said, and although he had not met a single man in the Resistance like those about whom the old man and others had spoken, he could understand why they chose to live as he had said they lived, when they found themselves free to fight other battles in the same war with different soldiers, different brothers in arms. He had seen it among the Romani who found him in the forest and who fed and clothed him as though he were one of their own. And, in truth, he was, though separated by the long road long ago. He understood now. For this and this alone he believed his fight was still far from here, and he could not stop until he had at least gotten to the place where he had lived once, because he wanted to help those who could not fight as he could. Allies, yes, but of a different land and rule and law altogether. He wished he could explain it, but he only knew that he could not return to anything or anyone he once knew, or answered to, until he had seen for himself that those who had raised him were able to fight for their own home, which was both nowhere and everywhere in these lands of constant fighting.

The old man nodded and asked if he meant the Roma people, and Becks said yes.

I have heard that they, too, have taken up arms. In the valleys. In what ways they can. You are the first, though, to have come over the mountains.

Then I have to believe I was guided here for a reason, Becks said.

Perhaps, said the man. Perhaps.

The next day, his morning meal different only in that they used precious wood in the hut to make a fire to brew coffee, Becks cinched up his pack and shouldered it and told the old man he was leaving.

The man nodded and asked Becks if he had everything he needed.

No, Becks said.

The blind man turned away from the light of the morning pouring in through the window of the hut and held his chipped ceramic cup with both hands as though it were a crystal ball he might gaze into, if he had sight at all in his eyes.

With the Matterhorn to the north, he said, follow the glaciers until you come to a high range. The peaks you see from there are Monte Rosa and the Jägerhorn. Make your way through the range any way you can. You will have crossed into Italy, and on the same line you will come to the headwaters of the Torrente Anza and this to the Toce. When you come to the lakes, you will have to be careful to stay on the Italian side. There will be soldiers at all of the border crossings. Go east when you can. South when you must. The third of the large ones is Garda. In Riva del Garda, in an alley off of the Piazza San Rocco, there is a small tavern called Il Nonno. Ask for Antonio. Tell them in Italian, *Il cieco mi ha mandato.* You'll get what you need. And God be with you.

WINTER DAYS OF WIND AND SNOW, THE TRAVELER PASSING through them guideless, gaunt, and alone. He climbs through the only *col* he can see that will offer passage through these mountains, between the two peaks of which the blind man spoke. When he picks up the river, he sleeps huddled against large rocks and covers himself each night with layers of pine boughs hacked from trees with a trench knife Jérôme had given to him before they parted, and he follows that river to another, and then to the lakes. From high cliffs that overlook the third, he makes his way down into the center of the town at the lake's northern tip and begins to search for San Rocco. His skis are still strapped to his pack and he doesn't know if this means he will look ordinary or suspicious. He sees the tavern as though he has been steered in that direction. It is dark and long past the mealtime and he knocks and a woman answers the door. He says he is looking for Antonio and that the blind one has sent him. She hesitates for a moment, opens the door to let him in, and closes it behind him.

HE LEFT RIVA DEL GARDA BEFORE DAYLIGHT WITH A SULLEN AND stale-smelling young man who was dressed as though he might be walking across town, even there in the winter. They hiked up into the hills and six hours later entered Rovereto. There he handed Becks off to another man, who spoke to him in Austrian German and asked him if he was the one trying to get to Hungary through Yugoslavia and laughed when Becks said yes. They continued on to Folgaria, a full day's walk, and did not stop when the sun began to set. They hiked in the evening dark along what the man called the Passo del Sommo into the hills and pine forests and emerged onto a height where an old and massive fort rose out of the ground. Fires were visible on the parapets outside, and this guide turned to Becks and told him that when there was cloud cover, there were no bombers, and so the men lit these fires to stay warm.

For three days he lived among six other men and his guide in the Austrian outpost of the Folgaria Plateau they called Fort Cherle, listening to them speak an Italian he couldn't understand, and being spoken to in a German he barely could. They did little but melt snow for water over fires they made with the deadfall of pine from the forest and brew coffee that tasted like the burned pitch of the pine. The bread was stale and this they ate with salami a runner brought in from San Sebastiano. No one thought to track a deer or even a rabbit, and when Becks asked if he could have a rifle to hunt for food, they scoffed at him and told him that was a good way to get himself shot.

On the fourth day, he left with another *zingaro,* as they called him, a man named Petalo, who told Becks he understood where it was he wanted to go, and that there were Roma, too, among the Yugoslav Partisans, and they alone knew the way into Hungary without detection. From the fort, they moved northeast, passing Lago di Caldonazzo and traveling along roads that skirted the base of mountains that offered passes through which they could continue east without a full ascent of the peaks of the distant Dolomites, until Mount Marmolada rose to the north of them. A storm was coming over the mountain and they remained there in an old farmhouse in the Val Venegia, where they built a small fire and cooked a scrawny hare Becks shot with his pistol, and slept on planks of what had once been bunk beds. In the morning they made their way into the town of Castellavazzo, on the Piave River, where they deliberated over whether they should trade the pistol or the knife for food, and they decided on the pistol. Petalo said there would be plenty of weapons among the Yugoslavs, but a knife was a tool for many things, including saving one's life.

They ate well that night on a supper of polenta and mushrooms brought to them by a husband and wife who ran a tavern called Il Portico, and with their packs stocked with salami and cheese for the journey, they crossed the Piave in the morning and continued east, Petalo telling him of an older brother he once had who fought and died in the Great War with the Austrians on the banks of the river they now called Fiume Sacro alla Patria, though there was nothing sacred about where they were going.

They walked out of the mountains along the torrente Cellina down to Lago di Barcis, where they hitched a ride on a Fiat 626 carrying mail all the way to Udine, and there they spent the night and rose before daylight and walked nine hours to the border of Yugoslavia. They slipped across the Soča River at the town of Kobarid with the help of the partisans who kept the Germans away, and slept in a barn at the edge of a hay field crisscrossed with white and empty drying racks like storks asleep in the snow. The next day they climbed in the direction of Triglav and stopped finally to rest in a hut on a ledge above the tree line overlooking the valley below.

In the morning, Petalo hiked into the forest for wood and returned to build a fire and boil water in a pan left there by travelers before them, and he and Becks drank pine-needle tea with a breakfast of Friulian soppressa they had bought in Udine. From the window of the hut, Petalo pointed to a small herd of chamois in the scrub and snow and lamented that they had neither the pistol nor a rifle, because there was nothing better than chamois roasting on a spit, though there was no time for a roast even if they had a rifle. The partisans would be coming that day or the next.

Becks asked him if he would be leaving then and sending him on to Hungary with them.

No, my friend, Petalo said. I'll be leaving with you.

You said this was as far as you would go.

I said this is where I would bring you. I needed time to watch and decide if you were who they said you were. If the story they told was true.

They, Becks said.

The old ones.

And Petalo told Becks that he, Petalo, was a young boy when the Austrian soldier they called Vinič brought the half-Rom baby to their *kumpania* on the Sajó after the Great War. He had just received word of his older brother's death on the Piave, a brother who insisted he fight for the emperor, against the strong counsel of the others who told him no emperor had ever given any Rom a reason to fight for him.

But my brother went, Petalo said, joining a Slovak Marsch batallion, and I only remember my mother kissing him good-bye on a day in autumn. We never saw him again. So when the soldier and the baby arrived in that spring of 1919, it seemed something so miraculous that my own brother's return became possible, as well. I saw in that baby a reason to continue to believe, even, as the years went by and the baby grew into a boy, when I understood finally that my brother was never coming home. I attached myself to the boy and to his *puro dad,* the man after whom my mother had named her son, but whom we called Meska, the only one interested in welcoming the *gadjo*-Rom into our midst, because he said God commanded us to care for the widows and the orphans.

For in you the fatherless find compassion, Becks said. I remember he used to say that.

Petalo nodded.

Often, he said. And when the old women would turn from you and make their noises and do all but spit on the ground you walked on, Meska would say to them, *And if we slit his throat right now, neither one of you crying out like frightened birds would be able to tell me which part of his blood was* gadjo *and which part Rom, would you?* Then he would take you and me by the hand, and we would walk down to the river, where he gave you a stick to play with, and I would ask him, *Are they right, Meska? Is it his blood that is* marime? And Meska would say, *No, Petalo. His blood is just blood, like yours and mine.*

Becks looked out at the sun in the east rising over the mountains and pouring in through the window of the hut as he listened. And when Petalo was finished, he said, I remember those days along the river with Meska. I remember how mean the women were to me. How kind he was. But I don't remember you.

Because when I was ten, Petalo said, my mother died and my father remarried and we moved to another camp along the Hornád.

And though I would see Meska when our camps came together, the rise of the Arrow Cross made it more and more difficult every year, until it was impossible. That was when I heard you had left. On a day when a group of men from Meska's *kumpania* coming back from Miskolc were murdered outside the camp, and the ones who did it left messages on the bodies saying the women and children were next. Our *kumpania* never stopped moving then, into Czechoslovakia, back into Hungary, sometimes to the edge of the Soviet Union if we needed to, until they found us, crossing back over the border of Hungary in the spring of '39. Those men who couldn't escape were sent off to camps.

You escaped? Becks asked.

And I've been fighting ever since. Eye for an eye. I've not reached the number yet. Nor have I many more to go.

There was quiet then between them, until Petalo spoke again.

I can take you to him. Meska. He's alive still, or was last I heard. His wife died some years ago and he remarried, the old stallion. I'm told he has a baby son, even though he must be well into his seventies. Yes, I can take you to him, he said. That will be our first visit. So that this journey will mean all the more to you when you two embrace again.

THEY STAYED ANOTHER DAY IN THE HUT, THEN HIKED OUT OF the mountains and followed the Sava into Ljubljana. On the outskirts of the city, they tucked into a bookstore, where a man took a photograph of Becks and told them to come back at midnight and he would have the papers ready. Petalo asked if he had any ration cards for food, as they had just come over the mountain, and the man gave them what he thought they might need for dinner and a drink.

In the morning they traveled east with a partisan named Ivo to the village of Hodoš, on the border, and there they slipped into Hungary through the forest and walked to Őriszentpéter, where they boarded a train for Budapest after their papers were perused by a soldier on the platform who seemed caught in a balance between suspicion and boredom, until the latter won out. The train pushed along the frozen length of Lake Balaton for miles in the evening twilight and terminated in Érd because Budapest was under siege. In Érd they moved south of the city and away from any Russian forces they might encounter, walking from one village to the next, past Miskolc to Sátoraljaújhely, where they spent the evening with a Romani man who had moved his family to the city when he found work in a factory there, and it was this man who told them that the *kumpania* in which Meska lived with his wife and young son could be found along the Bodrog now. And, in the morning, as it was Sunday and he had no work, he took them there in a cart large enough to be drawn by two horses.

SMOKE ROSE IN THE DISTANCE AS THE CART APPROACHED, AND Becks and Petalo jumped down and the driver turned the cart around and left. They walked the quarter mile to the encampment along the river, the outlines of vardos emerging, then their colors and quirks of shape, though all of them brought to rest, it seemed, by the cold. The excitement Becks felt as they approached slipped to caution at what the silence all about him spelled. Not a dog barked. Not a child laughed or yelled. Not a sound rose from the banks on which they were encamped and where these two who had traveled through war from the Austrian alps to the Danube plain found them, in the place where each man believed he would find a place of peace. They could see then what was there, what was left of the *kumpania,* the war having found them, too, finally. Petalo cursed, and the two of them ran toward the vardos, some having burned down to the wheels like boats caught fire and smoking now on a lake of dirt. The bodies of boys were sprawled in blood dried and frozen on the ground, holes of blackened red in the backs of their heads. Inside the vardos, women held their lifeless babies and lay in the same manner of death. From wagon to wagon Becks wandered, whispering the name of his grandfather, as though doing so would release some charm to protect him. But he recognized nothing and no one. No wagon painted or decorated in a way he remembered from his childhood. No one he would have known or grown up with lying among those dead. *Perhaps he isn't here?* Becks thought. Perhaps his grandfather had escaped once again, and he wondered only of where he might go, what he might do until the war was over, if it would ever be over, when he saw a large and older-looking vardo pushed right up to the banks of the river, so that its front wheels were sunken and listing in the sand. A hint of gold paint was all but scraped away by the years at the top edge of the roof, the shutters bolted next to the windows of the wagon a familiar robin's egg blue. The drape that covered the back opening of the vardo and faced him was the same drape he had seen for the first time when it had come off of the loom in Košice. He started walking quickly, then broke into a run, until he, too, was stumbling and listing in the river sand, and still he ran until he came to the old and now-faded drape, and he pushed it back. There was a woman he didn't recognize holding a boy no older than Bohumír at home, both killed by the same bullet that had passed through the child and into the woman's chest. And there, behind them, his head tilted too far back for rest, throat slit and clothes soaked in blood, was his grandfather, the son whose mother had christened him Samuel, arms at his sides, holding all and nothing of the *kumpania* he loved. Becks reached and clasped the drape so tight, it tore from the hanging rod, and he fell to his knees in the cold sand, crying out for the man.

4

A March rain pelted the window glass against the steady heat in the cab of the new truck as they drove from New Jersey through the Delaware Water Gap into Pennsylvania and the Poconos, then along Route 115 through Bear Creek to Wilkes-Barre. He spoke little and slept. Vinich asked him in Netcong and Stroudsburg if he was hungry and he shook his head.

I just want to get home, he said.

When they pulled into the drive along the orchard and Vinich parked, Becks looked out at the path of paving stones that wound through the grass and stopped at the porch with its granite steps and white columns and picture window trimmed in stained glass. It could have been the day he stood there for the first time. He got out of the truck and walked through the rain to the porch. Hannah came out with a wool blanket and wrapped it around him and they stood in that embrace and shivered and wept. Then she took her head from his shoulder and held his head in both hands and kissed him on a cheek rife with stubble.

I've got a nice fire in the stove in the kitchen and there's soup and coffee on, she said.

They left their coats and wet shoes in the foyer and he waited there for a moment as if to listen to the house. The ticking fusée. The settling boards. The rain outside running through the copper downspouts. He saw his reflection in the pier glass and turned away from it as he followed her down the hall and into the kitchen and pulled a chair out and sat down. She ladled soup into bowls for him and her father and poured coffee and set their lunch on the table. Then he heard the footsteps coming down the stairs and into the hall, steps small and slow and hesitant that stopped at the entrance to the kitchen. He turned from the food and saw his son and rose and walked to him and knelt down before the boy and took him in his arms.

I've missed you, my Bohumír, he said.

He spoke little to Hannah or Vinich that day, addressing the boy mostly, asking him questions about school and the farm in spring, telling him he knew it had been a cold one. The boy answered sparingly but never asked if he could be excused, until Becks went upstairs to rest and Bo remained in the kitchen, helping his mother.

It was long after supper, around the fire in the living room, the two of them alone, when she told him what she had known of the war from the hilltop there in Dardan, how in the summer of '44 his letters came less frequently and she worried what would happen to him in Europe with the Twenty-eighth, wondering why he would have left his position in the intelligence pool at all. Father Blok, not the radio, was their source of information about what was going on overseas, and she went to daily Mass as an excuse to find out anything about where Becks was in the fighting. In early September she received his postcard from Paris, where she knew the Allies already were, and she thanked God for it. Then nothing in October or November. She didn't know what to think or do, nor did Father Blok, nor Papa, nor anybody. On the day before Christmas, she received the telegram, reading it over and over so as not to miss a word. Then she put it down and gave Bo his lunch and tried to imagine a world in which he was not. She had it with her in the pocket of her cardigan there in the living room, and she unfolded it and handed it to him. He took it and held it, saw WESTERN UNION at the top, then leaned into the light and read THE SECRETARY OF WAR DESIRES ME TO EXPRESS HIS DEEP REGRET THAT YOUR HUSBAND CORPORAL BEXHET KONAR HAS BEEN REPORTED MISSING IN ACTION SINCE SEVENTEEN DECEMBER LUXEMBOURG IF FURTHER DETAILS OR

OTHER INFORMATION ARE RECEIVED YOU WILL BE PROMPTLY
NOTIFIED = ULIO THE ADJUTANT GENERAL. He folded it up again
and handed it back to her.

They sat in the quiet of the room before the fire.

But I didn't feel as if you were gone, she said after a while. As
if you were not. Here, I mean. In the world. And I told myself I
would wait. The winter was bad, going back and forth between
cold and thaw, with snow that melted and froze, so that everything had a kind of hard shell over it and looked gray and felt
gray, and still I waited. Until spring came and I started walking
in the woods. Some days I would leave Bo with Papa and walk
all the way to the bend and back, talking to you as though you
were right there with me, willing you to be, until it wasn't as
though I believed you were alive. I knew you were alive. I only
had to wait.

Then, in July, the end of the war in Europe already two months
old, she received not a telegram but a letter this time from the
commander in the Twenty-eighth Infantry, saying that Corporal
B. Konar was in the custody of the United States Army Military
Police and that he had been arrested, tried by court-martial, and
convicted of desertion in the face of the enemy, his sentence of
twenty-five years to life of hard labor to be served in Brooklyn,
New York.

And I cried and cried, she said. Not because of what they said
you had done. But because I knew now that you were alive.

He reached across the armchair and took her hand in his and
they sat like that without speaking until the clock chimed the hour.

It's late, she said. Let's go to bed.

She stood and removed the fireplace screen and pushed the
coals to the back of the hearth and replaced the screen, then
turned to him and watched him sitting with his eyes fixed on the
embers pulsing and flameless and dying.

Becks? she said.

He lifted his head.

Are you going to come upstairs?

He nodded and looked into the hearth and still did not move.

Did you ever see the bear? he asked. On your walks to the bend?

She looked where he was looking into the fire, then turned back to him.

Once, she said. Just a week before I received the letter that you were alive.

Tell me, and then we'll sleep.

So she told him how on that day in the summer, Jozef having taken Bo to the mill because the boy kept begging him to, she wrapped a lunch, put it in a rucksack, and set out walking all the way to the edge of the land. The day was warm and humid, but the air cooled as she moved through groves of oak and beech, swaths of false cedar like a green carpet at her feet. She watched for snakes when the path rose steeply toward the top of Rock Mountain, and she had to scramble with her hands in a few places where she had been able to bound as a girl, the tree cover light to nothing until she topped the mountain and hiked to the edge of the field and saw the old Younger house alone and abandoned. And she turned and walked into the woods in the direction of the creek and the game lands and down the back side of the mountain, where the air felt cooler still, and the moss thickened and the trees grew dense in the black ground.

At the creek she sat on the large stone and felt wisps of breeze push against her. She took off her pack and walked to the edge of the water, knelt down, and listened to it babble, then cupped her hands and splashed her face. She heard movement in the brush and stared at the bank on the other side, where a black bear emerged and sat down on the stones the way babies do, legs forward and tottering slightly. The two stared at each other, neither one making a move. You've come to tell me he's safe, haven't you? she said finally. He sent you. I know.

The bear sat with only the water between them, his nose poking and sniffing the air.

Tell him that I miss him, she said, and put her head in her hands and began to cry.

And when she looked up again, the bear was gone.

WHEN SHE WENT TO VISIT HIM FOR THE FIRST TIME IN THE Brooklyn Navy Yard jail in 1945, he was sitting in a chair behind a screen of wire two layers thick, and she sat down in a chair opposite him. His black hair was shorn to the scalp and his face was thin and his shoulders bowed. They said nothing to each other. Then he whispered to her through the screen, How's my Bohumír?

They never spoke about anything in those days except the boy. If they had to discuss the case against him, it was in the most terse and necessary terms, before he turned the conversation back to Bohumír and how he wanted to see his son, see how he was growing. For two years this went on, she feeling as though she were some weary messenger who flew from the mountaintops down to the gates of the city's hell to visit a soul not lost but dangling at the precipice of loss, her hand all that held on to him, until the day she had found out from the lawyer that his sentence had been reduced because of sworn testimony brought forward by a former army lieutenant in the Twenty-eighth who gave detailed accounts of Corporal Konar's unflinching conduct in battle in the fall and winter of 1944. Out of what she could only identify as joy, she told him first that she wanted to bring Bo with her to New York to visit him. He sat up and almost shouted *No!* Then he stood and walked back to his cell before she could even call for him to wait and tell him the other news. When she returned alone one week later, he was there behind the screen, waiting for her, and it was she who apologized, changing the subject only to tell him that he was going to be released. They would not overturn his dishonorable discharge because he was taken into custody by the Red Army in Hungary and had not turned himself in like other soldiers who had been found in France and Switzerland. But he would be free soon, and that was all that mattered to her.

He nodded.

I'm going home then? he asked when she had finished.

Yes, Becks, she said. You're going home.

When he walked out of the jail in 1948 and into the rain and the truck, and Vinich drove him from New York to Pennsylvania, the country had moved on in those years since he had stood in front of the man and asked for his daughter's hand in marriage. Years of war and work and waiting. A part of him wondered now if he and Hannah might let their life become again what it had been before, if it could be. Become the land and the work and the waiting for what each season brought, a struggle that seemed like no struggle at all among the goats and chickens in the barn, and the orchards and beds outside. Only the gelding Pushkin had not survived, and he missed the horse and longed for him every time he passed the empty stall.

In June of the long summer they had before them, he asked Hannah if she would walk with him to the bend again. Most days they only got as far as the rocky base of the mountain, where he would sit to rest before having to turn back to the house. Some days he made it to the top of the mountain and walked out into the field and looked over at the old Younger house as though he were studying it for some future purpose, but they turned around here, too, and went home, because he said he did not think he could climb back over the mountain if they went down to the creek bend now. Then, on a heat-broke day in September, still summer but with autumn in the air, the two of them emerged from the forest at the mountaintop and walked to the edge of the field, and she took his hand and they set off down that side of the mountain and crossed into the woods and sat in the cool shade together on the banks of the creek.

She never once asked him on their walks or when they rested what it was he had done in the war and why. And he never offered to tell. She spoke only of what was right in front of them, and he loved her for that. He had always wanted to tell Vinich that he, Bexhet, was wrong when he spoke once of having one heart in two worlds. There was only one world and he'd been given only one heart. It was the road he walked. The long road, the Roma called it, nothing else. Too long to see that it stretched out as if over a mountain, so that what appeared a new way or diverging path was the same path, the bend of it unknown until you came up and over the mountain. He could see that now. And for this reason the woods and mountain became his place of peace. When Hannah couldn't walk with him anymore, he would rise early from their bed and watch her sleep with her hands gently holding her belly, where their second child grew. Then he would slip outside and walk into the woods and up to the mountain, where the men he had known and fought with in other forests followed him along the path and over the stones with a silence like the ghosts they were, and he would speak to them and tell them he knew they had come to him because there was nothing and no one to fear in this forest. That was why he loved it. That was why he welcomed them, too.

One morning he found Bohumír awake and sitting in the kitchen with his dog, a black Lab named Duna, as though both were waiting for him. He whispered to the boy to put his coat on, and all three of them walked the path up the mountain together, the dog bounding ahead and back to them, the boy quiet in the dawn light as they trudged through the woods, until Becks asked if they could stop to rest.

The boy and the dog were inseparable, it seemed, and Becks asked his son how long he had had her.

I don't know, Bo said. I've always had her.

Becks nodded.

Do you know what her name means?

Mama told me it's a river. Is that right?

Yes, Becks said. I like watching her, your little river. She reminds me of a little bear.

A bear? Bo said, and began to look around where they had stopped on the stone ledge. Do you think there are any up here?

I'm sure there are, Becks said. This is a good place for them to live. But don't worry. They will hear you and your Duna and disappear long before you see them.

Good, Bo said, and they watched the dog scramble over the rocks and push her snout into the leaves that covered the forest floor.

Have you ever seen one? Bo asked.

Yes, Becks said.

Because you were quiet?

Because—

He stopped and was silent for a moment, as though considering his words.

Because I needed to see him, he said.

The dog circled back to Bo and nudged his arm and Bo pushed her away.

Do you understand? Becks asked, and Bo nodded.

He knew they should keep walking and so he stood.

Let's go, he said. Mama will start to wonder where we are.

Bo stood, too.

Papa? he asked, his voice hesitant now.

Yes, Bohumír.

Did you kill any Germans in the war?

Becks turned and looked at the boy and felt a rush of anger that made him want to scold him for his question, but he took a breath and let the anger pass and knelt down in front of him so that they were at eye level.

You don't want to hear about the war, Bohumír, he said in an even voice.

No, Bo said, and hung his head down. I was just wondering if they were bad men, that's all. When you were gone and I listened to the radio with Pop, he told me you were trying to stop the bad men and that it was hard because there were a lot of them. But it would be all right if you hurt them, because they were bad.

Becks breathed the forest air and steadied himself.

Your grandfather said that? he asked.

Bohumír nodded.

Well, son. There were some bad men. That's true. And there were some good men, too. It didn't matter which one you were, though. Everyone got hurt.

So you did?

Yes.

Because you had to stop them?

Because I wanted to come back to all of this, he said, and his hand swept across the expanse of woods that was bathed in the full light of the autumn morning as the sun climbed higher in the sky.

All of this, he said again. And to you. So that I could come home to you.

Bo looked into his father's eyes, not two feet away from him.

Okay, he said.

And they set out again, walking through the birch stands and false cedar groves to the edge of the field at a small boy's pace and looked out across the morning land, then turned around and headed back down the mountain toward home.

Becks made sure he walked alone after that, though sometimes he would find Paul Younger in the woods near the bend, the man looking as though he had woken up there and would be sleeping in the same place by the creek that night, as well. Younger knew where Becks had been and he addressed him when they met with a kind of respect that might be confused for indifference but was not. The first few times they only exchanged greetings, and Younger watched as Becks walked on by. On a day in early November, though, Becks lingered and asked him what kind of game he was tracking, and Younger told him he studied all of the game there on the land, as though it were a play in which no character had a small part, and Becks said he understood this. When he asked to what end Younger studied it, the man said for the pursuit of it, and the food that pursuit brought, and because, in the end, it was just plain beautiful. The more he studied it, the more beautiful it all became. And Becks said he understood that, too.

You used to hunt with Vinich and his daughter, didn't you? Your wife now, I guess, Younger said as an afterthought.

Before the war, yes, Becks said, knowing Younger was the kind of man who forgot nothing of what he saw in those woods. He looked down at the new Grenson boots he had bought in the summer and toed the leaf litter of the floor into the black ground.

Not now, though, he said to that ground. Not anymore.

Younger shifted and listened to the quiet.

You don't want to pick it up again? he asked. Because I could take you. Be your guide, I guess you'd say. It might help with the— you know.

There was in Younger's voice a note of kindness Becks recognized, and he was grateful for it. But he didn't answer, just stared at the ground, then looked up and around, the sun bright and the wind almost nothing at all, the field in the distance through the nearly leafless trees dried and golden where the itinerant farmer who worked that field had left it fallow that year.

I've known some guides, Becks said, and I'm sure you'd be a fine one. But I just don't think I've got it in me anymore.

I'm sorry, Younger said, the kindness still in his voice. Is it about being back and all?

It's not the being back, Becks said. It's the having gone. Anyway, there'd be no beauty in it for me, like you said. Not like there used to be. I don't know that I could even hold the rifle now.

Younger nodded.

You don't need to bring a rifle. I mostly just stalk and sight my scope. And watch. Been watching you. You're welcome just to walk with me anytime. Beautiful land here is all I mean.

Well, Becks said, and turned to the man. I just might. If not this winter, then in the spring.

Younger smiled and a long scar Becks could not remember seeing rose with that smile along the man's face, and he touched his hat and they parted ways.

AUNT FRANCES POSOL JOINED THEM AT THE HOUSE FOR THE *velija* feast on Christmas Eve that year, as she had each year since Helen Vinich had died, and during the years Becks had gone off to the fighting in Europe. He hadn't seen the woman since the wedding in 1940, and she still seemed to move within some state of elegant changelessness. She wore a black dress and a white wool cardigan and a string of pearls around her neck. Hannah placed her next to Becks at the table, away from her father, and she was as spare in her conversation with him as she was with everyone except Vinich, which is to say she spoke not at all. But Becks was glad for her quiet company and thought her reticence was a result of the pain it must have taken for her to talk out of her once-broken jaw. There was a scent about her, too, a floral scent that was no flower one would find in winter, and yet that's what it reminded him of. Winter. And he remembered then the smell of gardenia on Christmas Eve in the tiny village in France, the scent rising to him from the incense the priest swung in his thurible as Becks and the others waited in the back for the vigil Mass to be over.

Toward the end of the meal, after Father Blok had taken his leave, and the others finished the coffee Hannah served to shake off the brandy and white wine they had all been drinking for toasts and with dinner, Becks felt Frances Posol place her hand on his forearm, and he smelled the movement of gardenia in the air.

I'm sorry for the friends you lost there, Bexhet, she whispered from the corner of her mouth. Petalo and the others. They still remember you, the ones who survived. The boy, even. It is said he has a vocation.

Becks froze. If it had been Hannah, or Vinich, or the prison chaplain in Brooklyn, he would not have wondered how any one of these could have known that he had lost friends there, for they had all told him what they knew from what the documents of his arrest and the documents of the trial told when they had read them in order to find out what it was this man was said to have done when he walked away from one army of men and joined up with another. But this woman knew the names, and they were not the names of men from the Twenty-eighth. They were the ones from Košice. The ones he had known no longer than the length of Advent and had avenged, knowing it was his place at the table at which he now sat that he stood to lose when he killed for them. He had not heard Petalo's name uttered in over three years. And the boy he remembered now as one to be pitied, for the lad had learned hatred and vengeance at too young an age. No, he had mentioned these to no one. Not even the army lawyer, who could have cleared him at the court-martial simply with the names. He remembered Hannah mentioning that her aunt Frances had ventured into Czechoslovakia that spring and had returned at the end of the summer more reserved and aloof than ever, and he turned to look at her and wanted to ask her how it was she knew the names. But she rose and was gone from the table like the scent of a flower in winter.

He sat there alone after the others had gone, until Hannah came from the kitchen and into the dining room and asked him if he would go to Mass with her because it was Christmas Eve, and he said no. He was tired and needed to rest.

He went back to work at the mill in the new year, and in the spring of '49 a son was born and they christened him Samuel. And Becks believed for a time that he was not lost, that there was in the man a part of the boy who had come to the farm looking for the man named Vinich, the boy who fell in love with the girl who was the man's daughter, the boy who became a man there on the farm. Not in the war. A part (not all) he understood and accepted, for he knew what the war had done, and he knew, too, what the land—forest and field—might undo, could undo, repair, bring him back to, and in this he hoped, and wondered if he might find Paul Younger on that land again, and just sit with him, as he had offered. The man who had said to him long ago that one day he'd have to accept the death of the old bear. And Becks wondered how he, Paul Younger, knew what nobody, not even his wife, cared to know.

But how could she or any of them here know what it was for him to be there, back on the land in which part of his blood not only flowed but was spilled. The blood of men and women their age. The blood of old men and women beyond her father's age. The blood of children no older than their sons. Those whose memories were his blood as well, blood he had seen at their throats, as if to speak, and he knew that while all blood, like water, flowed into ground, memory did not so easily lie down. Did not pool wet and sticky on a vardo floor, or dry in the dirt of a riverbank, until it was recognizable no more. No, no number of names passed down could bring them back now. Memory, the thing fracted and upheld like a story within a story told in whole and in part, was not subject to the same loss, but, rather, partook of some immortality, and lodged there within the soul like the inhabitant of a house left alone at the top of a hill that one day would welcome the bones and muscle of the right man. A man who could keep bones and muscle and memory together, like a cobbler keeps a sole attached to the bottom of a shoe with whatever leather or sinew he has at hand. But he was not the man. Not Bexhet Konar. He missed them. The people who knew no land. And of them, he missed his grandfather most of all. And he would turn his back on them again, even the boy he had named after the old man, and go to Meska now, if he could somehow turn, or even just divert, the river of time. He knew this in his heart. He knew this when he heard the crack of the Weatherby one morning as he emerged alone into the field at the top of the hill, though it was spring, and knew the pattern of the man who had fired it, knew from the direction of the round that the man was sighting his scope, the one Vinich had asked—had wanted—to remain for all his days in the house in the field, but, like him, would not. The one who had asked him to wait and watch with him. His guide, he said he would be. Paul Younger. And Becks stood in the wake of all these echoes of voices and memories and rifle shots and walked down along the field to meet him, this man he knew was like him, this man he might talk to again, this man who believed he could show him the way to the peace and quiet of the forest, this man who knew the bear and foresaw death, the one Bexhet Konar recognized, even from a long way off.

A SETTLED PLACE
(1973)

Ruth Younger walked the hilltop ridge in her snowshoes and came out to the edge of the field as a small herd of deer disappeared into the hemlock grove. Iron gray clouds scudded low in the winter sky and wind from the northeast pushed against her. She watched chimney smoke from the house in the distance trace a flat line that dissipated along the roof before it could rise, and she remembered all her father had told her about the house his father had built in another time. The wealth and prosperity that had allowed it. The appetites, rage, and profligacy that had sent them out. The woods into which her father took refuge as a boy, where he found a world ordered and disciplined and just, in that it meted out what it had to offer according to how determined the tracked—man or animal—were to survive. Nothing else. She missed her father more than she missed the child born lifeless on the day her father died. And yet, she would survive. She, who was to become keeper of both the land and the house when she married Bohumír Konar in the spring, grandson of Jozef Vinich, the man who had acquired the land, all two thousand acres, piece by piece, they said, when the Great Depression hit, and who willed it upon his death nearly one year ago to the day to Bohumír, whom he had raised after the boy's father died. Willed it to him because Bo was capable enough to make it a place where a family might be raised again. Jozef Vinich had seen that. Believed in that. Believed, too, in the succession of land through a family by the firstborn, considering it a blessing that this firstborn was the most capable and not a prodigal. That one would not return, and Jozef Vinich, who had been a warrior once, too, in another war, in another land, went to his death believing that Samuel Konar, the younger grandson, the one who never knew his own father, the one who seemed most like Jozef Vinich and Bexhet Konar both, wouldn't be coming home from the war in Vietnam. And although Ruth Younger had once hoped that they were wrong, all of them, and that Sam would come back to her somehow and be a father to the baby that grew in her belly then, she knew when she had to commit child, father, and an aunt who was in the car as well, to the ground that the Konar boy she loved was in ground in another land altogether, and always would be, just as they said.

She looked up and saw snow flurries on the wind. It had begun. The storm. She bent into it on the steep slope of the mountainside and trudged down that mountain toward the house.

SHE HUNG HER SNOWSHOES ON A HOOK IN THE BARN AND CARRIED wood to the porch an armful at a time. When the rack was filled, she went back to the barn for one more load, entered the house by the kitchen door, and dropped the logs into the wood box next to the stove. She took off her knit cap and shook out the icy snow, removed her coat and draped it over a chair. Black hair that once reached to the small of her back still had not grown past her ears since they'd cut it off in the emergency room last June. She ran her fingers through what was there and walked into the kitchen. She lifted the cover plate on the woodstove, fed the fire, closed it, and put a kettle of fresh water on to boil. Then she sat down to pry off her boots and felt the ring scuff the leather as she tugged on the pull loop. She still needed to get used to it, a full-carat diamond that sat on her left hand like a single burdock seed on a sleeve in autumn. It caught in the threads of her mitten, nicked the edge of the stove when she fed the firebox, and gave her a blister when she shoveled snow. Yet she would sooner have it unravel her mittens, cover her hand with blisters, or slice her boots all to hell than take it off. She had not since the Saturday morning in January when she and Bo walked the same ridgeline and he took her by the hand and asked if she would marry him and live with him in the house he had spent the previous summer and fall rebuilding to make their home. It didn't matter that the accident and the birth had left her barren. They would be a family, the two of them, and find a way to put behind them the loss of the past year. He said all this and held the ring out to her there under the open sky. She looked at the diamond and back at him and said yes.

She tossed the wet boots from the kitchen into the tray by the door and splayed out the fingers of her left hand to admire the ring. As she did moments when she was alone. As though to be sure she wore it still, before those fingers curved into her hand again.

She made tea with the hot water from the stove and let it steep while she took a small cut of beef from the refrigerator and browned it in a pot with onions and carrots and potatoes, added red wine and broth, and put that in the oven on low and went into the living room. A fire in the fireplace after dinner would help him forget work and the mill and the drive home through the storm, she thought. She knelt down and laid some large logs in the hearth, a few stacks of smaller ones on top of those, then the kindling and tinder of cotton balls mixed with petroleum jelly, a technique for building a fire Bo had taught her, having learned it from his grandfather when he was a boy.

The phone rang as she was finishing with the tinder and she took her time wiping her hands with an extra cotton ball. Then she walked to the entryway, where the phone sat on a side table, and she answered it.

Ruth? the voice on the other end said. It's Hannah. Will you have Bo call me when he gets home?

Yes, Hannah. Is everything all right?

There was quiet on the other end of the line, as though they had been cut off.

Everything's fine, Ruth. Were you outside? I called earlier.

I went for a walk. I was trying to figure out what color ground I wanted to use for a new painting I'm working on, so I thought I'd go right to the source. Until it started snowing. It's really coming down now.

What are you painting? Hannah asked, sounding uninterested.

The high field, Ruth said. It's what I look at every day. I want to do four. One in each season. God knows, I've got the time.

She laughed, but Hannah said nothing, and Ruth asked, Are you still there?

Yes, Ruth. I'm here. Will you tell him?

I'll tell him, Ruth said, and Hannah hung up the phone.

It was dark when the truck pulled into the driveway by the barn and she looked out the kitchen window, snow falling hard and nearly sideways in the beam from the porch light she had kept on. He came in looking like he had rolled in snow from just that short walk from the barn to the house, and he smiled to see her waiting.

No one's going anywhere tomorrow, he said, and brushed the snow from his clothes.

They lit the fire after dinner and sat close before it in the living room and talked of the wedding they had planned for June, the Mass at St. Michael's, the reception in the orchard at the house, the guest list not growing beyond their few family and friends. He had wanted it here, at his house, had wanted to show the ghost of the man he still spoke to early mornings at the mill and evenings in the barn, where he went to work out a problem over the engine of the old tractor he kept, that he had done his part. That he was grateful. But Hannah asked if they would have it in the orchard instead, as she and Bo's father had done thirty-three years ago. It was Ruth who said yes to this, out of gratitude, she told Bo, for Hannah's having taken her in last summer when she had nowhere else to go.

Outside, the blowing snow mixed with freezing rain and sounded like a storm of sand as the wind pushed in blasts against the window. Inside, the fire burned warm and steady down to the beech logs Ruth had placed at its base. She put her head on his shoulder and looked at the ring on her finger.

Second thoughts? he asked.

She turned to look up at him.

The only thoughts I have, in no particular order, she said, are why does time seem to want to mess with us, and how did I get so lucky?

He pulled her in closer and stared at the fire.

I don't know. It may be as you say. Time messing with us. We all get to the same place in the end, though.

He stroked her hair from the temple down behind her ear and she could feel the calluses on his hand and fingers, remembering the day of the hurricane, the downpour at the creek side, when he held those hands out to her and she placed her child in them, and he dripped rainwater onto its forehead and whispered the words of baptism he knew somehow she and the baby both needed to hear.

I've got a share of that luck, too, he said.

THEY ARE GENTLE WITH EACH OTHER THAT NIGHT, AND EVERY night, in the bed he cut and shaped and turned at the mill. Gentle out of habit. Out of having had to wait for her to heal after the accident in the month of the flood. *He is still waiting even now,* she thinks, and knows he always will be waiting until she tells him she is healed. And she is hungry tonight. She has longed for him all day, ever since she watched him leave in the morning, as she does every morning, believing in some small part of her that one day he may not return, either, though he is only going across town. She moves from beneath the sheets then and straddles him and whispers to him as they make love, and they exhaust each other, then lie listening to the wind blowing down the mountain and against the upstairs bedroom window that faces east, wind with a ferocity that does not abate even as they fall asleep beneath the eiderdown in the cold room, and let morning come when it will.

SHE WOKE TO SLIVERS OF DAYLIGHT THROUGH THE CURTAINS AND the smell of coffee and breakfast and wood smoke. She went downstairs in one of his flannel shirts and found him putting slices of bread soaked in egg and cinnamon on the iron skillet. She could hear the muffled roar of the fire in the firebox and she sat down at the kitchen table.

You let me sleep, she said.

He nodded and poured a cup of coffee and placed it in front of her. She wrapped her hands around the mug and the ring clinked, and she sipped and held the warmth to her face and put the cup back down. He set a plate of the toast at her place and one at his and sat down across from her.

I meant to tell you, she said as she poured maple syrup on her toast and cut into it with a knife. Your mother called yesterday. She wants you to call her back.

About what?

She wouldn't say. Called a few times, but I was out walking. She must be lonely over there in that big old house. No one around anymore.

She wouldn't be happy anywhere else but in that house.

Maybe. But that doesn't mean she won't want some company every now and then.

Well, why don't we put on our snowshoes and go see her? A little thing like a winter storm shouldn't stop us.

You don't want to call first?

She's probably got a leaky faucet. Or is wondering why some light keeps flickering on and off, damned wiring in that place.

I don't know, Bo. That doesn't sound like Hannah to me.

Eat up and get dressed and we'll go find out.

They moved quickly over the snowpack that had fallen on the frozen crust that set from the freezing rain at the edge of the storm. Ruth walked out front, taunting Bo to move faster as they climbed the hill and tucked into the trees, leafless and limb-heavy, her pace quick and urgent almost, over Rock Mountain and down the path toward the farm, coming out by the orchard. She walked right up to the back porch and waved to Hannah in the kitchen window as she took off her snowshoes and leaned them against the side of the house.

The kitchen felt too warm as they came inside, the stove over-fed and the thermostat turned up.

Hannah seemed more distracted than happy to see them and offered them coffee and a slice of nut roll.

You didn't call first, Hannah said to Bo.

Do I have to?

I asked Ruth to tell you to call me.

I told him, Hannah. He wanted to come over in person.

Hannah looked back and forth at the two of them as though uncertain about which one to scold, then sat down.

All right. Better to tell you both.

They remained standing in the overheated kitchen and she looked up at them, puzzled now, it seemed, rather than angry.

Well, sit down, dammit, she said.

She paused, took a deep breath, and shook her head.

I don't know how to tell either one of you this, so I guess it's best just to say it. I got a call from the Navy Department yesterday morning. They've found Sam. He's alive. In a prison in Hanoi. They didn't know because the North Vietnamese were busy inter-rogating the officers, and because Sam hasn't said a word to any one of them since they captured him. They think he was wounded, but they know he can walk. That's all I know. All anyone knows. But there it is.

Ruth and Bo looked at each other and Bo turned back to look at his mother.

He's alive?

The question sounded to Ruth more curious than perplexing. As though Bo had stumbled on a problem that needed sorting out. Not one he could solve, like ordering board feet of timber, or adjusting the axial play of a saw, but one he could not. Like when his mother told him she spoke to his father when he came to her on sleepless nights and she sat up in bed and they discussed what had happened to the family since he'd been gone, and Bo asked in that same voice, *My father?*

That's what they told me, she said. And not just alive, Bo. There's something called Operation Homecoming that's a result of the talks in Paris. They're releasing the POWs. The air force is planning on flying transports right into and out of Hanoi.

Just airmen?

No, Bo. Everyone, she nearly yelled, sounding exasperated at his questions. Every American held in that prison, whether he walks out or they have to carry him out.

She didn't look at Ruth. *She won't look at me,* Ruth thought to herself. A strand of Hannah's thick and flax-blond hair was untied and hanging down over her forehead and into her eyes as she leaned forward and fixed them on her eldest son like some madwoman.

Your brother is coming home, she said.

THE C-141 FROM CLARK AIR FORCE BASE IN THE PHILIPPINES TO Travis Air Force Base in California landed in April of that year, 1973. Hannah was there to greet her son when he got off the plane with the rest—and the last—of the prisoners released from captivity in the place they called the Hanoi Hilton. Bo had wanted to fly out there with Ruth as well, but after days of silence during which she did not call once, Hannah drove over to Bo's house and told him and Ruth that she wanted to meet Sam alone when he arrived in California. She didn't know what he would expect, didn't know what she expected herself, and the Marine Corps officer in charge of information about him told her they wouldn't know much more than that he was alive until they checked him out when the plane landed at Clark.

So much has changed, she said to them both there at the kitchen table in Bo's house. He ought to see it slowly for himself.

And Ruth Younger knew what Hannah Konar meant was that so much had changed of what he left, and who, and what he'd find upon returning, leaving prison was going to be the easy part for Cpl. Samuel B. Konar.

THE APRIL LANDSCAPE WAS OF GRAY-GREEN ON WEST MOUNTAIN in Pennsylvania, across the Susquehanna River, as spring took hold of its forests. Closer in and the leaves of sumac and scrub oak covered the culm-piled hills that scarred the towns of Moosic, Avoca, and Dupont. Ruth watched through the windows in the arrival lounge as the Allegheny Airlines commuter flight banked in from the west and dropped down into the valley and landed on the far runway of the Wilkes-Barre/Scranton airport. Two weeks earlier, she and Bo had sat in front of the television in Hannah's house and watched the last of the C-141s land in California. There were cameramen and news anchormen who floated between the families of airmen and war protestors, and they saw Sam from a distance as he limped down the gangway in his uniform, and the back of who they knew was Hannah by her cardigan and long hair. Then the camera cut and an air force colonel gave a statement about how proud he was to have served and how happy he was to be back home. Ruth said Sam looked hurt, because he was limping, and Bo nodded.

Now, no television crews, no military families, not even protestors, just commuter flight 46 out of Philadelphia on the arrivals board as it taxied down the far runway and into the gate, the turboprops sounding like an industrial fan in a summer dance hall before the plane halted and the engines and propellers burped to a stop. A gangway rolled out and touched the plane, and a flight attendant opened the door. Passengers emerged one by one from the top of the stairway and walked down to the tarmac, a brief-case or a small valise in their hands, passengers who had done this every Friday afternoon for months and years of their lives, the work flight no different for them than the ride home to Clarks Summit, Kingston, or somewhere in the Poconos.

And then they were gone. The door remained open and Ruth got worried. She turned to Bo, who did not and would not show what was on his mind, until he motioned with his head for her to look back at the plane. She did, and Hannah and Sam emerged at the top of the stairway carrying a khaki bag. His hair was short and he was in uniform, but he looked smaller, Ruth thought. Aged beyond the age he ought to be. He paused at the top of the gang-way and looked left and right as if to make sure this was the place, then lifted his head up and limped one stair at a time behind Han-nah down to the tarmac.

Ruth wanted to run out of the terminal and embrace him when she saw him, but she waited for Bo, who remained inside as his mother and his brother walked through the doors. Ruth could see that Hannah had been crying, and would have believed it had she been told Hannah had not stopped crying since they dropped her off at the airport for her flight to California two weeks ago. She turned to take in Sam. He was thin and tired-looking, even in the crisp new dress blues someone must have tailored for him somewhere between the Philippines and Pennsylvania. But he was smiling, too, and he looked happy, and so she smiled, as well. For a moment she believed he would understand everything that had happened since he'd been gone, once they had a chance to sit down and talk about who they were and who they had become, though she wondered when or even if they'd ever get that chance.

He walked over to Bo first and hugged him.

I've missed you, brother, Bo said.

Sam leaned out and held his brother by the shoulders.

I missed you more, he said.

Then he turned to Ruth and neither one greeted the other. Neither one spoke. They embraced. Not the embrace of a return after a long time but the embrace of a leave-taking. As though it were here, in this moment, from which he would depart for war and not return, and her life would change without him. She, too, could not keep from crying now in that embrace, so weak and delicate he felt in her arms. Like a willow branch. *No,* she thought. *Like the empty shell of a locust.*

IN THE DAYS THAT FOLLOWED SHE DID NOT GO WITH BO TO THE house. She asked how his brother was doing when Bo came back home, and he told her Sam did little but sit and listen to the radio and occasionally take the old Dart out for a drive, though Bo didn't even know if he had a license anymore.

Does he talk? she asked. About what happened?

Bo shook his head.

I'm sure he's done all the talking he cares to do. You can bet the marines had a list of questions for him.

Did he do anything wrong, you think?

No. You heard what Captain Grayson said last year. Saved that platoon. He's just quiet about it, Ruth. Probably looking for the best way to put it behind him. I would be, too. He seems elsewhere, though. It's in his eyes. He asked me about Pop, and when I told him, he just nodded and limped outside to the barn, as though he already knew but needed to ask me anyway.

Must've been hell.

Can't have been.

Why?

No one's come back from Hell.

She didn't say anything to this. It was Saturday afternoon and she was making a list for a run to the store before it closed.

He asks about you, Bo said.

What does he ask?

Why you won't come over.

He knows, though, doesn't he?

He knows. That's no reason.

She turned back to the list and jotted down *flour, sugar, book matches,* and then looked up at Bo.

It was over between us even before he went missing. You know that.

I know it, he said.

And seeing him now doesn't shake my love for you in any way. You know that, too.

The alternative never crossed my mind, he said.

What about those second thoughts?

I wasn't thinking about him when I asked it. I was thinking about us.

I know what you were thinking, she said, and my answer is the same now as it was then.

She put the pencil down.

Hell or no hell, Bo, it can't be easy for him. Christ, it's not easy for any of us. But all right. I'll go see him. Still some things only I can tell him. And one place he's going to need to go.

She folded up her list and slipped it into the hip pocket of her jeans.

Do you trust me? she asked him.

Yes.

You and I, she said, her finger moving back and forth between them. You and I are right here, no matter who comes home. You got that, Konar boy?

On Monday morning, Bo dropped Ruth off at the house on his way to the mill and she sat in the kitchen with Hannah and drank coffee while they waited for Sam to come downstairs.

There was no conversation between them. Hannah looked tired, like she hadn't been sleeping, and Ruth asked her how she'd been.

How do you think I've been?

I don't know. Good, I'd say. After all this time, all the letter writing and calling congressmen you've done, and your son walks out of a prison in Vietnam and comes home. What else could you be wishing was different right now during Holy Week?

Hannah sipped her coffee and didn't answer.

I should go, Ruth said. We'll do this another time.

Ruth moved to stand and Hannah grabbed her arm.

No, she said. Sit down.

Ruth sat down again.

I've been wondering this whole time how you've been, Ruth, with Sam coming home from a war to find out his fiancée is getting married to his older brother. High school sweetheart, the two of you in love, against the wishes of your parents, the good times you no doubt had together. And you stuck with him through the arrest, the marines, boot camp, the war he signed up for. Twice. It just couldn't tear you apart, could it? You stayed right here, waiting to get what you wanted. I'll bet that visit to Honolulu was your idea. A little bit of R&R for both of you? You weren't about to have put in all that time and not get something out of it, right?

I told you last year, Hannah, Ruth said, in this house. What had been between us was gone because of the war. The weekend in Hawaii was his idea. He had to make sure.

Sure enough to give you a ring and propose. And in my day, getting yourself in the family way meant you were definitely going to say yes.

I did say yes, Ruth said. You're forgetting about the part where everyone was convinced, even the marines, that he was dead.

I never said he was dead.

What are you trying to say? It's all my fault? Ambushes, prison, floods. His baby dead in my arms? I orchestrated all that?

I'm telling you I know that when a girl can't get what she wants on the first try, she'll take what she can on the second.

Goddamn you, Hannah, Ruth said, and stood up so fast that she knocked her cup over and coffee spilled across the table.

Sam appeared in the doorway then, barefoot and dressed in old khakis and a long-sleeved shirt.

Something I missed here? Besides breakfast? he asked.

SHE DROVE THE DART DOWN THE MOUNTAIN WITH SAM IN THE passenger seat and they went through town and headed west for five miles until they came to the wrought-iron gates of Our Lady of Sorrows Cemetery.

Wait, he said, his eyes staring straight ahead through the windshield at the headstones that lined the sloping hill of the cemetery in their legion of shapes and attitudes of mourning.

She stopped, the clutch in and engine idling. His left hand reached for her hand, and after a moment he inhaled a long, slow breath and turned to face her.

This is the part about what I've missed, isn't it?

She nodded. You okay?

I should be the one asking you.

I'm no stranger here, Sam. Hannah and I used to come out every week, if you can believe that. Keep things clean. Talk sometimes. Most times just sit quiet. Pray, I guess. She's got other things on her mind now, though.

What'd you talk about?

You, mostly.

He looked through the windshield at the rows of headstones that lined the hill.

Who'd you pray for?

She looked out, too, then down at her hands and the diamond ring on her finger.

You, mostly.

She put the car in gear and drove slowly up the long road and pulled onto a berm of cinders where the pavement dead-ended at the trees and chain-link fence that marked the edge of the property. They got out and she walked around the car and took his hand and led him down the path to two headstones, one with the name Konar on it, where a marker on the ground read *Bexhet Konar,* and the other with the name Vinich, where there were two markers: *Helen K. Vinich* and *Jozef O. Vinich.* He stopped.

Bo told me Pop died in his sleep about this time last spring, he said.

I didn't know him, she said, but I sure heard about him from my father. Wish I had known him.

Sam knelt down on the grass and touched the stone with his hand, then turned his head to look up at Ruth.

He was everything to me.

She could hear the catch in his voice.

We can stay right here for a while, if you want to, she said.

I'll come back.

He stood and they kept walking along the line of graves to the last headstone, the name Younger carved in the granite. Beneath it a patch of grass grew around three markers, each with a name inscribed on it. The first two read *Paul* and *Mary.* Their child's name appeared on the last: *Clare Frances.*

She, he said, and looked at Ruth as if to confirm the truth of it.

We had a daughter, you and I.

She's not buried with the Konars?

We weren't married, Sam.

He approached and knelt down here, too, touched the marker and traced the letters of the names with his finger, then left his palm flat against the stone, as though it had somehow become attached. She watched the back of him, the once-square shoulders rounding, as if he were falling asleep, or giving up on something he had set out to do, the body slumping until he was almost prostrate against the ground, though his hand still touched the stone. He didn't make a sound.

She knelt down next to him and put her arm around him and

pulled him in close so that their heads were touching, his resting on her shoulder.

I'm sorry, she whispered.

No, he said, his voice determined but distant-sounding, like it had sounded on the night they were together after the judge and his grandfather both said, *Enlist or go to jail,* and he confessed his love to her on the porch of her father's house in the Flats, his promise to provide and his fear not that he would die in a war but that he would not die and not be able to keep that promise. Not be able to say *I am this,* and have it mean something, so that she and his mother and his grandfather most of all, it seemed, could say, *Yes, Samuel. You are.* His voice had sounded determined and distant then, too, and she'd held him, his body taut with muscle and strength, smelling of salt and sweat from having walked across town, and she'd believed this would be the man with whom she would spend the rest of her life. She held him the same way at that graveside, held him and waited for him to lift his head, square his shoulders, and rise. And she thought of Bo and her desire just that morning to be with him. As though the day could not move fast enough until she was home again.

IT WAS NOT QUITE NOON BENEATH A CLOUDLESS SKY WHEN THEY walked back to the car and drove out of the cemetery gates. She took a right turn onto Old Lake Road, and he looked out the rolled-down window at the hills, where the fields had been plowed and were already showing some vegetation. She glanced at him and remembered what Bo had said. *He seems elsewhere.* She looked out at the hills, too, and knew that if she were to ask him where, he would not be able to answer.

They came to a stop sign at an intersection empty of traffic.

Whatever happened to your car? she asked.

The Dodge? I don't know. Hannah told me in a letter I got

when I was at PI that Pop sold it and put the money in my bank account.

You never mentioned that.

He shrugged.

She sure was fast, Ruth said.

She sure was.

The road wound through hairpins that followed a creek and came out at the lake. A few pickup trucks towing jon boats on trailers drove by.

Trout season, he said.

They continued on along the lake, past houses and docks, and pulled into the parking lot of the Sunset. He seemed surprised the road had brought them to their old hangout.

Some things never change, he said, not without a tone of weariness, and she regretted the move to find some common ground that now must have looked to him like nothing more than forced nostalgia.

I didn't want to drive back to your mom's, she said. And this is the only place to eat outside of Dardan. I'm hungry and we can talk. What do you say?

Sure. A beer would be nice.

The restaurant was empty except for an old couple taking their time with a pizza pie. The hostess was someone neither he nor she knew. They sat at a table facing the water, the windows open and a breeze coming in, and he ordered a pitcher of Schaefer, then excused himself to use the restroom.

It was nearly twenty minutes before he returned. She asked if he was all right, and he said he just needed to splash some water on his face. He was not smiling, but he was not as distracted and edgy as before. They sipped their beers and he did not stop looking out at the water. As though he could not, or would not, look at her or even around at the place where they had met so often in the past and drunk with friends and laughed. Here he'd been like some benevolent ruler among them, their cars patient mounts in the parking lot, subjects whose only role was to play football or race those cars, though they would do anything this young man asked of them. And he asked no more of them than to sit and drink their beers, shoot some pool, and keep the songs coming on the jukebox.

Sam, she said, and he turned to her. Where do you go when you do that?

I'm sorry, Ruth. It's a lot coming at me, you know? His voice was level. Every day, Hannah treating me like an invalid, Bo not treating me any way at all. Today's been the toughest one so far. Christ, I just visited my daughter's grave.

It's why I've stayed away, she said. Not just because of Hannah.

I miss Pop, he said. I miss hearing his voice. He'd know what to do.

You don't know what to do?

He rubbed his shirtsleeve at the crook of his elbow and looked back out at the water again.

Mr. Younger and you are the only two I've wanted to talk to since I got off the plane. I didn't know you'd be at the airport in Scranton with Hannah and Bo. I didn't know about your father and the flood and the baby. The marine officer who debriefs POWs and fills them in on what's been going on at home told me about Pop because that's what Hannah told him to tell me. So I thought I'd drive down to your house for breakfast one morning, shake your dad's hand, have a coffee, talk about the weather and when we'd go hunting next, and you and I would either start over or keep going as friends. One of those two. Either one fine with me. Then I get back to the house and you and Bo go off in one direction, and Hannah puts me upstairs in my old room, the old lady meaner than cat shit, and I feel like I've gone from one prison to another.

Ruth listened until he was quiet again.

You want to hear about it from me, she said.

I'd like to.

She took a moment to collect her thoughts, then began, her voice steady, her words deliberate. She told him that after Honolulu she thought everything would turn out fine. A month to go of his second tour, her father telling her that guys as good as Sam Konar could make a career out of it, and it wasn't such a bad one.

You'd be what? she asked. A sergeant next. I didn't worry about you so much this time around. You talked a lot about Captain Grayson, so that when you said CAP, I thought you meant him, living in villages, no more jungle patrols. That sounded like something every marine came home from.

She paused and looked down into her beer but did not drink and looked up again.

I knew I was going to get pregnant that weekend. It's not that I wanted to. I just thought, *Well, what if I do?* All that stuff we worried about, fought about, never talked about, it wouldn't matter anymore. And for a little while, it didn't. Until your brother showed up at the hardware store and gave me the letter the officer had brought to the house when he arrived with a priest. Hannah wouldn't speak to me then, so I had no idea what was going on. Had only what you wrote to me, and I started to get worried when I didn't hear from you. I knew you wouldn't just say, *Hey, it's over. Time to move on.* I mean, it crossed my mind. I could have done that, too. But my father, at least, believed in us. Then, like I said, when Bo gave me the letter, everything changed. It all came into a kind of focus. Like time was being held back by some gate or dam, and no one knew when it would open, until it opened. Simple as that.

You didn't know I was alive?

No one did, Sam. You were listed MIA the whole time. I was the last one to see you, on that trip to Hawaii. The real question was, when would they just tell us where and when you had died, so that we could get on with our lives?

I don't understand it, he said. The company of NVA that captured me marched me for a while. I got shot in the leg. Clean through. Mostly muscle damage. One of the Vietnamese officers cauterized it with the barrel of an old French pistol he heated up in a fire. That hurt.

He reached down under the table and rubbed his leg where the old wound was.

But I'd be one-legged or dead right now if he hadn't. Then one day we came to a village and they put me in a truck with a bunch of other NVA soldiers, and they dumped me in the Hanoi Hilton. It was dry and getting pretty cold outside, so I reckoned it was winter. Past Christmas. Probably '72 already.

No one knew that, she said. It was Grayson who kept the case open. Refused to let them report you KIA, as he put it, until they had a body. Bo and I drove down to West Virginia to see him. Thinks the world of you. No wonder he didn't want to see you go.

I heard at the debrief that he made it home. You met him?

Spent a couple days down there. Bo even got a saw out of the deal. Ended up having to sell his truck, though.

So that's where that old piece of shit died, he said. What'd you get?

I didn't get anything. I just got angry, she said.

He shook his head.

That can't be true.

She looked at her ring and took a breath and looked up again.

I had a feeling about Bo even before I went down there, Sam. He was the only one in the days after you went missing who said more to me than *How are you, Ruth?* And he didn't even do that very often, for fear of getting your mother angry on top of her own grief. Even my father thought I should wait for you. And when he never shows? I asked. He just said you weren't like the others. Said he knew you.

He was a good man, Sam said.

He was everything to me.

She took a few sips from her beer and was quiet for a while.

So I waited, she said finally. We all waited. And while we were waiting, the rains came. A hurricane they called Agnes came, and in the middle of the night the baby came with her. I don't remember much of it. But I remember sitting on the ground in the woods in the morning, the sound of the rain and the creek so damn loud, and our daughter asleep in my arms after she had been pretty much knocked out of me by the car going over the bank and hitting a tree. That's what I thought she was. Asleep. *How can she sleep when it's so loud?* I thought. And then, like out of some dream, Bo was standing right there in front of me, and I just handed her to him and he poured rainwater over her head and blessed her, and said, *Now you can go be with your father.*

Her face wrinkled with the grief and memory of that day and her upper lip trembled and she started to cry and could not stop crying.

I knew she was dead, she said, her voice loud and unsteady all of a sudden between the sobs she tried to stifle with each breath. I knew our daughter was dead. And so were you. I wished I was, too, in that moment, and I would have been if Bo hadn't gotten me up the hill and into an ambulance. Drove through a goddamn river of water. I could feel it in the ambulance, the whole thing shimmying like we were driving on ice. Even had to make the last half mile to the mobile hospital in a boat. But your brother saved me. He saved me when no one else could.

She buried her head in her arms on the table and Sam reached across and touched her, reached his hand beneath her face and felt the wet of the tears and took her hand and held it, and she let him. The old couple tried not to look at them.

After a while she lifted her head and wiped her eyes with a paper napkin.

I had a concussion and a broken collarbone and ruptured spleen, she said in an even voice. I lost a lot of blood when the baby came. The doctor told me later that I can't have children again because of what they had to do inside me. And Bo was Bo, you know? In that way he always knows what to do. Never says how he knows it. He just does.

Sam nodded.

Do you love him? he asked.

I loved you once. I really did.

Do you love him? Sam asked again.

He's a good man. There's a lot I love about him, and he's asked me to marry him. So I will.

Sam turned to stare out at the bright sun emerging from a cloud as it began to arc down toward the mountain range that held the lake in the hollows of its old hills.

We were just too young, he said to that sky in the west, and turned back to her. When I proposed to you. It was only my way of holding on to something I was too scared to lose. Too scared of my own promise.

He looked down at her hand on the table and she covered the left one with the right one and could feel the protruding stone.

You still have the one I gave you? he asked.

No, she said quietly. I lost it in the accident. It's somewhere in the ravine.

Just as well, he said.

SHE PULLED OUT OF THE PARKING LOT OF THE SUNSET AND DROVE for a while along the remote and forested western shore of the lake. Sam asked her where they were going and she put her hand on his leg and he knew. When they neared the mile marker for Asa Pound's property, she pulled off to the side of the road and they got out and walked down the bank to the old dock, just like they used to. It was too early in the season for the Adirondack chairs to be out, but the sun was high and warm and they sat down next to each other, close, so that their hands touched, and they basked in the sun and stared out across the water.

Remember when we used to swim here? she said.

So damn cold, I'd swear my dick was going to fall off.

It didn't, she said, and leaned in to kiss him. He let her. She put her hand on his chest and could feel his heart racing.

It's okay, she whispered, and he turned then to face her and they embraced with a hunger she had not felt in years, but for the weakness she felt in him, the thin arms and hips as he pushed himself against her and she returned it, kissing him harder, arching her back and pulling him toward her with that hunger. She raised her arms and slipped her top off and started to undo the buttons on his shirt, and he said out loud *No*, fumbled with her pants and pulled them down, then pulled his own down and entered her, she crying out from the pleasure of him and the pain of a dock splinter slipping into her shoulder blade, the memory of their innocence lost in this same place, this same way, flooding back to her as she gazed into his eyes, pale gray and piercing, eyes that looked away for what they had seen, his face an empty silhouette against the empty bright blue sky, the man she loved somewhere other than here as he fucked her, and she cried out *Sam*, caught her breath, and held him tighter.

SHE SAW HIM AGAIN AT HANNAH'S FOR THE MEALS OF HOLY WEEK and Easter Sunday, pleasantries the only words between them. Then a month went by and he was not mentioned once by Bo or by Hannah when she called, so that Ruth had to inquire how his brother was doing on a Friday evening in May when Bo came home from work.

You can ask him tomorrow, Bo said. I invited him over for dinner.

Why didn't you tell me?

I tried calling you today, after I got off the phone with him.

I was painting. I didn't want to answer.

Well, there you go. I thought we'd cook out. All this time and he hasn't seen our place yet. I invited Hannah, too, but she said no.

Bo drove over to Hannah's in his truck on Saturday afternoon to pick Sam up, and the two of them came into the house while Ruth was carving a chicken. He had put on a little weight, not much, and she washed her hands and dried them quickly and gave him a hug.

I know there's a mountain between us, she said, but there's a car or two you can drive. And I know your mother owns a telephone.

Sam looked away, then looked back again.

Could say the same for you. I just figured, wedding coming up in a few weeks and all.

Let me get you a beer, Bo said, and I'll show you around.

She watched them as they passed through the kitchen twice, listened to their conversation as their voices carried from the upstairs and through the open windows of the house when they went outside to inspect the barn and the land up to the fields. Bo was measured in what he told of the work he had done on the house, the work he had paid others to do, his plans to continue planting winter wheat.

You have time to grow wheat? Sam asked when they had come back into the house.

I lease it out to a guy from Tunkhannock. He'll come and harvest this in a week or so. Let me know if you want to help.

I'll be all right.

Bo rubbed the back of his neck and tilted his head and looked at his brother.

I'll pay you. Unless you got something better going on.

I said I'll be all right, Bo.

Bo nodded.

What about you, Ruth? Sam asked. You don't work in this kitchen all day, do you?

God no. Your brother's a better cook than I am anyway.

You going back to the hardware store?

Mr. Levandowski wants me to, but it's been almost a year now.

Ruth's been painting, Bo said.

What, like walls? Sam asked.

Landscapes, Ruth said. I started classes with a woman in town last fall.

She's pretty good, Bo said.

The room upstairs with the door shut is my studio. It faces the field and gets light all day. I'm working on how to paint light in different seasons.

I'd like to see them sometime, Sam said, and Ruth knew he never would.

She set a table in the backyard with a tablecloth, candles, and good china, and an evening breeze pushed the mosquitoes and gnats that had been around that afternoon down into the bottomlands. Sam kept shaking his head throughout the dinner, saying how pretty it all was and how great the food was, and he told Bo that maybe he was right. Maybe he'd be better off moving over the mountain, and not just to harvest the wheat but to cut the grass and sweep the barn for them, too, if that's what it would take to get him food like this every day.

It's not every day, Ruth said, her tone flat as she glanced at Bo.

All right, then, every other day. Hell, I'll split wood and change lightbulbs for you if that's what you need.

That's enough Sam, Bo said.

Yeah, it is, Sam said. It's about enough.

I only meant, Bo began, and Sam cut him off.

I know what you meant. Lazy vet sits home all day drinking beers and feeling sorry for himself, while the rest of us get ourselves out of bed in the morning to work and put food on the table, right?

Bo put his head down and shook it and looked up at his brother.

What's wrong with some work? he asked.

Nothing. Go ahead and do all you want. I'll keep living off the money the old man left me and back pay the Marine Corps still owes me.

That and living in your mother's house, Bo said. If that's all it takes.

Or the house your grandfather bought from someone else and just gave to you when he died, Sam said.

They were all quiet then. Ruth noticed Sam had eaten little of anything on his plate, and she was aware all of a sudden of the difference between the two men who sat on either side of her, brothers still, and yet a mountain range apart.

I ought to go, Sam said.

No, Ruth said. No, I am not going to let the evening end like this. Bo, apologize to your brother.

She's right, Sam. I'm sorry. You know I think the world of you. What you've done and come through. I'm sorry, he said again.

Well, Sam said. You can't expect the world not to go on without you when you're sitting in a prison halfway around the world. Sometimes I need to remind myself of that.

A wind picked up and flickered the candle flames. Ruth rose without speaking and went into the house and came back out with two more bottles of beer and handed one each to Sam and Bo and sat down.

Drink, she said.

The brothers clinked bottles over the table, nodded to each other, and drank.

Can I ask you something, Sam? Ruth said.

Sure.

Were you ever scared over there? I mean, for all the time you and I talked about your going to Vietnam, you never said, *I'm afraid*, before or after. I can't imagine Vietnamese prison was anything like the Hilton they called it.

Bo looked at her and gave a little tilt of his head.

Sam took another long swig of beer and put the bottle down.

No, he said. I was never afraid.

It was a different voice entirely—both she and Bo could hear that—and Sam put his fork and knife on the plate of food he had hardly touched and wiped his mouth with the napkin in his lap. Then he sat back, looked first at Bo, then at Ruth.

I was scared sometimes, he said in that same voice. Like when we opened up in the firefight where I got captured. But that's adrenaline. Training kicks in fast.

Grayson told us how that happened, Bo said.

I'll bet he did. It was something. Not my first, but definitely my last. But even when I saw other men go down in front of me, I never thought about dying. I had never been so focused on what was right in front of me. Playing football maybe, but that wasn't life-or-death. Racing, I guess, was about the closest. And, excuse me, but when the shit's going down, it goes down fast and hard, and you just have to hang on and do what they taught you to do. Worrying about the bullet that's going to kill you sure as hell isn't going to save your life.

Bo sat and stared out at the field as Sam talked, as though studying the outlines in that field as they disappeared in the growing dark.

I don't know why I never thought to ask you, he said, then turned back to face his brother. I just figured you'd want to put all that stuff behind you, and you'd be happy doing the things I do every day.

You couldn't know, Sam said. I used to think about you and Pop a lot when I was over there. Jealous of you two getting to spend so much time together, running a business together. Probably fishing a hell of a lot more than I was, too.

Bo laughed.

Not hunting, though, Sam said. I did enough of that. Good thing you never took to it.

I just never wanted to, Bo said.

Sam nodded.

You know, Ruth, he said, our grandfather was a sharpshooter in the First World War. Conscripted out of his Slovak village in the mountains, where he'd learn to shoot with his father, and went to fight for the Austrians. He told me all of this when I was young and started hunting with him. When Bo had gone off to college. I used to look at that fingerless hand of his and remember him telling me he'd lost count of the men he'd killed. Days I thought, *Well, if Pop wasn't afraid, then I won't be.*

And Bo said, About a week before he died, he and I were sitting in the kitchen talking and having a bourbon. It was Good Friday, and he started telling me this story about where he was born and how his mother died, and his father took him back to the old country, where he grew up tending sheep in those mountains. He needed to hunt, and got pretty damn good at it. And that's where he left for the war. It was just after midnight when he was done with that story. You were still missing then. He must've been thinking about you. I think he was always thinking about you.

I would have liked to have heard that story, Sam said. But I feel like I got most of it in those times we used to spend together in the woods. I thought about our father, too, Bo. Becks. I remember nothing about him but what that photograph Mom has of him tells me he looked like. You remember that day Pop sent us down to Brookside to see old Aunt Frances?

I remember.

I had been out partying with the boys the night before, Ruth, and it felt like my head was in a vise and my tongue had fur on it. But there we were in her apartment in Brookside, nice place, and she starts telling us about how our father, Bexhet Konar, had fought for the French Resistance in World War Two, after he'd gotten separated from his unit in the Ardennes, and then traveled to the border of Hungary in the final months of the war, where he killed a bunch of fascists and saved a bunch of lives, and his name was like a hero's name over there. Just the opposite of what it was here.

Bo didn't say anything.

I thought she was making it up, Sam went on. Some old country nonsense about the Resistance and Gypsies. But Captain Grayson was a history major in college before he enlisted and went to officer's training. He loved that counterinsurgency stuff, and he said that happened a lot in France toward the end, the guys hollowed out from fighting for so long, getting lost and separated. They would make their way to Switzerland if they could, or fight with the French. Most were captured or killed by the Germans. But some got through. He told me that if she said it, and others remembered it, our dad probably did it. I wished I could've had something to remember him by, Bo. Then I could've talked to him, too. But mostly I talked to Pop when I was in prison.

You talked to him? Bo asked.

Sure. In the first few months I wouldn't tell the goddamn NVA anything more than my name, rank, and serial number. That was the code, and the old-timers used to bang out instructions to us in Morse, what to do, what not to do. I didn't know what the hell they were banging about when I first got there, but after a while I figured it out. So I kept quiet and let the officers do their job. When I did talk, though, it was to Pop, because his voice was in my head all the time, the stuff he used to say. He let me get arrested, you know? *No one in this family runs*, he told me, and held me there while the cops came back with their warrant. But mostly I'd just think of those times we had hunting and fishing.

He stopped and looked around at the night, his brother, the firelight.

Go on, Old Man, Ruth said.

The comment startled him.

Grayson told you that about me, didn't he?

She nodded, and he stared at a vase of wildflowers in the center of the table.

I talked to Mr. Younger, too, he said, and looked over at her. I didn't know he was dead, but it makes sense now. Around December, they moved a lot of the guys out of the city because of the bombings, but not me. And things got worse. I still wouldn't tell them anything, or go to their reeducation classes. They'd let the other guys play checkers, but they'd beat me in my leg and send me back to my cell, where I'd stare down the fucking rats, and I'd say out loud to your dad, *Mr. Younger, this sure as hell ain't a deer blind, and I sure as hell ain't walking home with a buck and my rifle.* And he'd tell me to wait, just like he'd taught me. Not get distracted. Not miss my chance. *If you need water, get some. If you need to eat, eat what you packed or reach out and eat the moss and the wintergreen berries right next to you.* And when

I'd shut my eyes, it was like I was home again, and I knew I was going to stay alive. There was another marine there who helped me out when I first arrived, a CWO named Frederick, who moved up to the Dogpatch with the other prisoners. I missed talking to him. I heard they chucked him into solitary, and I knew that he would die. He got typhoid, or something bad. It made me think a lot about the day I left that village in Quang Tri with Grayson and the other marines in our group, and how we went from doing something good to killing and getting killed by the same people in the space of one click. That about sums it up.

When they had finished their beers, Bo asked him if he'd like to head into town and see if they could find any of his old football buddies, or maybe a few guys who had spent time studying the shape of his taillights.

Nah, Sam said. I'm too tired. I don't need to see anybody around here anymore.

You thinking of leaving? Bo asked

I'm thinking of heading down to West Virginia to see Grayson. He and I could probably stand to have a word or two.

You want my truck?

Thanks, brother. I'm not going yet. And when I do, the bus'll be just fine. You can take me home right now, though, and let's say we try to get out on the town another night.

All right, Bo said.

Ruth, Sam said. I am stuffed and happy and much obliged for the hospitality. To the two of you.

She said good night and kissed him on the cheek, no more stuffed than he was.

THE WEATHER WAS DRY AND CLEAR ON THE FIRST SATURDAY IN June, as though they might have prayed for such a day, and Ruth and Bo were married by Father Rovnávaha in a nuptial Mass at the church of St. Michael the Archangel. Sam escorted Ruth down the aisle, then moved to stand at his brother's side. Hannah was Ruth's matron of honor.

The people who left the church when the Mass was over numbered only forty-six more than the four who were Konars now. Ruth and Bo were the last out. They walked into a small hail of rice and flowers and jumped into the cab of Bo's truck, which was parked in front of the church steps.

The white tent in the orchard was visible as they crested the rise of Rock Mountain Road and parked beneath an apple tree along the drive. Cooks had been at a roasting pit in the yard since five o'clock that morning, turning a whole hog slowly on a spit. Beer, champagne, and highball cocktails were available at a bar set up around the side of where the old smokehouse used to be, and the afternoon air smelled of honeysuckle, hickory smoke, and peonies. There was something about the light from the west in the tops of the trees, Ruth thought as she stopped and took in the image of the barn and the fire pit and the old smokehouse, and she wondered if she could paint it like a man by the name of Abbott Handerson Thayer had painted a mountain he loved in rural New Hampshire. She had seen his work in a book she took from the Osterhout Library one day. And today, she felt as though she could reach out and touch what had always felt slightly out of her grasp, and she and Bo walked up the driveway to greet the photographer.

When they sat down for dinner beneath the tent and the tables quieted, Father Rovnávaha blessed the food. Sam stood then and looked out at the Brookside relatives, Bo's coworkers from the mill, and the few people from town whom Hannah still called friends, and he wondered why their aunt Frances was not there.

When I was in a North Vietnamese prison, he said, I used to think of all of you gathered here today. This farm. That house. These hills. But most of all, I thought of this man right next to me. My brother. I thought of his strength always to remain. That's what got me through. And so I want you to know that Ruth Younger could not have found a better man to spend the rest of her life with.

And I want you to know, too, that my brother, Bo, is a man I consider one of the luckiest men alive today, second only to me, for having been born as a brother to him. There is not one of you here who does not know of this man's abilities and loyalty and strength, so what I am telling you now is nothing new. And while you no doubt would like to hear something new about me, I'll tell you only this: The Vietnamese were not all and not always enemies, and I had heard once from a villager I knew that the gods know best who will make us happy in life, and so they put those who will love us, those who will change us, those who will keep us happy, on our paths and in our way. If such gods exist, and with apologies to Father Rovnávaha, they are wise gods. I am convinced of that today.

He raised his glass.

To Bo and Ruth Konar. May their paths never stray from each other, or from us, those who love them and keep them and pray for them. *Na zdravie.*

The guests all raised their glasses and shouted *Na zdravie!* and drank. Ruth watched as Bo leaned into his brother when he sat back down, whispered something into his ear, and kissed him on the cheek. Sam blushed and the two started laughing. Hannah leaned into Ruth on her other side and told her she could not be prouder of the two of them, could not imagine her son happier or married to a more beautiful bride.

Ruth thanked her and thought of this woman who had taken her in the summer before and nursed her back to health when there was no reason for her to, other than her own desire, and she decided that she could not know what went on in the heart of Hannah Konar, but she would believe for her own sake that it was a good heart.

You made this my home, Hannah, she said. I'll always be grateful for that.

THE DINNER AND THE FOOD, THE DRINK AND THE DANCING, ALL went long into the night, and though she and Bo were happy to remain with those who were happy to stay and enjoy the party, they were tired, and it was Bo who asked if she would like to change and go back to their house before they left for their honeymoon in the White Mountains of New Hampshire.

You can change upstairs in Pop's old room, Bo said. Where you stayed last summer. Hannah will take care of the dress for you if you leave it on the bed. Wait for me there and I'll come and get you.

Thank you. She sighed.

She said good night to Hannah, who told her she had already put Ruth's suitcase in the bedroom upstairs, and she looked around for Sam but did not see him. One of the men from the mill told her he had seen Bo's brother going into the house, and so she took the small bag in which she had her change of clothes and went into the house by the back door. As she entered the kitchen, she stopped and listened to the sudden quiet. The party a distant echo outside. The tick of the wall clock breaking the hush. She needed to use the toilet, and she made her way for the half bath in the hallway just past the foyer, her bustled dress swishing against the wooden floor.

The guests had all been told to use the outhouse at the side of the barn, so she was surprised to see there was a light on. Hannah and Bo were outside still. The door was shut. She knocked, thinking maybe this was where Sam had gone. But no one answered. She knocked again.

Sam, she said out loud.

She heard movement and the clunk of an arm knocking the lid of the porcelain tank, and so she knocked again, then opened the door.

Sam sat on the toilet with the seat down, eyes closed, lips pursed. A red bandanna was tied tight around his upper arm and he held a needle deep into the crook of that arm, and she watched as a trace of blood backed up into the barrel of the syringe like the blossoming flower petals of a print her instructor had in the studio, and she tried to remember what it was called, the crimson rising, then disappearing in a rush back into his arm, as though that flower had grown, bloomed, and died right there like the flower of life. *That's what it's called*, she remembered.

He opened his eyes and stared at her, as though he couldn't be bothered by the intrusion. Stared at her standing in the doorway. Then he smiled.

Shhh, he said, and pulled the needle from his arm, untied the bandanna, and leaned back against the toilet tank, a dime-size circle of red blossoming now on his tuxedo shirt.

She closed the door until the latch bolt clicked, walked back into the kitchen, and sat down at the table. She listened to the clock tick, the sound of the quiet so loud in her head, and she thought of how she had longed for him once, like the drowning long for breath, but she had breathed her last of that love and knew he had, too, on a day at the Honolulu airport so unremarkable, it could be neither remembered nor recalled, only known that it had been so, and she would not expect or want that love to return now. And if it did? If he did? Walked down that hall and took her in his arms and held her like he had always done, days before and after the war. What would she say in that embrace? No. There was nothing she could or even wanted to say on this night in this house that she hadn't already said to an empty room, while he sat locked away somewhere in a prison cell, missing or dead, nothing more than the hush he had just whispered.

She dabbed her eyes with a paper napkin so as not to smudge the eyeliner and took a breath. Then she stood and walked down the hall past the bathroom door and into the foyer. Something in the pier glass made her hesitate, and she drew closer and saw the bride in the light from the lamps Hannah had left on in the living room. Makeup still intact. The longer hair styled and held back. And she remembered what she had come inside to do. She turned and walked up the grand stairs, holding on to the banister with one hand, the bag and the loosening bustle of her wedding dress with the other. The suitcase with her clothes for the honeymoon was upstairs in the room where Bo had told her to change and wait for him, and she willed him now to hurry. She was looking forward to sleeping in her own bed that night. With her husband. They had a long drive ahead of them in the morning, if they wanted to get to the big hotel in the White Mountains tomorrow evening by dinnertime.

THE SOJOURNER AND THE FATHERLESS

(Saturday, July 1, 1967)

From sunup, when they drove the new model Dart out of Dardan and across the river into Wilkes-Barre, until that same sun hung hesitant and red in the west, they sat in the top-floor apartment that was no more than a bedroom, a kitchen, and a sweeping expanse of parquet-floored living room with a window that looked out onto the Susquehanna River and Larksville Mountain in the distance, a sewing machine in the corner by that window the only article of any note in the room, the entire feel of the place cleaner and lighter than the humid river-mud haze that hung over the valley and was somehow lessened as they passed through the front French doors of the apartment building and climbed the carved and banistered stairs to the flat, where the scent of the rooms was closer to the chamomile tea she brewed and the lavender in which her customers from Forty Fort and Kingston packed the dresses they sent across the river by courier so she could mend them, or alter them, or make a second dress of exactly the same size and material altogether, Bo remembering when he walked into the apartment that the ancients had believed in an ether, a pure air through which the gods moved, and he thought, *This is what they meant* when she escorted him and his brother into the living room by the window, directed them to sit in armchairs with end tables on which two glasses of water sat on cherrywood coasters, and drew the drapes closed, as though some fisherman or drifting mariner on the river down which mariners never drifted might hear them through that ether, or see them through the window glass.

They didn't know why they had been summoned to Wilkes-Barre by their aunt Frances Posol, but they'd been told by their grandfather that if she wanted to see them, they must go. And so they arrived and went through the rituals afforded guests. The greeting in Slovak. The three kisses on the cheek (what their mother called the holy kiss, for its symbol of the Trinity and peace). The seating. The serving of tea, hot. And when she left them to go into the kitchen, and returned from the kitchen with her own cup of tea, she placed the saucer at the edge of the sewing machine, took a straight-backed wooden chair from behind the machine, and turned it to face the young men, brothers who, to look at them, shared nothing but the same parents and a childhood under the same roof of their grandfather's house. She thanked them for having come all that way from Dardan on a Saturday, when she knew there was work to be done, then was quiet as she sat and seemed to study them.

What they did know was that she had been born in the village of Pastvina before the Great War, two years after a man named Ondrej Vinich returned from America a widower with his young son, Jozef. And they knew, too, it was a mule kick that had left her mouth in the slack and menacing sneer that shaped what most people thought of Frances Posol when they saw her for the first time. The truth was, they had never not known this woman they called Aunt but who was no aunt, her presence ubiquitous in the house for Sunday dinners, birthdays, and religious feasts, always at the request of their grandfather. It was he, Jozef, who had used the word *beautiful* to describe the woman one day when Bo was a boy and he asked why Aunt Frances looked so ugly. *No, she is beautiful, Bo,* he said to his grandson. *There is no other word for her. You'll understand one day.* And he understood. Not that he, too, would use the same word to describe the woman, but why his grandfather did. Why he stood up for her, protected her, when it was his grandson who tried to demean her. It was not one day but over time that Bo came to understand the affection his grandfather showed his dead wife's cousin. Came to understand the whispered Slovak of their conversations. Came to understand the chaste and intimate way they embraced when they greeted each other, or said good-bye at the end of an evening, and Hannah insisted she drive Aunt Frances back to Wilkes-Barre. In time, he came to understand. There was no other word for it.

She sat before them now with her knees together and her hands resting on the lap of the dark blue dress she wore with the hem that reached just above her calves, a light white cotton cardigan on over her shoulders, buttoned at the first and second buttons, so that it covered the bustline of her dress. She asked how their mother and grandfather were, and Bo said they were fine. She asked about the new fruit trees in the orchard that Jozef had told her they had planted, and how they were faring in the heat, and Bo said they were well established and that they would be fine. Then she asked about Krasna, the black Labrador retriever that never left Hannah's side, and Bo said they were all fine and would be fine, then asked her, without masking the impatience he wore like a man who had his own work to do that day, why she had invited them to her apartment when their mother, their grandfather, the orchard, and even the dog were all less than an hour's drive from where they sat, a drive Hannah or Jozef would make anytime on any day to take her to the farm, where there was at least a porch and a breeze.

She pressed her hands down into the lap of her dress and sat up straight.

Because enough of the war has been brought to your house, Bohumír, she said. By him, by the stories of him, by the fact that he could not tell the story himself of what he had done in the war to his own sons. That's why.

Bo pulled at the neck of his T-shirt and shifted in his chair.

It's about him, then.

Yes, she said.

After all this time?

Time you needed.

She looked at Sam, who hadn't said a word since they'd arrived, the younger son, who'd never known his father, and she wondered if anything she said might change him.

Late night, Samuel? she asked.

Sorry, Teta. Party with my football buddies. They wanted to say good-bye before I leave.

Yes, for what was it your grandfather called it?

Boot camp, he said, and rubbed his temples with his thumb and finger.

And then what? Then you'll be walking right into this new war now, won't you?

Well, if I make it through recruit training, I suppose they're going to want me to fight. That'd be the point, right?

Would it? she asked. You're about to do what generations of men in your family have done. Left home to fight a war and returned home after that war, never mind how it turned out. If that's the point, then I suppose you're going to fight wherever they send you. If not, well then, you'll just have to decide how much fighting you want to do.

She turned to Bo, and he looked down at the floor, as he had always done since he was a boy because she had caught him staring at her. She took a sip of tea and addressed Sam again.

You never knew him, though, she said, so you can be forgiven for not understanding what it is your mother will not forgive, whom she will not forgive, for what was taken, though I tried to tell her years ago, when I only suspected, yet which I now know because of one who is alive still and speaks of him as a man whose fearlessness made others fear him, and this no doubt saved many, right up to the end. But to her, it doesn't matter. To her, the world is that farm, and all things begin from it and return to it, while she remains at its center, not in control of the paths that lead out and come back, if they do come back, war or no war, but certainly in command of them, shaping them while they are within her grasp.

And perhaps that is no different from anyone else's desire to alter an imbalance or injustice, just as it was your father's.

She waited, sipped her tea again, and placed the cup back on its saucer.

Never mind, she said. Hannah wouldn't listen to me, though I've told her I want nothing more than to give her some peace. *I have what peace I need*, she says, and I believe that and don't believe that, as is the case with so many things.

(But why the two of us, and why in Wilkes-Barre and not up here? Bo had asked his grandfather after their mother told him Aunt Frances wanted to speak to him and his brother alone, told him when and where, and that was the end of it. He'll be at Parris Island next month and I'll be hunched over those books at the mill, trying to find out how we're going to cover another slow summer without letting anyone go, and she knows something that will bind the two of us before he joins the marines and heads off to Vietnam? And Vinich replied, She knows more than she tells, because unlike the rest of us, who never wanted to go back to the old country, she does. I don't know why. I've asked her and she is as short with me as she is with anyone, the most she's ever said something that approximates Scripture. *I am the widow who is no widow, and yet still presses the judge.* Maybe she has news from some old Rom who reads palms, or a photograph she found, or she just wants to give the two of you money to show that the same is given to the first and the prodigal alike.)

He was no deserter, she said, as though the date were 1945 again. From the accounts I've heard, accounts it's time someone has settled with you, if *account* is even the right word, because enough of the stories and the sources have told of the same man among a group of Roma who created his own resistance against the Hlinka Guard and the Arrow Cross near the end. One who was neither Slovak nor Hungarian. And for no reason, it seems, other than retribution. Anger. Revenge. So, yes, what I mean is that I know something about your father that you could not know but which might—

She hesitated.

Not reform him. He was no criminal. Re-create. Re-create the man you have no memory of, Samuel.

She turned to Bo. And you no doubt remember not as a father, Bohumír, but as a walking ghost.

She gazed across the room and seemed to mumble out of the side of her mouth, though it could very well have been the trembling of the same mouth that remembered the kick, the girl too curious about the oddly passive mule, the pain so blinding she did not even remember the veterinarian who set the jaw, only being in the arms of Jozef Vinich.

Who am I to be telling stories now? she said as if to herself, then addressed Sam as though he were alone in the room. Will you believe it? I wonder. You? About to become a soldier yourself?

A marine, Teta, Sam said.

Yes. And did you join, or are they sending you?

I enlisted.

Enlisted, she said. Because of your girlfriend. Your Capulet, no?

My what?

Your Juliet. I've sat in your grandfather's library long enough over the years to have read more than the spines of his books. This girl. Ruth Younger. That's her name, right? Daughter of the man who shot your father, and whom your mother hates with a heart perhaps equal to your love, if you do love her, which is different from desiring her. Will you miss her more than your brother, your mother, or your grandfather, who gave you everything?

He didn't answer.

You will, for a time, and then you'll understand.

What are you trying to say, Teta? Sam asked, as impatient and uncomfortable now as his brother. I didn't have a choice. The judge told me if I didn't enlist and make something of my life, I'd be in jail quicker than coal down a chute.

We all have a choice, Samuel, she said, and looked at the floor again in that manner of the old (though she was not old) who gaze down when they want to recollect what is tucked away in a room somewhere inside the mind, the floor seemingly a place where they have lost and need to find again the only key that will open the room.

And you, Bohumír, she said, lifting her head as though Sam had asked her nothing, had said nothing. Who is greater? The strong one who stays and takes care to remain strong, or the one who is weak because he is drained of what strength he once had, strength he used for the journey, not the fight?

Bo didn't answer, either, and there was a tense silence among them, Bo thinking to himself, *All this time, not two words more than what command she was giving to me or Sam to do or not do, something we already knew from our mother to do or not do, and now she is like some oracle who won't stop speaking in that same voice through that crooked jaw until her audience is confounded or content. Pop couldn't have known what she wanted to tell us, how she would deliver it. He couldn't.*

You see, she said, I've heard the accounts for some years now, heard hints of them when I made my way back there for the first time in 1948, but then couldn't go anymore because it got too dangerous. Parts of the story have made their way here in the ones who have gotten out from behind the Curtain. Even they have your father's name on their tongues, every one of them, registered Communists or not. And you should know, young men that you are, what your father did in the war. Fight, yes, with a rifle and a uniform, as they all did, she said, and waved her hand in the air, so that the scent of chamomile and lavender moved with it. And all of this your mother knows about from him, and has read about in the reports from that same army, the weeks and months of advance into the winter, the attack in the forest, the counterattack by the Germans that everyone now calls the Bulge, and her husband left for dead. But not dead. No, quite alive. And wanting only to live. And so he moved and sought refuge in order to live. For her. For you, Bohumír. And you, too,

Samuel, in the way a man does not see but hopes and prays for what he might create in some future, with the help of God.

How? Bo asked with an uncertain halt in his voice.

Who knows how some men survive while others die, she said.

No. I mean, how did you go back? How did you get behind the Iron Curtain and into a Communist country?

She smiled now for the first time. Not just a lift of one corner of the mouth but a smile that showed her teeth white and polished, and it looked to both brothers as though this pained her more than speech itself, but she held the smile in place.

Look at me, she said. Do you think I am capable of no more than making my own breakfast and putting my shoes on?

I know what you're capable of, Teta, Bo said.

But they don't. The border guards. The customs officials. I fly from New York to Frankfurt and take a train into Czechoslovakia, the border crossing with its watchtowers and signs at the stations that say *Pozor! Haraniční pásmo* near the train tracks that seem to hover over the Czech forests of the borderlands so dark and beautiful, and the soulless guards who come onto the train and check your papers and your passport before it lurches into that forest and arrives at Pilsen and then Praha, towns and cities where they decide on their own if you are to be followed or left alone.

They leave you alone, don't they?

Yes. Now they do. Because everything I have is in order. The priest in the village has asked the head of the school to write a letter of invitation to me, with which I apply for the visa as a teacher, and I go. Everything is in order, she said again, and pointed to an upholstered suitcase in the corner of the room where they sat.

And all I take is that.

The two brothers turned and stared at the suitcase. As though it didn't belong. As though they couldn't believe that it had been there all along and they had missed it despite the sparseness of that room.

I've sewn a false pocket into the bottom lining of the bag, she said, and over that I place a sheaf of papers, written in Slovak, outlines of how I will teach the history and the progress of the Workers' Party, the factories, the collectives, twenty pages and more, so that if some bored official does choose to read, he may read, and if he does, the first two pages or so, he'll put them down after that and see it is housedresses and shoes and a woman's nylons that I'm carrying in the bag. And why would he want to touch these things? Why would he believe I have anything in the bag? He doesn't. He looks me up and down and I know what he is thinking, because he is quite eager to look away from my face. *Všetko je v poriadku,* he tells me, and I go.

Bo watched her, the pleasure she took in deceiving that adversary still visible, and he understood even more now what she was capable of.

Sam said, But you aren't bringing in dresses and shoes and nylons, are you, Teta?

She opened her mouth and exhaled and regarded the two young men before her, the separate imprints of mother and father on them both, the striking differences in hair and eyes. Bohumír, the inheritor of the father's line with his once long and manelike hair short and hueless black now, so that the eyes stood out in their unexpected and unsettling blue. And Samuel, the mirror of his mother, his hair flaxen and long (and he pushed it back from his face and around his ears then with the knowledge, perhaps, that it would soon be shorn to the scalp), eyes with their enormous and pale gray pupils from which few could look away.

Most, she said, never want to go back once they leave because they have found here what was hidden or unattainable there. Not out of ease or blessing but simply because they felt, or feel still, somehow, that the struggle is not futile here. But the struggle is futile everywhere, once one ceases to struggle. And I see and have faith in the ones who struggle there. So that is what I take, beneath the shoes and dresses and nylons. Beneath the pages of typed letters and courses and histories. I carry the means to struggle. The means to build and maintain a faith.

You take them money, Sam said.

I take them money, Samuel. I take not only from my excess but from my stores, and I give it to the priest in Pastvina, a man whose own life is at risk of imprisonment by those same corrupt officials more than my own.

How much does it cost to build and maintain a faith, Teta? Bo asked.

How much do I risk losing in the bag each time? That's your question, right? How much is an old woman who sews dresses worth?

Yes.

There is money and there is wealth, Bohumír. I sew money into that pocket beneath the papers. Thousands of dollars. If I had more, I would take it and give it, not to the people, not to those who have their food and their shelter and their souls given to them, but to the priest, the only resistance there is in that country now. And I do not ask where it is going or what it is being used for, because I know. I give him the money and I go back to the tables in the kitchens of my sister and nieces and nephews in Pastvina, where we say grace and have our meal, and I dole out the clothes I have brought for them, too, from America. You see, I wrap the Carhartt trousers and Levi's jeans for the men in my housedresses and women's underwear. I hide baseballs for the boys in my old boots. I once wrapped a teddy bear inside one of my girdles. And I bring dresses for the women, dresses I don't have to hide because I have sewn a false and plain material around them, which I remove before I give them to my younger sister and her eldest daughter, so that they emerge from all of their plainness like butterflies.

What would happen if you were caught? Bo asked.

I was, she said. The first time. I wanted to go on my own, so I didn't have the invitation. And I wasn't carrying the money then. I only had gifts and clothes hidden, things those officials didn't even care about in the end.

She crossed her legs and looked over at the curtain-drawn window and looked back again.

It was May of '48. The Communists had taken over the government in February of that year. I had gotten all the way from Praha to Košice. But on the train I knew I was being followed. At the terminus, two men came up beside me and told me the police needed to question me, and they took me into the station across the street. I was much younger and, foolishly, I played the fool. I told them I was a teacher of Slovak, I intended only to do that in their country, and that I would follow the rules to the letter. They laughed and opened my bag and laughed at what I'd brought, then took me into a back cell and laughed as they threw me down on a filthy mattress and lifted my dress and ripped off my girdle and—four of them. They laughed when they were done and told one another it was a shame I was so ugly. When I realized they were interested in nothing else, I stood up and limped out of the cell. I took my bag off the inspector's desk, zipped it closed, put on my coat, and walked out of the station. It was a beautiful day and I kept walking, though the pain was nearly unbearable and I thought I would pass out right there on the sidewalk. And when I couldn't walk any farther, I looked up and saw that I had stopped in front of a church. I sat in the nave and prayed to the patron of that church, Saint Elizabeth, until a sexton came out and asked me what I was doing there. And when I told him that I didn't know, that I had arrived from America and had just been released by the police, he knew. I began to cry in the pew at the back of that church, and he took my hand and led me down the aisle and into the sacristy, where I met Father Ostvald for the first time.

The young men sat in their chairs and did not make a sound when she was done. Did not even move, for fear of looking as though they were anything but humbled into silence by the confession the woman had just made to them.

I will tell you, she said, what I told your grandfather when I returned home months later. That with my innocence, I lost, too, my naïveté. They steeled me, those men. They showed me what could be done if I learned the language of the enemy. They showed me just how powerful a weapon revenge could be. And so I vowed to get my revenge.

You saw them again? Sam asked.

No. No one ever did. Not after Father Ostvald told some fellow prisoners of the Russians during the war what they had done to a Christian woman in the filthy cell of their jail. Two days later, those four didn't show up for work. They never showed up for work again, and the police they transferred down from Prešov never so much as touched my bag whenever I arrived in Košice and got off the train in that city. But that's not what I mean by revenge.

She sipped her tea and looked in the direction of the window as though she could see in the distance through the drawn curtains. Then she placed the cup down again, and put her hands in her lap.

It wasn't until Ostvald died almost five years later that I met the young priest for whom I carried the money, and who knew the stories about your father.

In Pastvina? Bo asked.

Yes, she said. He remains there, living in a small house, where he says Mass in secret, and working in the collective with all of the others, who know that if they betrayed this man of faith, they would suffer a fate worse than whatever prison or uranium mine he was sent to, and not at the hands of Communist officials, but at the hands of the villagers themselves, a fate that would involve the kind of suffering most would gladly end, because there are a lot of woods in those mountains. So, yes, I've heard the stories from the priest to whom I began to give my money to maintain the church, in Pastvina, and wherever else he sees fit, believing that he believes that the life he lives now is the one for which your father fought when he saw how others died.

She waited for more questions from the brothers, but none came, and she told them that, in the village, it was their grandfather the others still spoke of. The only one who returned from the Great War who was not maimed or vacant and who left for America because he was born there. And once he left, he would not send so much as a Christmas card back, though she didn't know to whom he would send anything after his old shrew of a stepmother died. But Jozef Vinich was the sun to which all the lilies of Pastvina turned when they admitted not just to wondering what life in America was like but to wanting to go there, still, even the workers in the collective, to find what Vinich found, to take as he took, not understanding there was nothing the man gained without having paid for it twice, accepted that price, and moved on, the man raised to be a hunter.

Your father is seen through that light, too, in the village, she said. But not outside. Not south toward Prešov and Košice and in the villages closer to the border with Hungary. This is where the train goes, from Praha east, through Bratislava and Brno in old Moravia, to Košice, as I've said, where the young priest comes to meet me at the terminus now and drives me north to Pastvina.

Why did you decide to go back? Bo asked.

I had always known I would go back. I wasn't going to let them take what they took for nothing. But what you're speaking of began in Wilkes-Barre, seven years later, when Father Hurajt at Sacred Heart Church came to me one day after Mass and asked if I was interested in—how did he put it?—*málo dobrodružstvo*, a little adventure, which made him smile at the time, the old saint. I asked him what he had in mind, and four months later I was in Czechoslovakia, where there were speeches and protests by the writers and intellectuals who came out into the squares all over the country to protest for free speech. And I heard again whispers about those who stood up to the Nazis along the border, defied the sympathizers among the Slovaks, and in the end killed members of the Hlinka Guard and its POHG in ways too brutal to tell in retribution for the brutality of that group's own brutality, so that there was a fear among the enemies that led to a kind of peace before the peace of nations for the people, yes, but especially for the Jews and the Roma, those who were hated and have always been hated in those countries of Europe.

But he was an American, Bo said. I remember looking at the photo Hannah keeps of them at his swearing-in ceremony, just before they were married.

That means he could not be Romani?

No, it means his allegiance was here. He was sworn to it.

You look at that photo next time and you tell me what you see beyond the flag at the courthouse that is no more than a prop. You look and you tell me you don't see a man who is—

Dark, yes.

Like you.

Yes, but no more Gypsy than I am.

So you say.

I do say. Because I know my mother and I know that farm. And I don't know what would have made him want to take up a cause, if that's even what it can be called, when he had sworn allegiance to a flag, had enlisted in the army under that flag, and had a family back home in the country that army protected. I don't know. I don't understand it. Especially not when I see what it came to.

She seemed to look at the young men before her anew and understood they would not understand the pull of lands other than the land on which they had grown up, because of their grandfather's and their father's own struggles to heal divisions within themselves that perhaps they knew or would know by the end were not wounds to be healed but scars to be held, as she knew, too, even when those scars brought a sorrow that walked along and peered into the valley of death itself, where others had already gone, where others were going even as they walked, and yet could not turn from the path entirely, could not and would not any sooner than the two brothers before her would turn from their mother now that their father was gone.

She nodded slowly and said, I had already seen him at the farm when I visited in the summers, and at Christmas Eve for the *velija* feast. But I remember when he came to Brookside with your mother and grandfather to bring food to us in '37. He already looked like he had left the old country and come here to stay, which was the work of your grandmother Helen, God rest her soul. Every year I wrote to family in Pastvina, never mentioning him, and the letters that came back always asked about the boy who had been in search of Jozef Vinich. The old stepmother, they said, screamed from her deathbed about how Jozef had robbed her of all she had left, and the boy was the devil he deserved. So they wanted to know if he had ever come, if he had ever found your grandfather, or if it was all some thief's ploy to steal a chicken or a sack of potatoes. But I never told them that he had come, and what he had become when he got here. I could see that your grandfather was fond of him, proud, even, perhaps in the way a father would be proud of a son who has learned to give of what's been given to him in this world. And I could see that your mother loved him by the way she looked at him, and listened to him, and stood near him, as though she were some flower that would wilt if it were placed too far away from the sun. No, I never wrote to anyone telling them that he had not only found Jozef Vinich but had been embraced by the man, and been given a home in which he didn't have to wonder when he would be awakened in the night and have to run.

Like him, I never thought to return, though it was the war that kept me away. I had plans of taking a ship across in the summer of '39, and then March of that year came and Czechoslovakia collapsed. I didn't know what I would find at those borders, if I even made it to those borders by myself. I spoke to your father of this, quietly, in your grandfather's library one Sunday only weeks before he and your mother were married, the changing borders, the armies that controlled them. Germans in the Czech lands, Hungarians taking what was once Slovakia and Ruthenia, and even Poland annexing land to the north of Pastvina. And he spoke, rather, of territories, rivers, plains, highlands, and mountains that he knew and had traveled through as a boy, as though he held some map in his imagination drawn long before there were even such things as armies and a people who moved the way water moves in one season, birds and seedpods move in another, which is to say, with the wind, for the sake of finding where for another season the land would be most accepting and sustaining. For a moment I could see that world, see the way in which he longed for it, not as a place to go back to in time but as a place that emerged once again, and those searchers on the road would find it in time. In time. But he seemed conscious, too, of what had been going on within the borders of Hungary, where in the past he had spent winters with his *kumpania* along the Sajó, and his voice rose with a kind of righteousness against those who were removing the Roma from their camps and long-held routes of travel with an impunity that was nothing short of getting away with murder. And so this was what he had to balance in his heart. Where and for what would he take up the fight? He had become naturalized, yes, and he was about to marry your mother, and yet no one through whom the blood of a people persecuted since before the time of Jesus could sit back and let happen what was happening to his own, even a continent and an ocean away. So, almost two decades later, as Father Ostvald learned I could be trusted, and then the young priest let small chapters of the story out, I was surprised only to find that your father suffered no small amount for acting with his conscience.

But how do you know that what this priest told you is true? Bo asked.

You see, Bohumír? Now you are full of questions. You may or may not believe that the man of faith can tell the truth, but I have no reason to believe he knows or tells anything else. Why would he? This was no story told once around a fire, night after night, about a man of no significance, then forgotten. Your father fought a battle in a war where the stories of those who also fought held out some promise, some hope, for resistance against an enemy, though that resistance is now mostly forgotten, because most had been captured and killed. But as the Roma themselves began to unwind from the spool of those fighters, the ragged, tenacious ghosts of a people hunted and thinned out as they drifted along on the slow wooden wheels of their vardos day after day, year after year, they found there was nowhere they could go where there was no war. And so they took up arms and fought, too, their ragged, ghostlike specters and insular language weapons themselves that could even a score so uneven, it would take a century of a world at war to even it. God forgive us when we are living only to even a score.

Bo waited to see if she had finished, and he said, If it's that kind of story, Teta, where is the truth in it, as you've said there is?

The way a story ends, Bohumír, has everything to do with the way it begins.

And she told them finally what she had been told by the priest and others who knew their father, and knew of him. How he had arrived in Budapest as the siege lifted in mid-February of '45, when all of the Soviet forces pouring in from their victories against the Nazis on the Eastern Front had their eyes on the German soldiers and Hungarian refugees, those they hadn't killed when they tried to make their escape, moving northwest toward Vienna. And Bexhet Konar, an American soldier separated from his unit during the fighting in Europe, made his way east with the help of a patchwork of Resistance fighters and partisans from France, through Switzerland, Italy, and Yugoslavia, into Hungary, which was uncommon but not impossible, toward the Sajó, where he expected to find those he had left years ago, those he believed perhaps the war had not touched. But they were not there. They had moved even farther east to the Bodrog, where it flows out of the old Ruthenian lands into Hungary, and so he followed, accompanied by another Rom they say he had traveled with from as far away as the Italian Alps. And there on the banks of the river he found the *kumpania* in which his grandfather was simply an old man enjoying the blessing of having remarried a woman young enough to bear him a child in his later years. All of them slaughtered. Mostly women and children, the old man the only man among them in the vardo where he lived

with his wife and child. Where and how they died bore the work
of the Arrow Cross, those wanting nothing more than to kill out
of a hatred for a people who wanted, in their innocence, to be
left alone.

And it was this anger, this rage, that drove him to do what
work he did, she said. As though he rose each day and went to
it out of a duty or obligation, your father, in the space of only
a few months, where he continued to kill those already on the
verge of defeat, because the Red Army would liberate the Hungarians and the Slovaks by April, and Germany would surrender
by May.

She stopped here and hesitated and wiped an eye. She seemed
to want to weigh what it was she would say next. Weigh how she
should tell it after she had heard it from those who remembered
and would always remember, because story is how they shaped
and lived and made sense of their lives. But especially from the
man who watched their father kill those whom he had watched
kill his family.

They seemed to know all about the bastard *gadjo*-Rom, she
said. His beautiful mother, his powerful grandfather, of whom
every Rom knew from the Baltic to the Black Sea, and the
unknown Hungarian officer father, the man who fell dangerously
in love with the Gypsy girl and died a hero in some great battle
of the Great War because this love was forbidden, though who
knows if he was a hero or a rogue. Their love was *marime* among
the Roma, taboo, and neither one would find a home among the
other's home, because that is how the story had to be told in the
wake of yet another war that erased all borders and boundaries
the Romani never acknowledged or believed in regardless, save
for rivers and mountains and the coasts of the sea. So the ori-
gins of the one who came to them were shadowy and mythlike,
too, and he was turned into more than a young man blind with
revenge. He was turned into the child of that forbidden love who
searched and searched in war for where it was he would find his
home, born into one country just after the first war, fighting for

another country in the next, found improbably in the forest like a man who had visited the house of the dead and come back, found and transported to the same people who had nursed him, when God opened his eyes in this world to the sorrow brought upon his people, so as not to forget the reason why the one who had raised him sent him away, not knowing that he would one day return without country or allegiance and kill those who had killed the only memory he had of peace among those who had lived before him, and would do so after him.

It was this vengeance he moved with, he and his brothers in the Resistance, though how many, no one really knows. It may have been only two. They knew where and when to avoid the armies. First the retreating Germans, who fought as they always fought, no matter what. To the death. Then the poor and undisciplined Romanian army, which seemed to revel in Hungary's bad fortune and collapse for having fettered its body to the Nazis. And then the Russians, who were advancing from the east as the Germans surrendered and withdrew, and this, remember, was happening all in the space of two months, so fast was the end unfolding. The Russians also held no love for the Roma, and so as a rule they avoided troops of any kind, unless they were in search of them. But first they went in search of those who had killed their own. They followed their tracks like a road they had made from the Bodrog right to the city of Sátoraljaújhely. And they found them. Drunk inside a tavern, their telltale armbands of the green arrows in a cross still on their shirts, six of them, young men too young to join the army, bragging to anyone who would listen about the filth they had rid their country of. Your father waited outside the tavern for them. Waited all night, they say, for the men who were given round after round of drinks because they had taken scarves and fabrics from the women they had killed and used these as proof of their labors, along with the blood they kept on their hands and sleeves and wouldn't wash off. He waited until the tavern shut down and they were turned out into the streets. And the next day they were found by the side of a creek that runs along the eastern side of the city, near the border, their throats slit, their eyes wide, and their bodies stacked in three stacks of two, each one on top of the other in the shape of a cross. Then they began to show up like this all around the city. Bodies of thugs who had somehow managed to avoid the army, their armbands prominently displayed. And others began to whisper that the same was happening elsewhere, in Miskolc and Nyíregyháza and even Budapest, these stacks of two in the shape of a cross, and that their killer, one man, could be in three cities at once because he was a spirit, a demon unleashed by the Gypsies and bent on death. But, of course, this was just superstition, or the guilt of a people, I suppose.

He was never careless. He killed only in small numbers after that. Or perhaps the Arrow Cross reduced the size of the groups in which they rampaged, because now they feared losing entire gatherings of men who would put on the armband and assemble and risk their lives for the lives they took. Your father and his men, if there even were other men, killed twenty in the end, it was said, because there were nineteen women and children in all, including the old man they called Meska, in the Romani encampment on the Bodrog that day. They took twenty in order to tilt the balance. Eye for an eye. And then one more of the adversary, in order to remind him there's another who still holds the knife.

Bo's head was down and he stared at the floor as he listened. Then he lifted it and looked at his aunt and turned to his brother.

I asked him once if he had ever killed in the war and he was honest with me and said yes. So that he could come home. And because he loved us. I was a boy and only meant Nazis. All of those images of the enemy that the comic books I had started to read had drawn in my mind. I never knew what he could have possibly meant. That he could have killed so many because he had seen so many die.

Yes, Frances Posol said. Yes. We think we're strong until we have to fight. Then we find out just how weak we are.

Sam pushed the fingers that had been massaging his temples through his hair.

But where was the weakness, Teta? In him. Where? he said in a voice too loud for the room.

Nowhere, Samuel. It's not a question of weakness or strength. The question is, What will you do and why? That's why I called you here. And to that end, I'm not finished, if you care to listen.

I'm sorry, Sam said. It's just that I don't want to think of him as weak.

He wasn't. Listen. What happened over the border in Hungary during that time only came to me through those who had heard the stories from others who could and would tell it when the war was over finally, and the stories managed to cross even that border with them, which was difficult. The Czechoslovaks and the Magyars have long memories, longer, it seems, than the empire in which the Hungarians believed everyone had to be Hungarian and under the Hungarian crown, so it was not a simple border along the plain of the Danube set up after the Great War. Ask your grandfather. He managed to avoid somehow the war fought there in 1919, even after he had survived a world war. But for all of what your father could do, he could not keep the Red Army from coming in from the east, and it was difficult for him and any man of fighting age to answer the question, *Why are you not fighting?* By which they meant with an army, victorious or defeated. So he slipped across the border into Košice, because there was word of a group of Romani left there in spite of the years in which the Slovaks' own Hlinka Guard did its best to rid the country of Gypsies. And this is where I question the story that he had other *men* with him, because I know that only one other man, whom they called Petalo and say was related to your father because he called him brother, was with him in the city when they arrived at the Greek Catholic church and were told the priest and his wife would feed them without asking questions. It was there that a new division of the Hlinka Guard, called the *Pohotovostné oddiely Hlinkoveh gardy,* or the POHG, arrived. These men were hunting for Slovak families who were hiding Jews still, as though time was running out for them, and someone had told these guards that they suspected the priest.

In the afternoon, on a warm spring day, in the courtyard between the church and the house where the priest and his wife and their son lived, two members of the POHG burst into the courtyard to arrest the priest and found your father and his brother in arms. Your father sat with his back to the door and it was Petalo who saw the men come in and raise their pistols, and he yelled *Chod' dole!* All three fell in time to avoid the bullets. Petalo sprang to his feet then and rushed them, killed the first one with his knife, and had the point of the blade to the chest of the other when the man shot him point-blank in the stomach with a pistol hidden in his coat. The gunfire must have alerted the other POHG in town that there was trouble at the church. The priest hid your father and Petalo, who was bleeding badly, but he, the priest, believed that the strong arm of Jozef Tiso, the priest who ran the country, would not be inclined to harm another priest. Until more POHG came and searched the priest's house and found Petalo and executed him right where they found him. Then they searched the house and found the Jewish family, a father and a mother and their daughter, brought them out into the courtyard, and brought the priest and his wife out into the courtyard, as well. And when they had finished with their long speech about how these Jews should have been sent to a work camp long ago, and how a priest himself should be at work for the good of the Catholic Church and the good of the nation, not for the sin of keeping Jews from their work, they lined all five against the wall of the courtyard and shot them dead and left their bodies in a heap. You can still see the bullet marks in the wall where they made them stand.

You've seen them? Bo asked.

I've searched them with my fingertips, she said.

And so how—

How did your father escape?

Yes.

Petalo knew he was going to die, so he let himself be found.

He thought he could save the priest's life. He thought wrong. Your father watched this from a broken window in the choir loft, which could only be accessed by a staircase hidden in the wall. The priest's son, a boy of twelve, had taken him there before the guards arrived, and the two of them sat without uttering a word and watched as the others were shot in the courtyard. The guards couldn't have known who else was left. They had killed three Jews, a Gypsy, a priest who proved to be no friend of the state, and his wife. It was time for a drink, no doubt, and they left.

And our father went after them and found them, Sam said. That's why you called us here, Teta, right? To tell us that. So we'll believe that story.

No, Samuel. You may believe what you wish to believe. I only called you here to tell you what I know. Your father found them, yes, and managed to lure them back to the courtyard, all with the help of the boy. The boy with nothing left, but who would become a man of faith nevertheless. When his tears were dried, he went out to the place where those same guards were drinking and bragging, and yet telling, too, of how they would fit back into their lives once the war was over and the Nazis left and the Russians left and they could get on with being Czechoslovaks again, as though they were the backbone of some good and grand design in that country. He, the boy, showed up at the tavern and told them to hurry, that there were others at the church who had come to take away the dead ones in the courtyard, and they could add to their work that day and be even greater heroes. These guards asked if those at the church now were Jews or Gypsies, and the boy didn't know what to say, so he just said, *Yes, hurry!* with a kind of impatience. And the guards stumbled out from the table and took their clubs and knives and pistols and ran back to the church as fast as they could, where your father killed them all one at a time as they entered through the gate. Shot them each in the head with a round from the Czech pistol the guard who had shot Petalo had been carrying. All but one of them.

And that one? Sam asked.

The boy shot. The boy of twelve. After the man begged for his drunken life and soiled himself on ground consecrated no longer because it was stained with the blood of homicide. Because this one was the man the boy had watched kill his mother.

And then?

Then no one else came to the church. No one else seemed to care what went on there any longer. The boy, who knew where every lock and every key in that church was, because his father had shown him where everything was, showed your father the crypt, and they buried there that night the bodies of his mother and his father, the Jewish family they had hidden for two years, and the Rom they called Petalo. All six laid to rest in the locked and stone silence of the crypt.

Frances Posol rose and went to the window and drew the curtains back. The sun had arced into the afternoon and it shone through the western-facing window now, the coal dust outside looking like clouded etchings in the glass, which would never be clear, and the Susquehanna flowed without seeming to move past those etchings.

All this time, she said from the window, and it's only water and tea I've offered you. Come. I've made a soup. We'll have lunch and then I'll show you the photographs I collected from over there. I would have suffered a fate worse than Petalo's if the police had ever caught me with them. But here I am. And after that, I have some ham and good whiskey we can enjoy with dinner. I won't let you starve here like you do at home. Come, she said again.

She walked into the kitchen and Bo rose and followed her. Sam, though, remained seated, and when she noticed it was only the elder son who had followed, she turned and walked back out into the living room.

Samuel, she said. Hunger only makes young men angry.

I'm not angry, Teta. I'm just wondering.

About what?

How it is you know, he said.

She shook her head and he said, Not because I don't know that you've been back there. I do. Pop told us. And not because I don't believe you have done things out of your own anger that are all of a piece in this family. I mean what he did. I mean the number of men. Can one man kill that many?

Oh, Samuel, of course he can. I know he did. And I know he felt both guilt and justification. Both of which may have been what killed him in the end. But come. That was a long time ago, and you have a long road of your own ahead.

She held out her hand as if to raise him herself, but he remained in the chair.

Yes, but how do you know? he asked, a note of pleading almost in his voice, and she brought her hand back to her side and thought, *He is just like him.*

Because of the boy, she said. Who he became.

She hoped he would not press her, but he asked, Who did he become?

Have you not been listening to a single word I said, Samuel? It was your father who begged him not to take revenge, begged that boy of twelve to give the pistol to the soldier ready to do what was about to be done, but the boy would not. He would not hand over the gun and even trained it on your father as he backed away and ran to the side of the thug he had watched murder his mother and put the last bullet that pistol held into the man's head. An orphan and a murderer now, the boy became a man in search of forgiveness and in need of it. He became what the sojourner and the fatherless all become in the end.

AND WISHED FOR THE DAY
(June 21, 1999)

1

That old bluetick hound we called Hector was just a puppy then and Grayson's only companion in the house when I showed up on the ridge in September of '73. A hunting buddy of his from school, who had found out he had a heart murmur when his draft number came up, drove by with the hound in the bed of his pickup. Grayson had just retired from the marines and moved back to Abas, and his friend presented the hound to him as if it were some kind of peace offering and asked if he'd like to get back out there, bag a deer or a turkey, or just shoot some squirrels. Grayson told him he had no desire to hunt anymore. Couldn't imagine there would be the same beauty in it as there was when they were boys and about lived in the woods, not after where he'd been. The man spit a stream of tobacco juice into the dirt and said, *Well, go on and keep him anyway, Burne.*

He told me all this as I stood thin and not a little ragged on his doorstep, Hector wagging and barking like, well, like a hound. I had just been given a ride up the mountain in the same pickup by the same man, the trip behind me having been considerably longer than the road to Morning Ridge, though Grayson saw me with only my AWOL bag and the clean pair of clothes I'd been given at the navy hospital in San Diego, and he said, *Damn, son! How long you been in town?* Not as long it took me to get there, I told him.

It was an Indian summer afternoon near the end of the month and hotter than a fox in a forest fire, but I had interrupted Grayson splitting cordwood, same place my brother had found him almost a year ago to the day. And he told me about Bo and a young lady named Ruth, who introduced herself as my fiancée, coming down for answers to the question of my whereabouts. He gave them details about the two tours I did with him, the preternatural luck he believed I brought to the platoon, and the ambush in which I had gone missing. If they were looking for whereabouts, Grayson told them, there was no *where* about it. I was in Vietnam, dead or alive, and he was going to put his money on the latter. I thanked him for not giving up on me and he started to speak, then hesitated, as if he couldn't decide whether to ask me about what had happened after the shooting stopped, or what had happened with my brother and my fiancée. Then he clasped me on the shoulder and said, *Let me show you around the place,* which took about a minute, the house little more than two rooms, a stone chimney, and a kitchen with a Franklin stove. It was home, he said, and had been since the day he was old enough to hammer a nail, cut a board, and snap a chalk line, and his father, newly widowed, bought the land and told him, *Son, we're going to build our house right here.* We ended up on the wide and covered back porch that looked south and west, like it was the last best view of the day, and that's where we sat.

Between the two of us, there had been the bond of the Corps. Always faithful, and never more so than when the fighting began and, weeks short, I stood at point and returned fire on the enemy that had attacked the Combined Action Platoon of which I was a part and which Captain Grayson had come to retrieve and escort back to Da Nang. I was twenty-two then and on my second tour, a marine corporal in the zone for sergeant. I had gotten engaged to Ruth Younger in Honolulu on R&R two months before, and I was looking forward to going home, getting married, and making a career of it. Move down to North Carolina, or out to California. And then, two years later, I was an empty shell of a man sitting on that porch with nothing but what I had still managed to keep in my AWOL bag, the sun setting and a late breeze just starting to stir. In time, when this ridge became mine, I would find that great heights of the Allegheny Range, like Spruce Knob and Thorny Flat, were out there, the latter visible on the high-pressure days of autumn, but neither sky nor range was discernible through the thick humidity and haze of that day as the sun set and evening came on. Birds called from the forest edge, bats swooped and siphoned mosquitoes in a clearing down there where the cordwood was piled, and a porcupine that had earned its peace with Hector whimpered from the branch of a pine.

I remember when then-Lieutenant Grayson told me on night patrol in the jungle once that his father used to say there is an intimacy with darkness some men discover when darkness is the only thing visible. It no longer becomes a beast to fear, or a threat from which to take cover, but a companion with whom one can sit and find peace. All that has happened in the daylight feels too loud, too distracting. It's nightfall that begins to quiet the noise and pare down those distractions, until there is only what matters sitting right in front of you. Then, when morning comes, it's as though the light that comes with it is light from the first day of your life. But it wasn't until the evening one year later, when the newly promoted captain had come home on leave to bury his father, that he sat on the porch built on this same ridge and understood then what the man had been talking about. When Grayson returned to Camp Lejeune, he was given command of a Combined Action Group and did a third tour in Quang Tri Province in 1970, when most of the marines had already left Vietnam. I had just re-upped, and he was the reason I went back for my second tour, which lasted slightly longer than I had anticipated.

I will tell you that as I sat there on the porch with my feet tucked under me and my shoulders straight against the wall of the house, the dusk and all of its sounds everywhere around reminded me of Pennsylvania. How much I loved the mountains there. How warm it got in the day. How cool at night. What that felt and sounded like. When my grandfather built his house on the mountain in Dardan, my mother told me you could walk into two thousand acres of forest and see for miles right down to the Salamander River, which cut through the center of Dardan. He was raised in the mountains, too. In the Carpathians of the old Austro-Hungarian Empire. And he told me once that of all the things he learned there from his father—how to shepherd, how to shoot, how to speak and read English—it was the man's presence that shaped him and taught him and gave him something, someone, to fight for when the fighting started. *I loved your father like a son,* he told me, *and so I promised myself I would raise you and your brother like my own in the wake of him.* The wake of him was my whole life, my father's presence a photograph on the mantel and my mother's secret bitterness for who he'd been and how he'd died. My grandfather kept his promise, though, and of all the things the old man taught me—how to shoot, how to drive, how to read spoor and people alike—it was his presence during those years that gave me someone to talk to in prison, when all around me there were only ghosts.

War took my father and my grandfather down off their mountains. A car took me off mine. The old man taught me how to drive the Ford truck at fourteen and I got my license the day I turned sixteen. When I was seventeen and had made enough money working at the mill to buy my first car, I bought the fastest one I could, a Dodge 426 Hemi, and that, one year later, was the reason why I had to enlist.

When I think back on those times, it's like cars were characters themselves, living lives right next to ours. Guys I knew ahead of me in school used to piss and moan about how they didn't want to graduate and get sent off to die in some politician's war they didn't believe in, and then they'd go out and get drunk as skunks and wrap their cars around trees, with them and their buddies in them. I once wondered if automobiles were capable of revenge, because I lost count of the number of friends I knew who died going faster than they knew how to drive. *Race car spelled backward is race car,* Ruth Younger always used to say when we heard that someone else we knew was gone, her way of telling me, I realize now, that it didn't matter how you lived, just that you lived, because we were all going to the same place in the end, and I wonder how it was she figured that out so early on. Anyway, I won my race. I beat a brand-new Plymouth Barracuda, but not the appearance before the judge, who said, *Son, it's time you did something with your life.* And they sent me down off the mountain one last time. All of them. My grandfather. My mother. My brother. And the judge. Only Ruth Younger came to the bus and cried when I left for Parris Island. And again, after my ship-out party and we drove to the lake and watched a waning moon rise from Asa Pound's dock. She made me promise I'd come back alive, and I kept that promise both times.

I told this to Grayson, when there was a porch here, and he just listened and swigged his beer and waited for me to break off, and then, into the chorus of nightfall, he said it sounded like the road off of that mountain came around to war for me, too. I nodded and said, I guess so.

I could have left it there, left it all unsaid and gotten on with why I had come down to West Virginia, to get away from the ghosts that walked the land in Dardan like they walked my cell in Hoa Lo, but I needed to say it out loud as much as I wanted Grayson to listen to what had happened after he lost me in that ambush. And what happened after they ambushed me at home, it felt like. Every fight comes to an end. You know it by the emptied-out adrenaline. You'll know it, too, son. I was emptied, but I needed to know this was it. No more twists and turns. As much as it was like a companion to me, I needed the night to be over.

I started with what he didn't know, which was everything

after the day we saw that first wave of VC swarm out of the jungle, firing on us, and all of a sudden dying there in the highlands of Quang Tri made sense to me, as though this was the direction in which the arc of my life would bend. But I dropped to my knee and shot the first man out of the bush straight in the chest and that thought melted away. I looked to Grayson for orders, watched Crawford crumble, and called my own men to tie in right, before a grenade went off and all I could see through the dirt and smoke was the captain on the ground.

I still thought we could repel them, and so I pursued, like we were trained to do. But the assault from both the front and the flank surprised me. There were Vietcong pouring out of the bush, and it was Vietcong I was firing at, but this was more than a guerilla attack, and I found myself alone and surrounded by NVA regulars emerging from the woods as though they had been waiting, their silence and quick moves more terrifying all of a sudden than the exchange of arms and grenade blasts. For the first time in a long time, I was scared. I turned to holler and wave off anyone who might have followed, and I felt my leg get kicked out from under me, even before I heard the round go off. And when I looked up from the ground, there was a man in those black pajamas the VC wore standing over me with his carbine pointed in my face. He kicked me, hollered in Vietnamese to get up, and I understood. I still had my pack on and I could see from the incline that the bullet had entered and exited my thigh without any great profusion of blood. *I won't die,* I thought, *at least not today,* and I lifted my head and said to the man, I would get up if you hadn't shot me, asshole. He raised his rifle butt and I heard a crack and he dropped to the ground. I looked over at where the round had come from and saw another squad of NVA regulars advance from the edge of the clearing. Four of them disarmed all the other VC, pushed them into the trees, and shot each one. *Wrong again,* I thought.

When I figured that would be my last day, too, on this Earth, another man in uniform, who looked like he just might be in command, walked over to me and said in English, *You were told to get up.* It was good. Deliberate. And I said to him that I'd already told the dead man on the ground over there that I couldn't get up. *Officer?* he asked. I pointed to the two stripes on my arm and shook my head, but he knew. He knelt down and pulled my leg out straight and studied the entry and exit wounds, then stood. *Do you know why there are only five of our guerilla comrades in that pile over there?* he asked. I didn't answer, and he said, *Because last night, while we waited for you, a tiger found the sixth one. Sleeping. He was their sentry. We have known of your propaganda among the villagers for some time now, thanks to the old ones. We were unsure of your troop strength, though. Tell me how many you are.* I didn't say a word. He called one of the regulars over to me, took a field dressing from a pack the man wore, poured iodine onto the wound, and wrapped the dressing around my thigh. *You are lucky not to be a prisoner of the guerillas,* he said. *They would keep you in a bamboo cage and feed you manioc and snake meat, if there was any left. But President Ho wishes us to treat our prisoners with leniency, not put them in cages, so they might see the truth. Now get up.*

I got on my feet and wobbled a bit, but I could walk. One of the regulars went into the woods and came back with a tree limb he fashioned into a crutch. I told myself this was what I would do until I was presented with an opportunity to do otherwise. I knew no one was coming to get me.

A few clicks later and it was near midday by my reckoning, the sun blistering and the air so thick, I felt smothered by it. The dressing around my leg was soaked in blood that dripped down the inside of my trousers and I felt weak. There were NVA regulars in front of me and behind me, each man moving in his own silence, so that there seemed to be a vow or some agreement among them. I didn't know why they shot those Vietcong. Something had happened between the two groups that I couldn't figure. Then we came out of the jungle and marched east along a ridge. I say *marched*, but I wasn't doing much of that by the time we got to where we were going. The land sloped down into a swath of grass and there was sand in the distance, a long and wide beach where waves appeared like beards that grew full and white before fading away into the shoreline. As we filed out onto that grass, I could see it was a full NVA company I was moving with. The regulars shifted their packs and stood at ease. I leaned against the crutch and tried to inhale the salt smell of the sea, but all I got was the smell of sweat and rot.

My leg hurt like hell and I was thirsty and ready to drop, so I tried to ask for water in Vietnamese to see what I would get, and a man who began barking orders at the others ran to my side and slapped me hard across the face. The officer who spoke English came over to me and said, *He thought you were speaking ill of our country.* I told him I just wanted some water, and he said that water and country were the same word in Vietnamese. *So be careful,* he said, and handed me an aluminum canteen. The water inside was silted and smelled of must, but I drank it all, and he didn't stop me. When I finished, I handed the empty canteen back to him and asked why his men had shot the Vietcong soldiers who had led the ambush against us. *Vietcong this month. The soldiers you call ARVN last month. I am sure their fathers believe they fight bravely, but they did not lead that ambush. They say they are our Communist brothers, but they are without discipline, and a soldier without discipline is more dangerous than the best-trained enemy. The one who shot you in the leg thought he was John Wayne, even after his lengthy reeducation. We needed them to draw you into the ambush. After that, we needed them not to be John Wayne.*

I told him we were only living in the villages with the people, and he smiled at me. *I do not believe that was what the French Jesuits would have called the vocation of a United States Marine. No. Your propaganda holds no sway with the people.*

He looked at my leg and called to a regular, who came over to him and listened to his instructions. The regular went back, retrieved a pack, and returned to the officer's side, knelt down, and removed her fiber helmet. She couldn't have been a day over fifteen, and I wondered how many men I had shot at were not men at all. If maybe Crawford had been killed by this girl. She began to work quickly, so quickly that I wasn't exactly sure what was happening. She had a Zippo lighter and a can of Sterno she must have taken off of some grunt, dead or alive, and she sparked that Zippo and fired up the Sterno like we were going to have Hormel for dinner. Then the officer took his pistol from the holster he kept on his belt, one of those MAS 1873s that the French had brought in. He pulled back the loading gate and half-cocked the hammer, pulled the ejector rod out, and removed the cylinder, then put the barrel over the lit Sterno can. It was clear to me then what he was going to do with that pistol. I tried to stand and he put his hand on my shoulder and said, *You won't make it the rest of the way if we don't.*

Why am I so important to you? I asked him. I'm only an enlisted man. He waved at his entire company, and said, *We are all enlisted. Enlisted in the struggle toward the peaceful unification of Vietnam.*

The girl reached back into the pack then and brought out a box of morphine syrettes, World War Two era, they had to have been, and the man snarled at her and shook his head. But she insisted until he relented, and she pulled on the wire loop, broke the seal, and pushed the needle into my leg. It didn't take long. From the back of that leg right up into the rest of my body, there was a slowly overcoming wave of bliss, and I thought the sky had never looked so beautiful. Then they pulled my pants down and he picked up some thick leaves to protect his hand, took the white-hot barrel of the pistol from the Sterno can, and shoved it into my wound. The sky went black and I could smell the stink of my burning flesh. The girl held me down, she was so strong, then rolled me over and the man cauterized the exit wound, as well. Then I passed out.

I don't know how long we stayed there. I came in and out of

consciousness and saw the girl each time looking down at me, stroking my hair, saying, *Blondie, Blondie.* It seemed close to night when she gave me another syrette, and I didn't feel a thing. I remember in my delirium I asked her what her name was, and she said, *Thien.* And I took that name into my dreams and slept at the edge of the jungle near the sea.

Eventually, we moved, though slowly. Two people helped me each day. One or another of the NVA regulars on my left, and the girl, always the girl, on my right. After a few days, it was the crutch and the girl, and we marched on again. Days, a week, I don't know. I just remember the constant wave of smells. The sea. The stink of men. The sea again. When she used the last of the syrettes, she wrote on the inside of the empty box and pinned it to the pocket of my combat jacket. The officer watched her, and when she looked up at him, he just shook his head and turned to move on with the others.

One day—I don't know what day—we came to a town. The smell of the sea had disappeared and the stink of men was everywhere. One of the regulars tied my hands tight behind me and the officer who spoke English loosened the knots so that I could feel the blood flow into my hands again. *Be glad,* he said to me. *We used to make the French walk to their prisons.* Then he took me by the arm and led me into the back of an old Soviet GAZ-63 with a group of NVA regulars, who laughed to see their traveling companion. Thien looked on. Then the truck bounced into the jungle and moved along a thick-canopied and well-maintained road, so that it seemed like we were flying now through North Vietnam.

On the empty box of morphine syrettes she had written, *This one is the horse among the locusts,* but I couldn't know that until I had gotten to Hoa Lo.

I didn't need to tell Grayson what that place was like, not with all of the attention Operation Homecoming had been getting. But there was a big difference between showing up as a prisoner in December of '71 and being one of the guys who had been there since the sixties. Most of the torture had stopped by then, or at least that's what I was told. But there are still nights I lie awake and wonder how you measure time in hell.

On the first day, I stuck to my training and gave them only my name and rank. One of the guards found the empty syrette box and handed it to another guard, and that was the last I thought I'd see of it. The last I'd hear of Thien. They stripped me and gave me a baggy red-and-purple-dyed shirt and pants to wear, then threw me into a cell. They didn't feed me until the morning of the next day, but because I wasn't an officer and wasn't willing to talk, even that food declined considerably over the coming weeks, and I believed it was there I would die, in that place where the war I fought was with myself. Believed it with a kind of faith.

One day, though, when I was limping to the latrine, another marine sidled up to me and asked if I remembered my Morse code. I nodded, and he said, *It's all in Morse.* And that night the tapping I thought was some kind of torture or gnawing rats was a slow and deliberate message for me, repeated over and over until I got it. *Eat stay strong.* I wasn't strong, though. And what strength I had was ebbing in ways I didn't even know yet.

They tapped out instructions first. The code. We maintained the rank we held at capture, and we conducted ourselves as American servicemen, regardless. No one gave anything. No one got anything. Not all of the prisoners were on the same page. Some of them had entered the NVA's reeducation program and began to come out against our continued presence in Vietnam and the war. Other officers and airmen were tortured and broken down until they gave recorded statements saying that we were foreign invaders killing women and children, and that America should go home and get out of Vietnam. They played these over loudspeakers in the camp, and you could tell the guys talking had been beaten, so empty-sounding were those words. I believed in the home part. But not the Communist propaganda. I know we were sent there to keep democracy in Southeast Asia. But that's not why I fought there. I fought because Grayson fought. I fought because Crawford fought. I fought for the marine next to me, each time, each tour. I don't think anyone really understands that. Sworn to God, country, and corps. And until either one or all of those three abandoned me, I sure as hell wasn't going to side with the North Vietnamese and their idea of where the truth was. In the bush with those dead VC, as far as I could tell.

I think they thought I might have been another Garwood, but I did nothing for them or their reeducation program. I stayed as mute as a panda for damn near a month. That's when her brother, Bao, showed up. I was in my cell and the door opened at a time of day when it never opened, and in walked a man in uniform, pressed and clean. He was not one of the regular guards. He stood looking at me on the ground, my prison clothes filthy, my food plate crawling with bugs, and he said in English, *It appears to me that my sister was wrong.* And he held up the syrette box.

He was the chief guard of the block, one I found out from the other prisoners could be merciful one moment and brutal the next. With me, though, it was like he was speaking to someone who was and was not me. The sergeant I had made contact with that first time kept telling me not to break, that this one was an evil bastard at heart, and to remember my family waiting for me at home. But I didn't think this man, Bao, wanted to turn me into a poster boy for communism. I held some connection to the girl, Thien. And it wasn't until he kept returning to my cell that I understood what that connection meant for me.

They came from a large Catholic family in the north, Bao and Thien, the last two children of seven. She was the youngest. Their mother was a seamstress in Hanoi, their father the manager of a rubber export business, a man who loved the French and hated the Japanese who had invaded their country in World War Two. He left his wife, two sons, and his job in 1940 to fight in Europe with the French. He was captured by the Germans, held prisoner for five years, and, when the war was over, returned to Hanoi, a man of skin and bones returning to a family no better off than he was, because they had had to fend for themselves during the time he was away and in prison. His wife nursed him back to health and gave him four more boys and the girl.

The two oldest brothers never forgave their father for having left them, and they despised the French. They ran away to join the Vietminh in 1952, and died in battle at Dien Bien Phu two years later. When the French left, their father left, too. Their mother stayed, though, to sew and cook and weep. That's all she did each day. And her children joined the People's Army when they came of age. Her three oldest living sons were members of the Twenty-seventh Battalion, which was wiped out by American B-52s. When word was sent to their mother that only her daughter and youngest son remained, she died of grief. Bao and Thien were orphans. They moved up from the youth army into the regulars, and went wherever they were ordered. Thien was taken in by the officer who spoke English to me. Bao was sent to Hoa Lo to work as a guard, so that there would be at least one man left to carry on the family name, which Bao had changed from his Christian name, Laurent Cheval, to Ho Minh Bao.

He did well there at the prison and rose to become a commander. The message on the box of syrettes was meant for him so that they would put me under his care, for the girl, I thought at first, but learned in time it was she who was taking care of him.

They did a lot of things to me there. One guard would beat me in the leg and yell at me to confess. Another one would pierce the thin pink skin of my bullet wound with a wire and let it bleed, before pouring rice wine over it and bandaging it up again. Then Bao would come in and talk to me about growing up in his village with his sister, whom he loved, and how they used to catch fish and take them to their mother, who would cook them over the fire and tell them stories about their brothers, who came to her at night and spoke to her. They beat me again the next day, and I began to wonder if Bao had ordered them to, so I asked him, and he said, *There are things we have to do, and things we want to do. If they want to beat you, they will beat you. What we have to do is always much harder.* This went on for a month, until I could barely stand, and the pain in my leg wound was unbearable.

Then Bao came to me one night and told me he could make them stop. Make them do what they had to do, not what they wanted to do. *And the pain,* he said. *Shall I stop the pain? Just as sister Thien did?* I said yes, and he pulled from his coat pocket a syringe, a tie, and a bag of white powder, and said, *This is better than those old shots of battlefield morphine. What do you Americans call it? Skeg, no?*

Skag, I told him. A skeg is on a surfboard.

Ah, yes. But Vietnamese skeg is pure, he said. *Not like American skeg.*

He was measuring the heroin into a spoon, and he had a Zippo lighter much like the one his sister carried. As he cooked up the dose, he said, *I have never seen anyone surf, have you?* And I told him I had, on the beach in Da Nang, where I watched a couple of marines from California surf on boards they had brought all the way from home. *Tell me about California,* he said. And before I could tell him that I didn't know much about California, that I was from the other side of the country, he had tied off my left arm, found a vein, and put the needle into me. I watched my blood flow back into the barrel of the syringe in a swirl of purple, and it felt like a thousand orgasms were coursing from my loins throughout my body. I closed my eyes and disappeared.

When I opened them again, he was standing over me. *How is the pain now?* he asked, and I could only mutter, No pain. He smiled and said, *Enjoy your place of no pain, and I will be back tomorrow.*

In the morning, they beat me. At midday, they brought me food. And in the evening, he brought heroin and spoke softly of his sister and his youth. A peace I never knew was possible washed over me, and I no longer believed I would die there.

If I had been released in those first months, I think I would have walked out of Hoa Lo prison and been fine. But two months turned to four, the same routine every day, and I could feel the cells inside me change. I used to think about how funny that sounded. The cells in my body. My body in that cell. The circle had closed, and I couldn't go anywhere but around it. That was when I found out why she had sent me.

One evening, Bao said he had no more *skeg,* as he kept calling it, and I felt myself panic. You don't get hooked right away, but after four months, I was a junkie for sure, and I needed a fix. Morphine? I asked him, and he said, *No.* For hours we sat in that cell alone together, hours that began to stretch out as though they were weeks. By the middle of the night, I felt myself getting sick, and he just watched me limp around and twitch, then writhe wide-eyed and start calling out for him to help me. He left when the sun came up, and the other guards came in and beat me. Just like they did every other morning. By evening I would have welcomed a beating. I didn't sleep that night, and the next day I received the same. Just when I believed this was what they planned for me, he stood in the faint daylight at the entrance to my cell and said, *What do you need, Blondie?* I told him I needed a fix. I needed the skag. *Do you need it, or do you want it?* he asked, and I howled at him in my confusion and pain. He walked to my side and began to stroke my hair, and said, *I will ease your pain, if you ease mine, too.* Anything, I pleaded. Anything. He just nodded, and said, *Tomorrow.*

When tomorrow came, the beatings were nothing to me. I was lost. Junk-sick so bad, I hoped they would kill me. That evening, Bao walked in, stood in the doorway, and didn't speak. I was curled up on my pallet, rocking and moaning and waiting to die. I watched him take a small bag of the heroin so white that it looked like Christmas snow from his uniform pocket and hold it in his hand, looking at it, studying it. Then he walked toward my bed and knelt beside me. He took my arm, held it out straight, and tied a filthy bandanna above the elbow. Then he scooped a dose into the spoon, cooked it with his Zippo on the cell floor, and drew it up into a syringe. He held my hand in his hand while I looked on with the eyes of a man hungry for what was just out of reach, and he put that spike in my arm. I watched the purple swirl of my own blood flower and disappear, and my suffering was over. This god had delivered me, and I could see him smile as I fell back into the place of my high.

When he was done, he put the heroin and the needle and the spoon away and began to take off his uniform jacket, shirt, and trousers, folding them and placing them neatly at the entrance of the cell. Then he crawled naked onto my bed, reached under my arm and across my chest, and held me, whispering something in Vietnamese to someone who wasn't there. I could feel him become erect and push himself between my legs, and I thought, *If this is what I have to endure to feed my own desire, then I will.* But, as though he was ashamed of what was in his thoughts, or this was all the closeness he, the commander, would allow himself to feel, his body relaxed and he fell asleep there next to me. Chaste, or fearful, or wanting only that much, I never knew. I only knew that I wasn't the one he was whispering to. In time, I fell asleep, as well. And that is where and how we both slept every night for months after, the two of us together on a pallet bed in a prison in Hanoi, what we needed and what we wanted both close and far, far from there.

Early winter of '72, it had to have been, B-52s were dropping bombs so close to us in Hanoi, they moved some of the prisoners up to a place called the Dogpatch. Bao didn't send me, though. He kept me on the heroin, and I let him sleep where he wanted, his desire not for me, I realized, but for the sister he had lost and wanted to find again, though to love her was no longer possible. She had touched me, he said, so I was the only way he could touch her now. The beatings stopped, and there were nights he would lie next to me, whispering until first light, so that I couldn't sleep, either, nor, at times, did I want or care to sleep. And none of the other prisoners knew.

And then early the following year, they announced we were going home. Just like that. The NVA wanted to make it into a grand gesture and send the airmen, officers, and the admiral home first, but we stuck to the code. We got released according to how long we had been there, or no one got released at all. I was going home last, but I was going home.

On the morning of my departure from Hoa Lo, a guard brought in clothes for the bus ride to the airport. I wasn't thinking about the fact that I was an active-duty United States marine with a full heroin habit. I was thinking about no longer being in that prison. I was thinking about seeing my mother and my grandfather and brother again, and waking up in the house where I was born. Bao came in after the guard had left and picked up the clothes, put them back down, and said, *The bus will be leaving without you today.* I asked him what he meant, and he said that he could not let me leave. He would tell the delegation that I had been reeducated and wished to remain among the Vietnamese. I became furious and told him that was a lie. The bus was waiting for me and I would be on it. *Not without this*, he said and held out the same small plastic bag.

I don't know where my rage came from. Maybe I could see him now for who or what he was. But I had a seat on a C-141 at Gia Lam Airport, just a short ride from where I stood, and I was going home. I ran at him, so fast that he had no time to react, to drop the bag and protect himself, and with one move I grabbed him by the head with my hand over his mouth so that he couldn't yell, and slammed him hard into the wall. His legs gave way and he slid to the floor.

I didn't want to kill him. I just wanted to go home, and he stood in the way of that. I suppose he believed we had forged a bond together, and that my desire for heroin was greater than my desire for home. But he was wrong about the heroin.

I checked his pulse and, though he was unconscious, he was

alive. I could leave him and he might stay out cold until I was gone, or he might come to. Either way, dead or alive, the guards would find him and I would be seized, and there would be no release for me then. I needed to be on that plane before he woke or was found. So I took the baggie and the works he kept in his uniform, cooked a dose, and shot up, so I could think straight. The fix would get me to the Philippines. And when I looked at Bao on the floor and held the hands that had overcome him in front of my face, I knew I couldn't bring myself to spend another moment in that place. I knelt down and cooked up another dose and gave it to him. Then I cooked up another one and gave that to him, as well. I shot him up three times and kept the rest of the heroin for myself, in case I might need it later. Then I watched him as that shit plowed through his body like a bulldozer made of lotus flowers, watched him twitch and nearly come back to life, his eyes even opening once in a quick and distant terror before they glassed over again. And he was gone.

I dragged him onto the pallet, put his uniform coat over his shoulders, my striped pajamas over his legs, and made it look as though he was sleeping. Then I put on the civilian clothes they had brought for me. When the guard opened the cell door and looked over at the commander on my bed, I nodded and made the sign of a man sleeping, folded hands holding up my tilted head. The guards knew. He smiled and winked and led me out of my cell and into the compound.

The heroin you get in Vietnam, the heroin Bao shot into me while he spoke softly in Vietnamese to some memory of his sister, is pure heroin. My only fear on the bus ride to the Hanoi airport was not that I would be found out for having killed a North Vietnamese prison commander, but that I would have to go from the skag they sold in Vietnam to the brown junk you find on the streets of every city in America. I know, because I found it. And how long would it be before I ended up busted and in another prison, my family thinking they should have left me in the one in Vietnam? But once I got on the plane, it didn't matter. At Clark, in the Philippines, they listened to the account of my capture, took one look at my leg, and gave me all the morphine I asked for. At Travis, in California, the navy doctor there did the same. He even gave me some for the plane ride home to Pennsylvania. And I traveled the whole way with the small bag I had taken from Bao. After that, I found smack everywhere in Wilkes-Barre and even got myself a dealer in the town of Luzerne, closer to Dardan. I was set. I just had to figure out what my life would look like now that everything and everyone I had known before I left for Vietnam had changed and gotten on with their own lives without me.

2

Eventually, I knew I'd have to come down to number one Morning Ridge to see Grayson. To let him know I had remained faithful, as he had, to the belief that I had not died somewhere in Quang Tri, that I had just gotten lost and it was only a matter of time before I was found. For two months, though, I waited. And the day my brother and Ruth Younger got married, the same day my former fiancée realized I was a junkie, was the day I figured it was time. I packed my seabag, put my works and my stash in my AWOL bag, and headed to the bus station in the early light of day, bound for West Virginia, or so I thought.

I was on the bus out of Wilkes-Barre when I went to sleep, and I woke up just as we came to a halt in a station dock and the driver hollered out to us, *Columbus, Ohio, people! We'll be here for one hour.* I rubbed my eyes and stretched my arms, and it never dawned on me that we were too far west for a bus going to West Virginia. I was still a little high after having fixed in the middle of the night by toilet light, the rocking so bad as the old hound barreled down the highway, I almost spilled what I had cooked up in my spoon, until I figured out how to wedge myself between the sink and the door and let my body move instead of trying to remain rigid, like being on a ship. I'd have to fix again somewhere by the time it was evening, but I reckoned we'd be in Richmond by then and I could find a park bench or a restroom.

The air-conditioning on the bus was making me cold and I wanted to get my jean jacket, so I stood up and walked down the aisle and stepped out and onto the dock and went to the side of the bus, where I asked an old man who had just lit a cigarette if he could open the luggage bay so I could retrieve my seabag. He looked at me and nodded and rolled up his sleeve, where he had a tattoo of the 2/4 on his forearm, then pulled the latch, and said, *Go on and get your gear.*

The bag wasn't there. On its way to Richmond, I thought, and then remembered the driver had said Columbus, and that this bus was supposed to go from Harrisburg to DC. I'd gotten on the wrong bus and the driver had let me. I showed him my ticket and everything, punched right through to Richmond with the change to the local for Ripley. Now all I had was my AWOL bag and three hundred dollars I'd gotten for my hunting rifle and two shotguns. I kept that in a billfold, along with my new driver's license and a Case knife Ruth had given me for my eighteenth birthday and I had found in a dresser drawer at home. Hannah had wanted to make a withdrawal for me from the money I had in my bank account to buy some traveler's checks, and I said, What the hell do I want traveler's checks for? I'm going to West Virginia, not the West Indies. She said you never know and bought me two for a hundred bucks each. I went inside the station, and the woman at the ticket booth listened to my story, shook her head, took the ticket, then handed it back to me. *You're on the right bus, honey,* she said. *Says right there. Ripley.* Ripley, West Virginia? I asked, and she said, *Ripley, California.* She paged through a book on the counter in front of her. *Bus'll drop you off at the convenience store in Blythe. That's the closest we get, but it must be close enough if they went and gave you a ticket.* I asked her how much I'd paid for the ticket, and she looked at me funny and said, *A hundred and eight dollars. That's about right for a bus from Wilkes-Barre, PA, to California.* Your grandmother had bought the ticket for me and never wondered why it would cost over a hundred dollars to go a little over three hundred miles. I asked if there was a bus to Richmond, Virginia, coming along anytime soon, and she said, *Tomorrow morning. Bus to DC. That's the one.*

I thanked her and walked outside. I had enough heroin for a

couple days. I could cut that with some distilled water and push it to a third, but I'd be hurting. I didn't even know if I could find a dealer in the town where my brother told me the captain lived on the top of a mountain, but part of me imagined I'd get clean somehow. The nonjunk part at least. The rest of me knew how to find it when I had to. Knew where I'd find the users. I could tell who was a dealer just by looking at him. Richmond. Ripley. Abas. It didn't matter. California, even. Hell, that sounded better. I went back inside and found out that the bus was a long haul to Los Angeles, and that it would change bus and driver in Tulsa, Oklahoma. After that, straight through, with thirty- to forty-minute stops for food at breakfast, lunch, and dinner. I asked the same woman if I was ticketed right through, and she said, *You sure are, honey. Right to Ripley. Thirteen hours by the schedule, but, you know. It'll take longer'n that. Next stop'll likely be a quick one in Indianapolis.*

I just kept looking back and forth between my bag and the bus, then bought another ticket from Ripley to Los Angeles for fifteen bucks and went back out to the loading bay, where the man with the tattoo stood and smoked. He offered me a cigarette and I waved it away, and he said, *Where were you in-country?* I told him Quang Tri, two tours, but that I'd wound up in prison on the last. He nodded and said he was glad I'd gotten out, because he'd heard it *wasn't no picnic* over there, then asked me where I was headed. And I didn't know what to say, so I told him I was still trying to get home.

A half hour later we were rolling out of that bay and onto Interstate 70 into a hail of wind and rain, the bus slowing down and speeding up on the highway, the wheels slipping so badly, I could feel the back of the bus fishtailing and see the lane markers flashing under us when I stood up to look out the window. I heard a long horn blast and felt the bus kick up cinders from the berm, and I walked to the front and asked the driver if he had somewhere to get to they all didn't know about back there. The man's face was gray and pockmarked and he reeked of hair oil, which I could see had saturated the brim of his driver's cap. *You just go on and sit down and leave the driving to me,* he said. I told him I was leaving it to him, and that's what had gotten me and the other passengers worried. Rain was pelting the windshield so hard, the wipers could do nothing to disperse it, the entire world beyond it visible as though through plastic sheeting fogged with breath. The man turned his head all the way around to look me in the eyes, holding them there, the bus drifting and drifting into the oncoming lane, until the bastard sneered and said, *This ain't the first storm I've driven through, and it won't be the last. Sit your ass down.*

We stopped in more places along the way than just Indianapolis. In the town of Springfield, Ohio, I swear I watched an angel got on the bus, but when I closed my eyes and looked for her again, she was gone. In Dayton, a couple of hippies boarded, long hair and peace signs on chains around their necks, on their way to California, I guessed, looking for roles as extras in a movie they hoped was about them. Or maybe just taking the bus to Indianapolis. Six people got off there, and no one got on.

I held out as long as I could on that leg of the interstate, the driver no better on dry roads than on wet, and I fixed in St. Louis. I looked around in the bus station for anyone who seemed like he had junk to sell, but all I saw were passengers waiting to move on to another town, east or west, and drunks who may have once been like those travelers but were no longer able to move on. I gave up looking and bought coffee out of a vending machine and hoped I'd get what I needed in Oklahoma.

It was night by the time we pulled into Tulsa, and I could smell that driver, a giant of a man, leave the bus. I still had enough heroin for a day, but I didn't want to get caught in the middle of America somewhere sick and mindless on a Greyhound going west, so I grabbed my bag and went into the station, looking for the only food I'd need. And I found it this time. Past the cafeteria and the vending machines. Past the ticket booths. Past the family with one fake-leather suitcase, waiting on who knew what bus was next. Past the kid not much younger than I was, washing his hair in the restroom sink because he was going somewhere that kept him on a bus longer than a few days. I found my men hanging out by the storage lockers. They nodded, and we all knew, and the crew moved outside to a park near the station, where there were trees for cover and benches to sit on in the hot, dry summer night there in Tulsa. I paid the man who had what I needed and I cooked that food and put it straight in a vein, the old familiar pleasure of it washing over me, like the feel of a homecoming, one you've been waiting on for a long time, even if you haven't.

I stayed there a week and bought straight from the place the dealers bought, the back door of an artificial limbs store near a dubious entrance to that park. Looking back, I could have stayed there two weeks, three, the rest of my life. It didn't matter to me. But the man who ran the store, an old Greek to whom I always brought a cup of coffee as part of our transaction and who knew where I had been, asked me one day where I was headed, and I looked around at the street and the park where the trees had that wilting, hot summer look to them, and the benches where the other junkies were just sitting or sleeping, and I told him I had been on my way to California but that I wasn't so sure anymore. I fished my bus ticket out of my bag and showed it to him. I always carried my AWOL bag, so that it became a joke with the other users, one of them a former marine who called me Baggins. The old Greek looked down at it, then back at me, and told me it was time to leave. I looked to see if there was anyone else in that park around us, but all I saw were those trees. All right, I said to him, and reached for my billfold to buy enough to keep me fixed all the way to the coast, but I had used up most of what I'd brought. The man smiled and shook his head and gave me what he could with what money I had, then threw in an extra cap just because he liked me, he said, and because he could tell that I had once fought bravely. Then he walked back into his limbs store, and I walked through the park and into the station, where they were calling out the gate for the bus to L.A.

When we rolled into Amarillo, the driver took his time getting back on, and when he did, he said the bus wasn't going anywhere for a while. Alternator belt broke and we'd have to wait for another one, though bus or belt wasn't clear. By then, I couldn't stand to smell myself. I went into a bank and cashed one of those travelers checks, then started walking, looking for what, I wasn't sure, until I saw it. A motel in the only place I could find as I ghosted around that town, the sun going down and the temperature with it. It was a place called the Sicily, the guy behind the counter a fat old Texan with an eye patch and breath like he ate rotten jerky all day. But he took my money and gave me a room, and that's all that mattered. I was bone-tired and needed to sleep.

I took a hot shower and washed my shirt, underpants, and socks in the sink, then hung them up to dry on a chair in the corner of the room. I wrapped two thin white towels around myself and sat down on the bed and remembered I hadn't eaten anything since the bus had stopped in a town called El Reno, where I'd bought a burrito from a street vendor and stuffed it into my bag. It was still there and it was good, even cold, and I picked up the phone and dialed the front desk to see if the one-eyed Texan could tell me where I could get a beer, but it rang and rang and no one answered, so I hung up. I thought I might fall asleep to the television, but it was eleven o'clock and the only thing on was the news, so I shut it off and tried the front desk again. The man answered and I asked if he had a beer he could sell me, and he belched into the phone and said, *Not anymore.* So I asked him if he knew what time the bus left for California, and he said he knew for a fact there was one every day at six-thirty in the morning for Los Angeles. I hung up and knew I wasn't going to sleep.

I crawled out of bed at four-thirty and fixed. From the window, the streetlights outside looked like tiny strobes through the blinds. I had nodded off and slept in all but my shirt, and this was still damp when I went to put it on, so that it sat against my skin now like a nervous sweat.

The man at the desk moved and sounded like he had been

drinking all night. I backed away from him and bought a candy bar and some crackers from a vending machine he had in the office. And when I asked if he would call a taxi for me, he growled, and I told him to forget it. I would walk. He said, *No one walks to the bus station from here,* and I said, I guess I'm no one, and limped out of there.

It was still dark and there was nothing open in town and I walked past blinking stoplights and empty streets in the direction I had reckoned the bus station was, after looking at a map of the cities of Texas that I had slipped under my jacket when that desk clerk wasn't looking. When I came to the corner of South Monroe and Fourth Avenue, it was six o'clock and there was no one inside but a man at the ticket desk, who was flipping from one country-and-western station to another on his AM radio. I asked him where the six-thirty to L.A. would come in, and he pointed to gate number three and went back to his music. I went into the restroom, locked myself in, and sat there until I heard the call for the bus on the intercom.

The sun was high and bright by the time we were out of the city limits and barreling across the Panhandle Plains. I looked out at the landscape of red and brown, and down at the map, identifying the tablelands and Canadian River, then back out at the breaks of that river dotted every now and then with a lone farmhouse or windmill, and I wondered if living beneath so much sky and in the path of so much wind would make a person go mad with jealousy for those who built homes in places where the wind might be considered a gift. I dozed off to the whispered Spanish of a Mexican mother one seat ahead of me pointing out cloud formations to her young son, and when I woke, the bus was pulling into Tucumcari, New Mexico. The driver let me get out to buy a cup of coffee while he checked tickets on four new passengers, and then we were back on the road.

In Santa Rosa, the highway crossed a wide and muddy river with banks of cottonwoods and salt cedar, and the young boy shouted, *Mamá, look! El Río Grande!* She laughed and said, *No, hijo. Not yet. This is the Pecos River. In the olden days, when they called this the Wild West, they used to say there was no law beyond the Pecos. Only the strong dare come this far.* He got quiet and whispered, *Were there monsters?* She laughed. *Not monsters, hijo, just men. But men who would do bad things. They could take another man's life, and his soul,* she said, and pointed to the boy's chest where he sat in his seat across the aisle from me, and I was so taken by this that I looked out, too, and wondered about the monsters that were trying to consume me. Wondered if I would escape them one day, east or west of the Pecos. It was strange land we were traveling into, land in which a river had to have some supernatural strength for it to be flowing over ground, where it looked as though so little water would never flow for long before it disappeared beneath the rock and dirt. And in the river-beds, where all kinds of trees grew, and the distant mountains, where vast stretches of conifers grew, the green of those living things was like no green I had ever seen. Not in Pennsylvania. Not in Vietnam. They had a hue to them like sage and old copper, so that everywhere there appeared a quiet and ongoing battle for what God had, in His wisdom, doled out in small and precious proportions, when life emerged at the moment of creation, and endured these long eons later.

It was afternoon when we crossed the Rio Grande Rift and passed through the Sandia Mountains, where breaking clouds revealed a white and snowcapped Sandia Crest, mountains I had never seen the likes of, and I wondered at their sheer faces and sudden lift from the floor of the Plains and desert, like the sharp edge of metal that's been pierced by a bullet in the geological equivalent of an ambush from the night before.

At the station in Albuquerque, the driver told us the bus was scheduled for a thirty-minute layover and we should take the time to stretch and get some food, but not wander too far. I sat down at a lunch counter and ordered a bowl of chili from a waitress who looked to me in the plainness of the day like some goddess among mortals. I was in that place where the initial intensity of my fix had leveled off, but I wasn't yet on the downward slope of need toward the next one. She brought me a bowl of green chilies with pork and white hominy, and I was hungry for the food. When I had finished, I looked up and saw she was watching me with a hunger all her own. The last time I'd even been approached by a woman was at a bar in Dardan, where a drunk high school girl with a fake ID said she wanted to know what it was like to fuck a marine who had been in Vietnam. Her breath smelled of too many beers and menthol cigarettes, and I told her she wasn't ever going to find out. But this woman behind the counter, whose desert tan glowed like daylight beneath her white blouse and yellow apron, became so bewitching to me that I could feel something of the old need stirring in me again.

Her name was Kira, she said, and she was finishing up her shift. *Isn't that your bus leaving?* she asked, and pointed out the window as she took off her apron. And there it went. The old hound. Its brakes hissing off and on as it navigated the turns out of the bay and into the side-street traffic of Albuquerque, rocking back and forth as it accelerated in the direction of the sign for Interstate 40. I shook my head, not because it wasn't but because I didn't care.

After she changed out of her uniform, we got into an El Camino and drove to her place on Montoya Street, a brown adobe-style house beneath the shade of cottonwoods so old, they looked like their limbs ached. A calm but sharp-eyed dog waited for her on the porch, one that reminded me of Krasna, the black Lab I had known since I was a boy and who had been shot by a hunter while I was in prison, my mother told me. But this dog was sleek and gray and looked more like a wolf at rest for a short time than a pet trained to stay. *This is Chula,* Kira said to me, *offspring of a bitch and a coyote, and neither the pound nor the coyotes would have her, so she lives here with me. All of the beautiful ones come here, but this one is the only one who has stayed.*

She lived among relics of some past inside that house. Artwork hung on every wall, artwork so raw and tactile, it was as though each piece had been created with what colors and threads and wood and stones of the earth could be gathered in the arid and sage-hued dirt that was right outside under the cottonwoods. There were paintings of the mountains that rose in the distance, icons she called retablos of saints whose lives I knew nothing of, tapestries of hunting scenes with animals and women hunters. On small tables throughout the living room there rested varicolored sculptures large and small of figures beautiful and grotesque that looked to have been formed from the same adobe clay layered onto the walls of the house. Each piece drew me to it, as if I understood why I could not understand these things to which I was drawn. And when I turned away from them, finally, and saw her emerging from a back room of the small house, she had changed and put on a wrap of linen gauze, beneath which her breasts rose and her skin shone like that of the goddess I believed she was. And I wanted her. Even high on smack, I wanted her like that desert outside wanted the rain.

She was not gentle with me as we made love, knowing this was both what I longed for and what I feared. The afternoon light had slipped into her bedroom window from the west, the house cool beneath the shade of the trees, the air dry, so dry, I was nowhere I knew. Her breath smelled of cinnamon, her skin like desert sage, and all the pain inside my leg, my heart, and my mind began to subside, like the end of a firefight, when it's over, and you're calm, and you're alive. Not shaking yet. Just alive. It was like that. And for that moment I wanted to get clean and live there in the desert with her for the rest of my life.

But junk gets into your cells deeper than love ever could, and she let me fix, so that I wouldn't get sick. Then she brought out some tequila and magic mushrooms she'd sliced up and placed on a bread she called *sopapillas*, and we ate them on the bread with honey. When the room started to brighten and the colors of all her paintings and retablos and sculptures intensified, we rose and went out walking in the New Mexico night, toward the Sandias, their peaks black against a sky lit with stars and a rising moon in the east. We moved toward them as though drawn, as though they were stairs to what lay beyond in those stars, and I was unflinching in my approach to those mountains. I heard coyotes yapping in the distance, stopped, and Kira stood next to me and took my hand and said, *You've had only shades to guide you, and they will, one last time, but not in this place. It will be hard to purge yourself, Samuel, but God will hear your cry, just like the others, just as you heard His at your birth.*

God, I said, and stared up at stars so thick, the mountains were like a jagged outline of black curtain across them. What God?

Don't you believe? she asked. And I was silent in the presence of that curtain, because I didn't know what to believe.

In the morning she cooked what she called *huevos rancheros* for breakfast, and although I rarely had an appetite after I had just shot up, the eggs covered in red salsa looked and smelled so good, I ate more than I had eaten of any food in months. After she cleared the table and fed Chula, she said, *There's someplace I want to take you, and I don't know how long we'll have to be there. We'll stay as long as we need.*

After an hour driving north on interstate 25 in the old El Camino, we came to Santa Fe and took the road through town and kept climbing up 84 toward Española, then east. We were going to a place she called Chimayó. A place, she said, where the santos dwell, and the dirt itself heals and takes all lost travelers home.

There was no town to speak of, save for the church, a walled adobe structure with two bell towers, and a door in the courtyard carved to look like a heart with wings bleeding beneath its own crown of thorns. I recognized it from every holy card of the Sacred Heart my mother used to bring back from St. Michael the Archangel, but on this door of some ancient wood, the heart itself seemed to pulse with blood beneath its worn and hand-smoothed finish. This was El Santuario de Chimayó, Kira told me. We walked to the sanctuary itself and she took my hand and pushed at the plain wooden doors there and we entered.

It was after noon, but the church was as quiet as a midnight vigil. No priest. No sexton. Our steps echoed on the wooden floor and we walked into a small room my guide called *el pocito,* where a tiny round pit of dirt lay at the center, and we knelt before it. *The dirt heals,* she said, and sank her hand into the sand, lifted it, and let it sift between her fingers. *But there is more beneath the ground, where those who have gone before you can be found.*

She took my hand and held it palm up, and with a knife kept in a tiny scabbard on her leg, she sliced the soft flesh of my palm and let the blood drop into the sand, put her hand to my chest, and said, *Stand.*

When I did, there was a sound like a small wind rising from the dirt, and there appeared with it what I might call ghosts, simply to tell you of them, but *ghosts* would be too weak a word, too thin, too inexact. They were spirits, true, but ones that glowed as though more alive than any living thing I had ever seen and ever will. Out of that little round pit they rose, all people I've known. The first were boys from school who died on the roads in their cars, or by their own hands with their hunting rifles. Then came the men from my first tour. Sikora. Daniels. McManus. Eyes down, limbs like feathers, dressed in a garment that was some strange and constantly changing cross between camouflage and a burial shroud. Then I saw her. Thien. She drifted up and raised her eyes to look at me, and I said out loud, How? but got no answer, until I saw every single NVA regular and the officer who marched me to Hanoi rise up behind her and drift off into the afternoon darkness, and I knew how. The bombs so unrelenting that winter, we heard them and feared them even in our prison cells. Then, prone still, his eyes closed and his hands folded and holding up his head, Bao drifted out of the dirt and into the air to join his sister without a sound.

I wanted to go then. I wanted to stand and get out of that place, but Kira held my arm, and said, *This is why.* And I saw Ruth's father, Mr. Younger, rise, his sister Mary, with whom I had sat down to meals of venison and beer more than a few times. And then a child. No, less than a child. A baby so young and new, her eyes seemed barely opened.

Who is this? I asked Kira, and she said, *Your daughter, here with the others because of your brother's love.* And I watched her as she, too, rose like an angel, her garments exactly what I would have thought an angel wore. Her eyes didn't need to open. Her entire body shone with a light that made me realize it was not I who was seeing her, but she who was gazing at me with a knowledge of where she was that outshone all the others, she who never had to carry any of the weight the living are called to lift in their lives.

Behind her was my grandfather Jozef, his face mirroring mine, I know, for the sheer joy that came to me when I saw him. And this one spoke, saying only, *Your father is here.*

And there he was. A man I recognized in the same instant I would recognize my brother, so like each other were the two, the black hair thick and with a glint to it like a broken-off piece of coal, even in the beard I was told he grew when he came home from the war, and Bo had grown, too, now, the mouth round and full behind it, the teeth white and set like small columns of granite, and the eyes as blue as the New Mexican sky under which we had driven to this place. Yes, it was my father. And if a spirit of the dead can be said to smile, he did for me, and said, *How I've longed to see you again, Samuel. How sorry I was to leave.*

But why here, why now? I asked him, and he said, *Out of our need, all of us as real, and as fleeting, as that need. Let go of your prison, Samuel. Look for the night while it is young, facing your east from a western shore. There you will find the day you've wished for.*

And then he was gone. They were all gone. And I was lying in the dirt of *el pocito*, Kira standing over me, her wrist wrapped in bangles adorned with green turquoise, her hand reaching down to take mine and help me up. I ached with the sickness that was returning to me, returning and reminding me of what I needed there in the dirt and dark, though it was full daylight outside. And she said, *Come. The priest will be here to say Mass soon.*

We left the room and the church and got into her car and drove through the small town, where I could see there was street skag to be had everywhere I looked, the men who used it and sold it drifting in and out of view like the spirits I had just spoken to, and she said, *Not here. There are nothing but lost souls outside of the sanctuary.*

We drove back to Santa Fe and toward the east side of town, past the Church of Christo Rey and up into a canyon along a dried-out riverbed, until we came to a house tucked among plants of yellow and gray-green she called chimisa and sagebrush, a house built beneath the shadow of an oak that looked as though it grew out of some wager it had made with the desert. *We are here for one thing,* she said, *and when we get it, we leave. They will want you to stay, and they will draw you to them, but don't listen to what they have to say. This is not a good place, but it is the only place I know. When your strength gives out, remember what your father said.*

It was already afternoon and I was beginning to feel that slide into wanting to do nothing but get my next fix. Inside the house, it was cool and there was music playing, beautiful music, and I looked around for a hi-fi or turntable somewhere, but I couldn't see one. The room in which we waited was spare and clean and bereft of everything but two windows, a couch, and a few chairs. The doors that led to other rooms were closed. The kitchen was open, and that's where a man and a woman stood, two who looked at the same time younger and older than I was, and I realized the music was coming from them, like a conversation, and they spoke to Kira this way, only their words were sung. When I looked at Kira to see how she would respond, it was not with the soft and level voice she used with me, but with a loud and commanding tone and a look on her face of distance and wariness. The others smiled, though, and came out of the kitchen with everything I needed for a fix, which they did for me as they sang and Kira looked on, the spike in the arm, the familiar thud to the back of the legs, the feeling not of warmth but of being emptied into a fullness, like after making love, and I wanted to forget where I had just come from, forget what I had heard my father say, and remain here with these two who sang and cooked up smack like songbirds.

When Kira came over to lift me off the couch, I resisted and told her I wanted to stay here longer and rest, and the others seemed to sing that request to her as well, and for the first time I saw an anger rise in her beautiful brown eyes. She cradled me like a baby, so that the silver necklace she wore rested on my forehead, and the singing stopped. I had no idea she was so strong, and she carried me like this out of the house and into the car, then went back to the front door and took a leather pouch from the two, who suddenly looked as haggard as the junkies I had seen in Tulsa and on the street corners of Chimayó. She ran to the El Camino, turned the ignition key, and drove fast down the canyon road and out to the highway south to Albuquerque.

It was night by the time we returned to her house on Montoya Street. She made supper and we went to bed, where we made love for the last time, her body pulling me out of the indifference to the body my addiction always made me feel, and offering me a glimpse of pleasure I once knew, and might know again one day. At dawn I packed what little there was to pack in my AWOL bag, and she gave me the pouch she had taken from the two at the door of the canyon house. Inside were three papyrus envelopes of heroin. Not just street smack. Heroin as pure as what Bao shot into me, and she said, *You'll need this for what night remains.*

3

One summer when I was a boy and my brother, Bo, was preoccupied with school and going off to college, my grandfather asked me if I wanted to come out to the orchard to see a comet visible in the night sky. It was August and we sat in a place where there was a break in the trees and looked to the horizon until we saw that comet hanging among the stars like a white dry fly we used for trout on the Upper Salamander. And when it had dropped below the horizon, we didn't move. We lay there on the grass for hours, gazing up at the blanket of stars until well past midnight, not even my mother calling out to us to come inside. And I discovered then that there is a quiet to the middle of the night that is different from the chorus of birds, insects, and animals that come out from evening to dark and retreat in the graying predawn. In the hours of dark just past midnight, on nights where there is no wind or rain or moon, nothing moves or makes a sound. Nothing hunts or is being hunted. Everything is at peace and at rest. I discovered this for the first time on that night of the comet, and when I broke the silence to ask my grandfather why this was, he said, *There is never no sound, Samuel. Listen closely and you'll hear the sound of the lost.*

When the Greyhound to L.A. pulled out of the Albuquerque station the day I said good-bye to Kira, I was in a window seat at the back of the bus, and I stared out of that window as the sun rose higher on the desert, the mountains to the south and to the west always at a distance, ever approaching and never reached, the land unchanged in its resemblance to a place where only old prophets might wander in search of the horizon. We didn't stop for lunch and I didn't care. I watched as rainstorms swept across the land in patches so dense and black, I could see where the rain began and ended. Sometimes the road itself split in half, wet on one side, dry in the sun on the other.

We left Flagstaff, Arizona, just after eight o'clock in the evening, the light of a nearly full moon shining above the forest and mountains of the high desert and into the darkness of the bus. Four seats ahead of me, two men who had gotten on in Winslow occupied a space around them that the other twelve passengers on the bus made an effort to stay away from. They weren't junkies, but they were addled and odd. One was loud in his speech and mannerisms, his voice rising and falling from whispers to shouts as he spoke to and argued with his companion, his arms and hands choreographed to follow, and, from the way I could feel the vibrations in my seat, his feet, too. His companion, though, sat as quietly as if he were indifferent to or unaware of the other's outsize expressions. If I hadn't seen his head turning on its swivel like an owl hunting in the dark, I would have guessed he was asleep. But he wasn't.

How long I had been sleeping myself, I didn't know. The canyon skag, as I thought of it, had a longer, evened-out high to it, and I was happy to find that I could sleep and wake up not needing to fix, at least not yet anyway. I had been dreaming of Kira, dreaming of her body next to mine, after the nightmare of the shades rising from the dirt in a back room of a church. I stood to stretch and saw the two men in front of me stand together in that moment as well, and I knew something was wrong. The twitchy one of the pair moved quickly in that dim light and started to yell out loud that he had a gun and he was going to shoot anyone who didn't give up a wallet or a watch, and he began to make his way up the aisle. He did have a gun. It was a big old .357 and he either knew how to use it or he didn't, and I figured he'd do more damage with it if he didn't. I slid down into my seat and took the Case knife out of my pocket, opened the long blade, and watched the quiet one. He started sliding into the seats of passengers, some sleeping, some awake, and fleecing them before they could even voluntarily give up what they had. It was a good ploy. The loud one instilled fear. The quiet one stole in the distraction of that fear. Then he noticed me, or remembered me, the quiet one, and he turned and started to walk to the back of the bus. I could see his feet, and I could smell him, too. I have smelled the sweat of a lot of men, dirty ones and dying ones, and this one smelled like he might feast on both. I watched as he reached for the top of the seat in front of me and peered down into mine, smiled a tight-lipped smile, and held out his free hand palm up, his fingers waving in a *Give it to me* gesture. And just as I was about to push that knife up in the direction of his sternum, the bus swerved hard off the road and he fell toward me, his hand now palm out to stop his fall, and that's where my knife went.

The scream was like the scream of a child waking from a nightmare and finding the monster right there, so high-pitched and sustained, there was no other sound on that bus. I pulled hard to get my knife back, and he pulled his hand close to his chest, blood pouring down his arm, his mouth wide open as that scream kept pouring from it, his teeth filed down to points, so that he looked like some weird piranha, and he ran down the aisle toward his partner, who had his gun pointed at the driver. *Stop this fucking bus!* he yelled out of his own confusion, and that Greyhound skidded hard onto the berm and careened against the guardrail, sparks flying past the windows. The driver threw the door open and those two jumped out into the Arizona night.

We all stood there on the side of the highway in the flashing lights of the state police cruisers, until sometime toward dawn, the sky just starting to grow pink in the direction from which we had all come. Then a replacement driver arrived and we boarded and were on our way. I fixed in the bus station in Needles, California, and four hours later we were in L.A., where I got a local to Long Beach, because L.A. seemed too big for what I needed. I could fix twice more with what I had of the canyon skag, after which I'd have to score whatever I could find. I needed food and sun after that bus ride, and I was in California.

I started walking down Long Beach Boulevard until I came to the water, where I asked some hippie chick if there was a good beach nearby to hang out on, and she said, *Hitch on up to RAT Beach, man. You won't get hassled there.* So I did, and from San Pedro I got a ride up the coast in a '64 Pontiac GTO, and the driver dropped me off in Torrance and I bought some food from a vendor, who told me it was Friday. Then I walked down to the beach they called RAT and just sat there and watched the surfers and the kids and their moms.

I tried to remember what that shade of my father had said to me in Chimayó. *Look for the night while it is young, facing your east from a western shore.* If it even was my father, or some hallucination, some desire I had deep within me and the drugs let me see. But Kira was real. The blood in the hinge of my knife from another man who'd tried to rob me was real. The heroin coursing inside my veins was real. Why shouldn't that visit with those lost souls be just as real? I was filthy. I smelled like a bum. And I had on me only what I had left Dardan with. I stripped off my shirt and waded into the surf in just my pants and swam into the deeper water and floated there, washing everything and nothing off of me. Maybe it was the cold ocean after the warm air. Maybe the realization that I could go no farther than where I was. I was high, but I was tired. Tired and remembering summers I used to swim out at the lake with Ruth, our bodies wanting and needing nothing but each other, and I knew, too, that by the evening there was only one thing I'd be wanting more than anything or anyone I loved, either now or a long time ago, and I could feel the tracks in my arms stinging from the salt in the sea.

I slept huddled near some rocks on the beach that night so that the cops wouldn't see me, then woke and fixed and walked down to the water's edge barefoot, the sun coming up over the hills and the haze in the east, nothing but dark ocean in front of me. My pants were wet and rolled up to my knees and I had my shirt on.

If I started swimming, I thought, I could get pretty far, farther out than I was the day before, out past the waves and the surfers, and I could keep going until I couldn't turn back and the clothes weighed me down. No casualty officer this time, no chaplain, no report of a marine KIA in a firefight in some province no one could pronounce. Just a guy who didn't want to fight anymore.

Then I saw this girl, a young girl, skipping down the beach. She was carrying a bucket and she picked up rocks and shells and inspected them and put them back gently in the water, until I realized she was doing this to the crabs and things that got washed up on the sand. She came very close to where I stood and didn't seem phased by me at all. I watched her pick up crab after crab and return them to the water. Then she looked up, saw me, and smiled. What are you doing? I asked. *I'm saving the sea creatures,* she said. There was a long stretch of hills behind her, and miles of the California beaches ahead, and I said, That's a big job you've got. Can you save them all? And she walked around me and over to some crustacean struggling at the tide line, picked it up, and placed it in the backwash of a wave. *I saved that one,* she said.

Her name was Laila, and she told me she was five years old and did this every Saturday with her mother and father, who were walking not far behind, because their job was to save what creatures she had missed. She pointed down the beach toward those hills. *There they are,* she said, and took my hand so quickly I had to catch my breath before I pulled my hand away. She furrowed her brow, looked confused, and said, *Come with me to meet them.* I said no. I couldn't go. She asked why, and I said, Because I'm sick, and I need to get well first before I can be with people. Her face lit up then, and she said with a kind of cherubic calm, *That's what my father does. He makes sick men well.* And she grabbed my hand again, her grip strong and unwilling to let go this time, and we started walking toward them while she told me she knew the minute she woke up this was going to be a good day.

From a distance, they were the kind of couple who walks the beach hand in hand without saying anything to each other, or at least not seeming to. *Who am I to be meeting strangers like this,* I thought, *high on smack, and looking like a homeless bum who slept on the beach?* I was glad at least for the ocean bath I'd taken the day before, so that the smell of where I'd been did not precede me. And as soon as we were in shouting range, she hollered, *Daddy, I found him!*

I couldn't believe then who her daddy was, the man standing right in front of me. Grayson couldn't believe it, either, when I told him, but I could see in the light of a hurricane lamp he had lit for us there on the porch that he was smiling a big goddamn smile when I did. It was Doc Moore, the corpsman from Grayson's platoon on my first tour. I remembered when he had tried to save Sikora, tried to stop the bleeding from the chest wound, and watched as his friend's life ebbed away. And there he was, shaking my hand on a beach in California in front of his wife and daughter. Then he looked closer at me, like he had the day Sikora died and I helped him strap the body to the skids of the Huey, and he seemed to know. He pulled me in tight and whispered as though he were about ready to cry, *Don't worry, Konar, we're gonna get you out of here.*

We sat on the beach while Laila went about her rescue efforts, and I asked him how it was he had gotten here. The odds that we would meet again like this were themselves astounding, and he said, *Maybe not.*

He told me that, after his tour, he left the marines and decided to go to medical school. He got his degree, and had just started his first year of residency at Balboa Hospital in San Diego. His mother lived in Palos Verdes, and so on the Saturday mornings he had off, they'd drive up the coast to visit her, and his daughter always loved walking on the beach because of what she found there. No, he didn't think the odds were that crazy at all. The real question was why I, a Pennsylvania boy, was sleeping on a beach in California. So I told him what I could, in what little time we had before his daughter came running back to where we sat with her bucket, and he just nodded and said, *You're not the first,*

*Konar, and you won't be the last. But the good news is that I
know exactly what to do, if you want me to. Your call.*

I was still thinking this might all be some crazy dream or hallucination, but we got my stuff from behind the rocks and went
over to his mother's house that morning, where I got a shower
and some food, and he told me to fix with what I had so that I
wouldn't get sick before we got back to San Diego. The next day,
he had me examined at Balboa, where they gave me some new
clothes, but I didn't stay there. For all it wanted to, the VA didn't
really know what to do with the men coming home from Vietnam with more in their seabags than they had bargained for. Doc
Moore had a friend on a team at Mercy Hospital that specialized
in drug addiction recovery. He told me it was expensive, though,
and I told him I knew who to call. And all your uncle Bo said
on the phone that night was, *You just tell me where to send the
money, brother. I love you.*

I can't tell you all of it. I can tell you it wasn't easy, and I was
sick as a dog while they let me go through my withdrawl, some
of the darkest nights I remember. Worse than Hoa Lo, truth be
told. All of those souls from the dirt in Chimayó standing around
the edge of the bed and looking at me night after night, just looking, while I searched for my own need to get right with that war
inside. And after a while—I don't know how long because time
messes with you—those souls left, and I woke up one morning
and heard birdsong and felt hungry. I asked for a cup of coffee
with milk, like my mother used to make for me. And coffee never
tasted so good. I managed a few push-ups on the floor of my
room, like I used to do in my hooch between patrols, and that
night I went to sleep tired, staring out the window at the stars.

I started walking around the grounds and in the park. I met
with counselors, and therapists. One of the people I had gotten to
know on staff was the chaplain, a Jesuit named Father Al Schiera,
who had been at the University of Scranton. He and I had some
long talks about CAP and the ambush, the prison and the junk.
But we often just sat and talked about fishing rivers and creeks in

Pennsylvania, like the Delaware, the Lehigh, and the Loyalsock, and he said he wished he had known about the Upper Salamander. I told him I could take him there, if we both ever made it back to Northeastern Pennsylvania, and he wondered out loud if that was really where I wanted to be? *Lots of places to fish, Sam. It seems to me like those waters have gotten a little too muddy, don't you? Tell me something. Which did you enjoy more? Catching a bunch of fish in the same old fishing hole, or finding someplace new and working it until you hooked into a beauty?* I didn't need to think about that too long. I told him about the time my grandfather and I headed out to the Tiadaghton State Forest in Central Pennsylvania. I was fifteen, it was late fall, and we fished Slate Run for two days. Some of the meanest and most beautiful woods I've ever had to get through to catch some of the meanest and most beautiful trout I've ever seen in my life. We slept on the ground, ate what we caught, and then walked out. No more than ten words passed between us in those two days, but I learned things about the old man, just watching him. How balanced he was when everything was pared down to the basics. Steadied. Never quick to react. Accepting of what was given to him as well as taken away. And I changed that day. I set out to become him. And although part of me had, the part that was a good marine, a good part of me had not yet. The part that had gotten lost, in the prison and the junk. That's what I was looking to find again. A place where things were pared down. And I could accept what I had been given, as well as let go of what had been taken away.

Father Al nodded as he listened, and when I was done, he spoke of consolation, the feeling when we're making a discernment that a certain direction is good and right. *Like water on a sponge*, he said. Desolation, the feeling that something was not good, not right, felt like water on a stone, going off in every direction and none of it sinking in. Discernment was an exercise of the heart, he reminded me, one where the struggle between the good and the not good was real, and we had to navigate both in our lives, moving forward with that knowledge. *Knowing that you will be asked*

to relinquish as much as you would like to retain, Sam, may be
the most important lesson your grandfather ever taught you.

One morning, October already, I guess, Father Al knocked on
my door and walked into the room looking like a character out
of a Nick Adams story, and we drove out of the city and up to
Cuyamaca Lake, where he knew the rangers, and we fished that
day for some beautiful trout. We were in a little place in the Four
Corners eating dinner when I told him I had come to the realization on the water that day—though I had been thinking about it
all night—that I wanted to go to West Virginia and find Burne
Grayson. I had been home in Dardan and I had found home to be
something it was not anymore, and maybe would never be again.
And San Diego was too far from anything resembling home to
me. What I needed was to close the loop on the one person who
had told the rest of the world that the loop was still open, that I
was still out there, and they just had to wait and have faith in me.
Father Al smiled and said he would make a few calls and see what
he could find for me in the way of transportation. Two days later
he came by to say there was a Jesuit brother of his at Loyola who
was on his way cross-country to teach philosophy at Wheeling
College for a semester, and he could give me a lift right to Abas,
if I was sure that was where I wanted to go. I said it was, and that
I would be grateful for the ride. It was a long and twisty road out
west I had traveled. A straight road back east with a professor of
philosophy seemed like the right one this time.

When I had finished telling Grayson about where I'd been since
he last saw me, I expected him to offer me a ride down the mountain and get back to his cordwood and long conversations with
Hector, the dog. I didn't know where I'd go after that. There was
always work at the mill, if I had to. And there was a woman in
New Mexico I could try to find again, if I wanted to. But I was
tired, and I was emptied, and my honest hope was that he'd say,
Why don't you take some time and hang out here for a few days.

The sky outside that morning was starting to gray in the east
and a small chorus of passerines had begun to rise from the

trees. The hurricane lamp he had lit sometime before midnight was nearly empty of oil and I could see the wick flicker and start to smoke. He stood and turned it down until it went out, then stretched and said, *Damn, son, you have not had it easy.* I tried to stand, too, thinking it was time I took my leave, and he said, *You got somewhere you need to be?* I said I didn't, and he said, *Well, set yourself down, then,* and after a while he asked if I could still buck firewood with a bullet hole in my leg. I told him I could timber it, buck it, split it, and burn it. I just didn't run so fast anymore. He said, *No need to be fast anymore.*

The dawn turned into something resembling light. Grayson went inside and began rustling around the kitchen, and I must have dozed off, because after a while he came out and shook me awake and handed me a big steaming mug of coffee with milk and sat back down next to Hector. We didn't say anything more as I drank and listened to the morning come to life, the mountain sky autumn pink now in the east over my shoulder, Venus sitting low and barely visible on the horizon, and it was like I was seeing it again for the first time. Like the day I had been wishing for. Wishing for a long, long time.

THE MOURNING HOUSE

*S*am Konar sits at his desk in the study of the old Victorian
he and his wife have called home near the campus of West
Virginia University, in Morgantown, for twenty years and enters
the last of his students' grades into his grade book. There is a
skiff of snow on the ground from a squall that passed through in
the night, but the morning is dry and cold and he has laid a fire in
the fireplace. He dreamed of his friend Burne Grayson the night
before, as he does every year at this time, the man bearded and
wearing the flannel shirt he always wore when he split wood at
his house in Abas, and he said nothing to Sam in the dream, just
placed the index finger of his nonfiring hand on his upper arm
for the sign to move the squad leader forward, and the image
vanished. He hears a knock on the study door. It's his daughter,
Helen, and she hands him a letter, the return address a forward
operating base in Afghanistan and Lt. B. Konar USMC written in
his son's neat block lettering above it. This came yesterday from
Burne, she says. The sight of his son's handwriting reminds him
again of the dream, and he thinks in that moment he should drive
down to Abas and tell the boy's namesake how the lieutenant is
doing, that he's up for captain, but he catches himself, puts the
letter in the drawer of his desk to read out loud at the dinner
table, and turns to his daughter, who smells of tack and leather
and is still wearing her riding breeches. He asks her if she's been
out at the stables this morning, and she tells him they're taking
old Dante to a farm in Tennessee. I just wanted to say good-bye,
so we went for an early ride. He nods. You all right? he asks, and
she says, I'll get by. He has come to love the Appalachian lilt to

her voice, just as he loves it in her mother, and he asks, Where is Mama? At the hospital, she says. On call today. I saw her leave early. He nods again. I remember now, he says. Tell David and Mickey to pack for Uncle Bo's. It'll be cold in Dardan. We'll all have dinner together tonight and leave tomorrow. Grandma Konar won't want us to be late for her feast. His daughter leans over and kisses him on the head. I know, Daddy, she says, and closes the office door behind her when she leaves. He wants to read the letter now, but he knows what it says, the quotidian details of the Marine Corps officer writing home to his mother and father. The news a father wouldn't want to get would not get to him by his son's hand. He puts the envelope on the desk and picks up a postcard of the Cranberry River he bought at a visitor's center when his son had just graduated from Annapolis and the two of them went fishing. He taps the edge of it and thinks he should take his two younger boys fishing there in the spring. Hike into the backcountry like he used to. Teach them how to love the woods at night.

THEY WERE RAISED BY MEN WHO KNEW THE MOUNTAINS AND the outdoors. One motherless. The other fatherless, though lucky to have a grandfather take up the role of father to him. And they came from different eastern states—West Virginia and Pennsylvania. Geological cousins, if not siblings. That seemed to be connection enough.

They never would have met on any field—football, frozen high meadow with deer in the offing, quarter-mile strip of mountain back roads in their cars—other than war. The Marine Corps took them both to Okinawa, Japan, where in the early spring of 1968 PFC Samuel Konar was assigned as a rifleman to E Company, Second Battalion, Third Marines after his Infantry Training Regiment at Camp Geiger, because they needed boys in Vietnam. He had just turned nineteen. First Lieutenant Burne

Grayson was the platoon commander, his second command of a platoon in the 2/3 and his second tour of Vietnam. He was twenty-seven. He had landed in Da Nang in '65 on his first tour, at a time when not every second lieutenant got out alive. He did, and still went back, and something told Konar he should be glad to be with a veteran of the campaign.

Thirteen months in-country, on patrols along the DMZ in Quang Tri, and in the brief, elusive firefights with the PAVN, the lieutenant brought a kind of knife edge to his bookishness, and the private first class could see this. He had seen it in his grandfather, had heard that his father was once the same, so he felt at home among this warrior class. For his part, Grayson saw the private through a commanding officer's lens of obliquity. Admire a man too much, believe in what he could accomplish in the jungle, and in the Corps, and that man would be KIA and strapped to the skid of a Huey in a week's time. Let the Fates have their way, and maybe, just maybe, there would come a time and place.

And yet, Burne Grayson could see that Samuel Konar was different. He carried with him something of what the Greeks called the *mákarios*. The blessed. The fortunate. Translated into a marine on the ground in Vietnam, it meant damned good luck. He seemed always in conversation with the source of it, too, and whispered on patrol in a way that never upset the platoon, from Grayson right on down. Even hard-ass gunnery sergeant Boots Hogan waited for it, listened for it, and got spooked when he didn't hear the kid talking to the old man, as Konar called him. After Hogan was wounded in a firefight and got sent back to Hawaii, the new gunny gave Konar no end of grief when the whispering started, even after Grayson told him about the private's talismanlike pronouncements. Gunny shut him down quick. Until on patrol one day, Konar insisted to the point of nearly shouting, *Goddamn it, Sergeant, I'm begging you not to take another step!* The sergeant did and the trip wire was a dud, but that man thought long and hard about his life here and in the next on his way back to base, and in his tent for the next couple of days, leaving well enough alone when the platoon went out on patrol again.

They had lost three men in the summer of '68 supporting Operation Kentucky in the area around Con Thien. Private First Class Sikora, Lance Corporal Daniels, and Corporal McManus. Thirteen months later, on the flight to Hawaii, Grayson found himself seated next to Konar on the C-130 and told him he took hard the body count on this tour. On his first tour, he had three wounded but no KIA, and he wondered out loud about the ways of men and war. Konar wondered out loud right back that if the lieutenant found any other way, he'd appreciate knowing about it. Grayson laughed. *The mákarios,* he thought to himself. When they discovered their connection to the mountains, they talked about hunting and fishing. Konar told Grayson about the street racing that, for all intents and purposes, was the move that put his ass in Vietnam, but he had no urge anymore to ride that quarter mile flat out, and he was thinking about remaining a marine when his three years were up. Grayson told Konar about his university study of counterinsurgencies in campaigns, from the *Histories* of Herodotus to the Bavarian hunters who had become sharpshooters for the Germans on the Western Front. He had a theory that lethality required symmetry, and that was how he conducted the movement of his men. That, for all intents and purposes, was what put his ass in Vietnam, but he had no desire now to go back to the books, having seen just how lethal symmetry could be up close. He'd remain a marine for as long as they'd have him. Konar said he wished he could be that widely read but only had the history of his grandfather to rely on, a man raised in the Carpathian Mountains in the Austro-Hungarian Empire and conscripted into a Slovak Marsch battalion of the Austrian Landwehr, where he became the same hunter-sharpshooter the Germans trained, and plied his trade along the Isonzo River and in the Italian Alps. The old man? Grayson asked. The old man, Konar said. I wish I could meet him, Grayson said. That can be arranged, Konar replied at the time.

BURNE GRAYSON MADE CAPTAIN IN THE SPRING OF 1970. HE had buried his father just months before and was visiting Camp Lejeune, where he sought out Samuel Konar and asked him if he wanted to re-up, like he had said. Grayson was being tapped by Lt. Col. John Keenan to command a Combined Action Group in Quang Tri, and he wanted Konar to go back as part of a Combined Action Platoon in the group. Grayson knew the private had made E-4 and was Corporal Konar now. What he didn't know was that, back home for a two-week family visit, Konar had already told his mother, his grandfather, his brother, and his girlfriend that he had signed the papers for another three years in the suck.

The Combined Action Groups operated independently of the infantry, and Grayson was taking his CAPs back into Quang Tri and the villages of South Vietnamese women, children, and old men at a time when the marines had all but pulled out of the provinces south of the DMZ. Captain Grayson and the group he commanded now had a new mission. The counterinsurgency of hearts and minds. And Corporal Konar believed in it because this man, this mentor, this believer believed in it first. Konar read *Street Without Joy*. He studied Vietnamese, and the science of making wells, which led to the discovery of tunnels at the end of his time in the village in 1971. But their mission was not to search and destroy. It was to divide. The locals from the Communists, NVA and VC. And on the morning in October, packed up and heading back to base, two weeks short to a man in the group, Konar's platoon the last to pull out with the others Captain Grayson was collecting that day, the ambush they could not see coming, could not repel, and could not divide changed the hearts and the minds of every marine who believed he would go home thinking he had done something in-country those months and weeks and days.

THE AFTERNOON KONAR APPEARED ON THE STEPS OF THE HOUSE at 1 Morning Ridge in Abas, West Virginia, the former POW's wraith-like body was both a haunting and a liberation for Grayson. The corporal's long-held status of missing in action looked more and more like a defeat for the former captain as each month of the war dragged on, so that, seeing him there that evening, broken as he was, but alive and free, Grayson listening for hours by lamplight to the nightmare of what the man had gone through in the aftermath of jungle, prison, and coming home, made Grayson—there was no other word for it—proud that the man had showed up on his doorstep. When the morning came and he asked Konar where he was going next, Konar looked out at the mountains visible from the heights of Morning Ridge and said, I don't know what next is.

The winter was mild and Konar found work as a hunting guide with an outfitter in the small town of Kenna. He brought back wads of cash that he put in a large mason jar in the kitchen of Grayson's house and taped two labels to it that said FOOD on one side and COFFEE on the other. He shot whitetail deer, boar, and the occasional turkey. But by March, after more than a few trips out with fat men from Charleston in brand-new upland jackets who talked too much and wanted to know how many gooks Konar had killed, he was tired of everything about it, most days dreading the sight and sound of a man pulling a trigger. Just like Grayson said he would be. Konar came back one weekend with the last wad of cash he stuffed in that jar and said to Grayson, You were right. Just ain't no beauty in it anymore.

Neither man needed the money. Grayson lived on what he'd saved from his officer's pay, and the inheritance his father had left him, which was considerable. Konar had the money his grandfather put in his bank account before he died, back pay as a POW, and a disability check he received every month for his leg wound.

Come spring, they fished, driving down to the Cranberry River in Grayson's Bronco with Hector the dog, and hiking into the backcountry, where they would camp for days, living on fresh trout they caught and squirrel Konar shot in the head with the .30-30 he still brought with them on those trips, because his grandfather had taught him that a bear in the spring is not a bear you can reason with, or likely run from.

They hiked in as far as a full day of hiking would take them, to a place where the Cranberry ran deep and cold and unseen by all but a few. Grayson told Konar how he and his father used to fish this section of the river when he was a boy, camping in the same spot they had chosen on the ground beneath a gnarly beech, and mapping out the future.

As though we could, Grayson said.

Konar told him about the section of the Salamander on his grandfather's property.

Trout in it big enough to swallow Hector.

And you don't need to get in a car and drive to it? Grayson asked.

We'd walk it. From the house. You could walk all day in that part of Pennsylvania and still be on Vinich land, Konar said.

Grayson shook his head.

What are we waitin' for?

Plenty of trout streams between here and there. Don't you worry.

They never spoke of the ones they'd lost on those cool spring nights by the fire they built. Fathers, grandfathers, brothers in arms, a daughter. Never spoke of life anymore from 1965 to 1973, as though it were a receipt to place in a jar and set aside. They only looked forward. Not as though it were something they dreamed of, for neither one put much faith in that, but of what they were yet capable of, might yet accomplish with what stock remained with which to work. Konar had been wondering about school. When Grayson spoke of history, it sparked something in him he had not felt since his grandfather had told him stories about growing up in the old country. He wondered, though, if it was too late. If he was too old.

Never too old, Grayson said.

What about you? Konar asked.

Grayson stared down at the fire and Konar could see the flames in his eyes.

Don't know, he said. I'm here now. Tomorrow I'll fish, if I wake up. That's about how I feel about it.

Konar told him he sounded like the naval airmen in Hoa Lo who went to the Academy and quoted the philosopher Epictetus in their never-ending discourse of Morse code.

You must resign yourself to remaining in this post in which the gods have stationed you, until you're called home, Konar quoted.

There you go, Grayson said.

IT WAS WHEN THEY WERE BACK FROM ANOTHER TRIP ON THE Cranberry in early May and passing through Abas that Konar saw the blue '62 Dodge pickup in the lot of the Phillips 66 station.

That's my brother's old truck, he almost shouted.

It is indeed, Grayson said, and told him how it had broken down the morning Bo and Ruth were set to leave Abas, like everything they had come to that town for. Roddy towed it. Told him it was warped cylinder heads and gave him two hundred and fifty dollars right there on the spot.

Two fifty? Konar said. Fucking robbed him.

Well, he did put some work into it, Roddy did, Grayson said. Shaved down the heads, got new tires, fixed it up nice. It ain't no workhorse anymore, but it's a good truck for getting around town.

Konar nodded.

Pull over, will you? he asked. I always used to rile my brother and tell him he ought to get rid of that piece of shit, but it was like he was devoted to it. Heard he even drove it through a flood once and came out the other end.

I don't doubt it, Grayson said.

Looks kind of lonely in that old filling station all by itself.

Roddy drives it, Grayson said. Not much, though. Tell you

what. He runs a poker game, if you think you're good enough to get it back. That could be some fun.

Oh, I'm good enough, Konar said. The question is, will he agree to put it on the table?

Depends on what kind of cards he's got. And what kind of cards he thinks you've got.

Two months later, Konar a regular in the Friday-night games they held in the back of the diner, it came down to him and Roddy, and Roddy was either bluffing or holding a hand good enough to want to stay in no matter what, despite the fact that he had little left with which to play the hand.

How about that pickup truck? Konar asked. The one you stole from my brother.

Shoot, I didn't steal nothin'. I paid cash money for it.

Well. I'll play you for it, Konar said.

Why? You ain't got no truck to bet.

Konar looked at Grayson, who ever so slightly placed the index finger of his nonfiring hand on his upper arm for the sign to move the squad leader forward.

He does now, Grayson said, and threw the keys to his Bronco on the table. Roddy laughed like an idiot, fished the keys for the Dodge out of his pocket, and threw them on the table.

Konar's hole cards were a seven of spades and a jack of hearts. The flop showed a two of diamonds, an eight of spades, and a nine of clubs. He knew Roddy had three of a kind. The man laughed too much to be bluffing.

The river was a ten of diamonds, and Sam drove his brother's old '62 Dodge pickup back to 1 Morning Ridge that night.

LUCY GRAYSON, BURNE'S YOUNGER COUSIN ON HIS FATHER'S SIDE, came down from Morgantown that summer and took the job she took every summer waiting tables at the diner. The morning they stopped in for breakfast and Grayson greeted her like he knew her, which he did, Konar could not take his eyes off her.

Lucy, where's Ashley these days? Grayson asked.

I don't know, Burne. I just started this weekend. Classes only finished up on Friday. I'll tell her you were asking about her, though. Didn't know you were still seein' her.

Seein' her? That's what you call it? Grayson said. I'll look for her when I see her.

I'll tell her that. When she and I go get our nails done.

Funny, he said.

She was small, with straight blond hair down to her shoulders that she let fall and didn't tie back. Hazel eyes a little bigger than you'd expect. And a sprinkle of freckles on her nose. She let the Appalachia come out in small doses when she spoke.

Lucy, this is Sam Konar, Grayson said. A buddy of mine from up around Pennsylvania. Sam, Lucy is my cousin. Our dads were brothers. She's studying premed at Morgantown.

Sam stood and held out his hand.

It's nice to meet you, Lucy Grayson.

She took his hand and they shook, and Sam could feel the strength in that handshake her frame belied.

My, my. A real gentlemen, she said. It's nice to meet you, too, Sam Konar.

Sam sat down again and Lucy turned to Grayson.

Burne, you keep bringing boys around here like this one and I will have to change my opinion of you.

I don't bring boys around here, Lucy, Grayson said.

Well then, there you go.

She flipped her order pad to a clean page.

Now, what can I get y'all?

They started eating there regularly after that. Konar's choice. When Ashley moved to Charleston that summer after her mom got sick, Lucy worked every shift, the manager slow in looking for someone else to help cover the busy times. And still she always came by the table, no matter how busy it was, to tell her cousin he ought to get over Ashley, that she knew he was more partial to his hound than to anyone or anything walking upright, and Grayson agreed.

Days when Konar went into the diner by himself, Lucy still came over, inquired about her cousin, and wondered out loud if the two of them weren't some kind of a club.

Rotary, Konar said. You didn't know we were founding members, did you?

She laughed.

I've got to get back to my tables, she said.

He asked her out after that. She had a day off on a Sunday and they went swimming at Audra State Park. He knew, once she saw him in shorts and with his shirt off, the road map of hurt on his body like it was printed by Rand McNally, she'd either stick or quit. She asked a few questions as they lay on a rock, drying in the sun. Not as many as he thought she would. It wasn't until she invited him over for dinner a week later at the place she rented on the road to Spencer and dinner turned into a late-night conversation that she asked him about the scars and the bullet hole. He told her what he could, what he thought she'd want to know, figuring she'd find out more when the time came, if it did. She listened to him, clinically, it could be said, training for the profession she aspired to, as she was wont. But he told her, too, about the wounds she could not see beneath the skin, wounds from the prison and the heroin, from the return home to the loss of his grandfather, his fiancée, and the daughter he never got a chance to meet. It was the way he told it, the way he unfolded each loss and folded it back up again, as though it were a dress shirt he would not need to wear but would keep in a closet nevertheless, that began to soften her, and she cried as she listened. When he was done, he held her. No sound in the room where they sat but the sound of crickets coming through the screens from outside. He asked her if she would like to go back to the swimming hole with him tomorrow, because it was supposed to be a hot one, and he knew she had the day off.

They went to the swimming hole at the state park as often as they could that summer, waking early on a morning when she wasn't going to work, coming back late to her house, exhausted and falling asleep in their clothes on the bed, their bodies smelling like mountain water and pine needles. When she worked, he tinkered with the truck, perused fishing catalogs with Grayson, and waited for her. Like he hadn't waited for anyone or anything in his life.

KONAR AND GRAYSON HIKED INTO THE CRANBERRY RIVER backcountry one last time in August, the days hot and the water low, so that they had to keep a sharp eye out for timber rattlers coming down out of the hills to the water, and they stepped around a few. But they still caught trout in the deeper pools in the early mornings and when night came on.

It had been almost a year since Konar had shown up on the porch in Abas, Grayson reminded him around the campfire, trout fat sizzling as it dripped from the grate onto hot coals. Grayson scooped the fish up and placed them on camp plates and handed one to Konar and the two dug in.

You were cleaned up, Grayson said, but weaker'n a newborn pup. I could tell. I was worried about you. I wondered if the need would come back and make the man weak again. I've seen some boys in Abas and a lot more around Spencer. They are sad-looking sons of bitches.

Konar nodded.

I might've been them, back in Dardan. But I'm not going back there.

Cousin Lucy, Grayson said.

Konar nodded again.

I'm happy for you, Grayson said. She's a good girl. Smart as hell.

What about you? Konar asked.

Shoot, I don't need no one. I got Hector, my fly rod, and gas in the Bronco.

Konar laughed and they put their empty plates on the ground and were quiet while the fire cracked above the steady burble of the river flowing just below where they were camped.

Seriously, Konar said.

Serious as a preacher on a Sunday.

I guess I been letting you alone up there on the ridge for too long this summer, haven't I?

Don't be a fool. You're not obliged.

Konar looked at him through the firelight.

I'm not obliged. I am in your debt.

Ah, now don't go gettin' all misty on me over there in the dark, son. Hector, go on and give that boy a lick on the face so he can see how good you and I got it.

Hector did what he was told, until Konar had to push the hound right the hell off him, and the two of them were quiet again.

She's going back to Morgantown in a few weeks, Konar said finally. She wants me to go with her.

So go, Grayson said.

And do what?

Oh, I don't know. It's a college town, right? So how about you join the fire department, or deliver mail for the goddamn United States Post Office. C'mon, Sam. If there's anyone who can give that girl a run for her money in the smarts department, it's you. Use my address for the in-state tuition and study whatever the hell you want. History'd be my bet. Have the Navy Department start sending those checks here and you'll be good to go.

You really think so? Konar asked.

I know so. Why else would she be asking you?

SHE HAD A SINGLE IN A DORM FOR THE YEAR, HER LAST AT THE university before she applied to medical schools. Konar bought a futon and put it on the floor next to her bed, but once the semester began, they might just as well have been living in separate dorms on separate parts of campus, so rarely did he see her, except on weekends, and even then, after pizza for dinner on a Sunday, she went back to the library, or the lab, or somewhere else schoolwork waited for her. One Friday evening, he went to the chemistry building, where he knew she was, and searched the halls and found her. She looked shocked to see him at the door. Her partners—a short, smileless young woman with Coke-bottle glasses, a concert T-shirt, and jeans, and a boy (Konar thought of him) who looked the part with his Mountaineers varsity jacket, Duck Head chinos, and penny loafers—eyed him from their table across the room and asked Lucy if everything was all right. She didn't introduce him. He told her he thought she might want to take a break and go see *Chinatown*, which was playing on campus, and she said she couldn't. Told him she'd be back late.

He didn't enroll full-time. He took two classes, not knowing what he would find or how the work of a college student would suit him. He used Grayson's address in Abas as his own (he had begun collecting his disability pay there, just as Grayson said he ought to) and enrolled in Ancient Greek History and The Greek Philosophers. He read the *Iliad*, the *Histories* of Herodotus, *The Peloponnesian War* of Thucydides, the dialogues of Plato, Aristotle's *Ethics*, and *The Discourses* of Epictetus. He was put off at first by the size of some of the books and the amount of reading assigned, but once he started and immersed himself in them for long stretches, he would be surprised to look up from his reading and his solitude and find the daylight was gone and he had not in that time thought once about where Lucy Grayson might be on campus.

He tolerated the lectures. He had been a prisoner of war, he told himself. He knew how to focus. His history professor asked questions in the middle of class, getting everyone in the hall to wake up, and more often than not Konar had the answer, or offered an answer, or would raise his hand to ask a question of his own when the man had paused to let a particular point sink in.

The philosophy lecturer was drier than a popcorn fart, and that angered Konar, because he loved the ancient texts and stories and thought there was more the man could do to make all of the eighteen-year-olds basking in their parties and their privilege sit up and listen.

He was at a bulletin board one day in October, looking for his midterm exam grades, when he heard someone behind him make a joke about grandparents going back to college. He turned around and could tell the two undergrads played football. They had the necks and the legs, and were probably good backs or defensive ends.

Don't worry, boys, he said. I'm sure you failed this one. Just like your grandparents, from what I can see.

The bigger one stepped up.

Fuck you, old man, he said. Get out of my way.

Konar didn't even wind up or get in a stance. He put a little pressure on his back right foot and sprang with enough force in his punch to drop the kid with it. His friend jumped to the side and held his hand to his mouth, while the other one rolled around on the ground, his face covered in the blood pouring from his nose.

Konar looked down at him.

You need to show some respect for your elders, he said, and walked away rubbing his hand, which had started to hurt a little bit.

Lucy showed up at their dorm room after class that afternoon and told him the entire campus was talking about the old guy who laid out some kid for no reason.

Old guy, Konar said. That's who I am now? Fucking Eddie Haskell is lucky I've got my reasons for only breaking his nose.

You'd better hope the campus police don't show up here, Sam.

Konar sniffed.

They won't call the police. They'll make this into what it wasn't for all their frat buddies and point to the guy limping around campus who got in a lucky shot.

Sam, what is it? she asked. Is it just about thinking you're not cut out for this? Something you're not allowed to have?

It's what it isn't, Lucy. I came down here to be with you. And I'm not.

You came down here to go to school, Sam. To change the direction of your life instead of sittin' in Abas and splittin' firewood for the stove all winter, waitin' to go fishin' again in the spring.

She was talking fast and he could hear the Appalachia come out of her, the long *i* in *fire*, and he wished it was summer again.

I came down here for you, too, he said. Can't I do that? Can't I do two things at the same time? Go to school and be with you?

She sat down on the edge of the bed and shook her head.

I'm working my ass off, Sam, so that I can get the grades to get into the medical school here, and I'm afraid that if I give you any of that time, and I don't get the grades, don't get in, I'll resent you.

I wouldn't let that happen, he said.

You wouldn't, but I would, she said.

He looked down at the floor.

So, is that it? he asked, and turned to her. We're quits until you get your grades, and get into school, and get out of school, and keep at it until you wake up one day and you're Dr. Grayson? And where am I in that scenario? Because that sounds to me like everything and nothing to wait for, depending on which side of the waiting you're on.

She didn't say anything. She shifted her body on the bed, and he didn't know if he could walk away, even if she asked him to. But he would if she did.

How'd you do? she asked. On your exams?

Ninety-two in philosophy. Ninety-eight in history. How'd you do?

I did what I needed to do, she said.

He moved onto the bed and sat down next to her.

There's always going to be something coming down the path, Lucy. Friend. Foe. Sometimes both. All you can do is work with what you've got and move on to the next, if you can. I've never been in a situation where I was better alone. Not even prison in Vietnam. The last man I killed, I killed so that I wouldn't die in that place alone. I'll head on back to Abas after finals. I don't know that this school thing will work out for me anyway.

She sat holding his hand.

What will work out for you?

I don't know yet.

She pushed her hair behind her ears and lifted his hand to look at it in the overhead light, and he winced.

You'd better get that taken care of, she said.

I'll be all right. You bandage it up and we'll just give those boys a better story to tell at night. I'd rather they keep looking over their shoulders for me.

She stroked the swollen hand softly and raised it to her heart and placed it there at the center of her chest, and after a while they lay down on the bed and slept.

ALL SEMESTER LONG, HE AND GRAYSON TALKED BY PHONE EVERY Sunday night at nine o'clock—Grayson's idea. He told Konar to have the operator call the pay phone at the diner from the pay phone in the dorm and say, Collect call from Jack Crawford, and Grayson would answer, leaving Ma Bell to foot the bill. They'd catch up on the goings-on of the week, which meant Konar did most of the talking about class and school and life in Morgantown, which meant he ended up talking about Lucy and how she seemed a different person altogether up there.

She is a different person altogether, Grayson would say. That's what you ought to be sticking with her for.

When Konar asked how he was doing, Grayson would just laugh and say he and Hector were doing fine.

Waitin' on Christmas, my friend. Waitin' on Christmas.

Well, I'll be there, if my room's still open.

Room, kitchen, whole damn house, Grayson said.

HE DIDN'T MAKE THE CALL THE SUNDAY BEFORE HIS FINALS AND only saw the time that night when he looked up from his notes because they were closing the library at twelve. The next day he bought a stamp and a postcard with a Mountaineer on it at the student center before he went into his exams, addressed it to 1 Morning Ridge in Abas, and wrote, *Sorry I missed you. In the library until dark-thirty. Driving down Friday the 20th. Sam.* On Friday morning, he left a note on Lucy's pillow that said, *Merry Christmas, Doc. I love you,* and drove the pickup out of Morgantown down I-79 to Route 119, missing her already but feeling the weight of his time at school lifting as he listened to the radio, A Hard Rain's A-Gonna Fall filling the cold of the cab until the college station turned into static and the song disappeared.

TWENTY-FIVE YEARS LATER AND HE WAS DRIVING BACK TO Morgantown with his son after a week in the backcountry of the Cranberry River, where they'd been fishing and camping, the young man a second lieutenant now, just out of Annapolis and on his way to leatherneck training for Marine Corps Ground. In a small gift shop in the town of Buckhannon, he found a postcard of the Cranberry River and bought it and tucked it into his jacket pocket. They weren't far from Spencer, he told his son, and so they drove over to Abas and up to the ridge, and he parked the station wagon where he'd always parked the old truck. A fair amount of oak and maple saplings had staked their claim since he had been there last, but you could still see the western sky unobstructed from the ledge of rock on which a father and a son had once built a house where Samuel and Burne Konar now stood. The June air was crisp and sweet that morning. They sat down on the ledge and Sam Konar told his son about the day he hitched a ride from the filling station in Abas right to the house that once stood in this same spot, a day into which he had emerged after a years-long night of hell, and he didn't just mean the Hanoi Hilton and the stories midshipmen could hear told when some of the old guys returned for seminars or visits to Annapolis. The bluetick hound he called Hector was just a puppy then, he told his son, the story unfolding from there, like he had wanted to tell it for the past ten years of his son's life. Just never had.

It was near evening when he finished and Burne stood and stretched and sat down again. Crickets moved in the dirt and leaves and a pair of barred owls lifted off one after the other from the branch of a large spruce and swept down into the forest.

So, you own this land now? his son Burne asked.

I bought it along with the house after he died. Your grandmother gave me a small loan, let's just say, and your uncle Bo came down for a couple of weeks and the two of us cleaned it up and cleared brush around the property and then went fishing on the Elk at the end of the second week. When Bo went back to Dardan, I sat here and read with Hector. In the fall, I returned to school in Morgantown and to be with your mother.

What happened to the house?

Lightning strike, they say, but who knows. I found a pack of Zig-Zags when I was kicking through the ashes. Probably some kids getting high who tried to light a fire in the Franklin stove.

Burne nodded and looked down off the ridge in the direction of where they'd just been.

A week out there, and you never said anything. Were we close to where you found him?

Pretty much the same spot.

Jesus, Pop. You are one tough old bird.

Not so much anymore.

They were quiet then and listened to the sound of nighthawks.

Why'd he do it? Burne asked finally.

Why? his father thought, and remembered the note he had found on the table in the house when he pulled in with the pickup that Friday before Christmas of '74. *The gods have called me home, Old Man,* written in that meticulous block lettering learned somewhere from someone. Remembered how fast he drove out to the trailhead of where they'd always spent those days on the Cranberry, the pain in his leg as he managed a limping quick time along the trail, the hound sniffing and waiting, sniffing and waiting with an impatience greater than Konar's ability to move with anything resembling speed, then the tent pitched in the clearing on the riverside, the body buried deep in a sleeping bag, blood from the opened wrists cold and coagulated on the tent floor, both forearms bare and white and perfect in the cold. The lethality of symmetry.

Just a guy who didn't want to fight anymore, he said to his son, and exhaled quietly, a man himself exhausted by the questions to which he had yet to find any answers on the threshold of the mourning house.

NO NIGHT THERE

(December 25, 2004)

Snow has been falling all day outside her window and she can see it is falling still through the curtains of light from the streetlamps in the parking lot of the nursing home and the streetlamps visible from her window out on the road, but when she tries to remember what the snow looked like in the daylight hours, all she can think of are winters when she lived in the house her father built and in which she raised her sons. The terraced land at the top of the mountain blanketed in white. The limbs of the fruit trees in the orchard heavy with ice, like thin men with gray beards. Cold seeping in from the edges of the window. Warmth radiating from the ironblack stove. But the windows she can reach for and not quite touch from where she sits up in her bed are sealed tight. The vent beneath them pushes dry air no matter what time of year.

Her sons were here today. She knows. The smell of wood smoke and cedar from the wool they wore still lingers in the air. She has known that smell all her life. And on her bedside table, along with the scentless food she has not touched from dinner, is the note Bohumír wrote to remind her of their coming. *Today is Christmas Eve, Mom. Sam is here.* Bo comes to see her every day, whether she calls him or not, from his house on the other side of the mountain, where she thinks he still lives with his wife, though she has not seen his wife in a long time, and isn't even sure if she can remember her name anymore. But Sam was here. Because it's Christmas. Sam lives far away, teaches college there, and has children whose names she has forgotten. All but one. Helen, the girl named after Hannah's mother. The girl who loves horses, she remembers that much, and how she used to sit beside her at the *velija* feast in the dining room of the old house every Christmas Eve and help her serve the food and listen to the priest and answer the questions Hannah asked about the girl's horse, and her studies, and sometimes, as she got older, if there were any boys she liked, so that the girl, Helen, would blush and say, Boys don't like me, Grandma, and Hannah knew that was not true. She misses those days at the house when everyone sat around the table and ate her food and drank her wine and wished one another a blessing for the New Year. Or simply said, *L'úbim t'a.* She can almost smell the freshly cut tree in the living room. *Where is Father Tomáš?* she wonders, and lets the scenes of the funeral at St. Peter's Cathedral in Scranton come back, the last time she had left Dardan, a young bishop saying the Mass, the other priests crowding the altar, the pine coffin at the chancel steps, and she says out loud in the room, Oh. But her boys, they were here. Bo, bearded and blue-eyed. Sam, as clean-cut still as the day he went off to join the marines. Yes, he fought in that war and she doesn't know why. She only knows that he did things he would not speak of, and it took time for him to forgive himself, just as his father had, and her father had. Just as she had. Needed the time to forgive. *But why?* she thinks. *Why did he come today? Because it's Christmas?* And she remembers why. Not just for Christmas but with news. News of the boy. His boy. *What is his name? Burne. Yes, like Sam's friend. His friend who died. Sam's Burne is somewhere far away, too, in a city, the name another name for a chimney, I think, or something like it. Yes. There is a war there. Another one the boy has gone to. Isn't there always a war?* she thinks, and sighs and sees the tears in her son's eyes, and she remembers. Sam came to tell her that his son, her grandson, wouldn't be coming home to see her. Not anymore. And she said, Oh Sam, I'm so sorry. They said that about your father. And about you. And now your son, too. I'm so sorry. And he: Yes, Mom. But there is no question about the missing anymore. And she: Oh Samuel, Samuel. She remembers, tears rising to her eyes then as they do again now. *But he will be buried just up the road. Sam's boy. At Our Lady of Sorrows. With Papa and Becks, and so I will be able to see Sam more often when he comes to see them all. Bo I see every day, and he is a blessing to me. But Sam, Sam was lost once and is found, and I will see him now, and his family, such a big family that I can't remember them all, except for his daughter, the one who loves the horses.*

She turns the light out on her bedside table and the room is lit by the streetlamps in the parking lot of the nursing home, and the streetlamps out on the road. *He'll just be up the road, the poor boy,* she thinks, and lays her head down on her pillow and breathes in the wood smoke and cedar that she can still smell in the room, still wants to smell, as though she were home in her own room in the house her father built, the one in which she raised her sons. And it is moonlight now coming in through the window as the snow falls and her head rests on the pillows of the four-poster bed. She looks at the foot of it and sees her husband, Becks, who has come to sit, as he often does when she has questions or is grieving and needs to talk. And she tells him about their grandson and their son's own grief for the boy, and she knows some part of him blames himself for letting the boy follow in the footsteps of his father, after he tried so hard to convince him not to go. Of fathers, I should say, shouldn't I, Becks? And then her father is there, too, though both are standing now at the foot of the bed in the bedroom of the great house, and he says to her, as he always said to her in the morning when she was a girl, Hannah, it's time to go. And she knows. She knew when she saw the moonlight and the snow in the orchard, and the wood smoke and cedar smell would not leave the room. Then the boy. Burne. He is there, too, and she has not forgotten how handsome he is, and she sighs as though breath itself were leaving her, and all she can think to say with this breath is, Your father loves you so much. But the boy does not speak, his head down, as though in mourning far deeper than the grief he knows lives on in the ones he has left behind.

And she rises from her bed, the room neither warm nor cold. She is dressed in the clothes she always wore. And all four now stand at the door. She looks back into the room and the window and the moonlight that is shining in through the thin drapes she has not closed. The snow has stopped falling and the night sky is clear. She sees the note on the table and thinks, *I will miss them, too.* And she turns, no one to call out to her through the darkness, no one to see her leave in the night, she who all her life asked the Lord for them.

GENEALOGY

Jozef Ondrei Vinich. Born March 1899, Pueblo, Colorado. Son of Ondrei and Alzbeta Sabo Vinich. Emigrated with his father to Pastvina, Austria-Hungary, in 1900 and served in the Austrian Landwehr 1916–1918. Captured on the Piave River, Italy, June 1918. Prisoner of war from June 1918 to November 1918. Returned to America summer of 1919. Owned 2,000 acres of land in Dardan, Pennsylvania, and a home on Rock Mountain Road. Died in Dardan, April 10, 1972.

Helen Posol Vinich. Born September 1903 in Wilkes-Barre, Pennsylvania. Daughter of Stefan (oldest brother of Frances Posol) and Susan Hudák Posol. Married Jozef Vinich June 4, 1921. Died in Dardan, April 1938.

Frances Posol. Born August 27, 1902, Pastvina, Austria-Hungary. Daughter of Pavel and Hortense Posol. Emigrated to United States in 1922. Lived in Wilkes-Barre, Pennsylvania, until her death in August 1994. A plaque in the nave of the church of St. Joseph the Worker, Pastvina, Slovakia, commemorates her generosity to the Church during what it calls *decades of struggle behind the faithless Iron Curtain.*

Hannah Vinich. Born February 22, 1922 in Dardan, Pennsylvania. Only daughter of Jozef and Helen Vinich. Married Bexhet Konar May 1940. Died in Dardan, December 25, 2004.

Rev. Tomáš Rovnávaha. Born January 23, 1922 in Scranton, Pennsylvania. Served in United States Army 1942–1945. Ordained a priest in the Diocese of Scranton June 1948. Died in Scranton, December 2, 2001.

Bexhet Samuel Konar. Born spring 1919, Hungary. Emigrated to Dardan, Pennsylvania, 1933. Married Hannah Vinich May 1940. Served in United States Army 1941–1945. Imprisoned for desertion 1945–1948, Brooklyn, New York. Died in Dardan, April 4, 1949.

Bohumír Joseph Konar. Born March 8, 1941, Dardan, Pennsylvania, to Bexhet and Hannah Vinich Konar. Owner-operator of Endless Roughing Mill. Married Ruth Younger June 1973. No children.

Samuel Bexhet Konar. Born March 22, 1949, Dardan, Pennsylvania, to Bexhet and Hannah Vinich Konar. United States Marine Corps from 1967 to 1973. Two combat tours of Vietnam with the 2nd Marines 3rd Battalion. Listed *missing in action* from October 1971 to April 1973. Returned to Dardan April 1973. Married Lucy Grayson August 5, 1977. Professor of History, West Virginia University, Morgantown, West Virginia.

Paul Younger. Born 1910, Dardan, Pennsylvania. Son of Walter and Cora Younger. Died June 23, 1972.

Ruth Younger. Born January 2, 1950, Dardan, Pennsylvania. Only daughter of Paul and Judith Younger. Married Bohumír Konar, June 1973.

Clare Frances Younger. Daughter of Samuel Konar and Ruth Younger. Born June 23, 1972. Died June 23, 1972.

Burne Grayson. Born July 2, 1941 Charleston, West Virginia, to Charles Lloyd Grayson and Charlotte Booth Grayson. BA History, West Virginia University, 1965. Commissioned United States Marine Corps, September 1965. Died December 22, 1974.

Lucy Grayson. Born December 13, 1953, Charleston, West Virginia, to Joshua Cole Grayson and Virginia Wilson Grayson. BS Pre-Medicine, West Virginia University, May 1975. Married to Samuel Konar August 5, 1977. MD, West Virginia University School of Medicine, May 1979. Pediatric surgeon, West Virginia University Children's Hospital.

Burne Andrew Konar. Born 1978, Morgantown, West Virginia. Eldest son of Samuel and Lucy Grayson Konar. Graduated Annapolis 1999 and commissioned United States Marine Corps. Listed *killed in action* commanding Alpha Company, Fallujah, Iraq, November 19, 2004.

Helen Elizabeth Konar. Born 1982, Morgantown, West Virginia. Only daughter of Samuel and Lucy Grayson Konar. BS Veterinary Science, West Virginia University, 2003.

Michael Bexhet Konar. Born 1985, Morgantown, West Virginia. Son of Samuel and Lucy Grayson Konar.

David Joseph Konar. Born 1989, Morgantown, West Virginia. Youngest son of Samuel and Lucy Grayson Konar.

ACKNOWLEDGMENTS

Although this is a work of fiction, the author wishes to thank the following, who were consulted for the purpose of weaving certain true events into the narrative, and who also offered just damned good advice: Warren C. Cook, Thomas P. Krivák, Rev. David C. McCallum, S.J., Rev. William Hart McNichols, Virág Sárdi, Joseph Schick, Michael Silitch, and James E. Wright. They have been generous with their knowledge and time. Believing, too, it is true that books are made out of books, in addition to the many works of fiction and nonfiction, articles, and documentaries that were perused in the course of writing this novel, the following were indispensable for their subject matter and authenticity: *The Centurions*, by Jean Lartéguy; *Crossing*, by Jan Yoors; *The Deserters*, by Charles Glass; *Dog Soldiers,* by Robert Stone; *Enduring Vietnam*, by James Wright; *The Hebrew Bible: A Translation with Commentary*, a three-volume work, by Robert Alter; *Junky*, by William S. Burroughs; *Novel without a Name*, by Duong Thu Huong; *P.O.W.*, by John G. Hubbell; *The Sorrow of War*, by Ba'o Ninh; *Street Without Joy*, by Bernard B. Fall; and *The Vietnam War*, a film by Ken Burns and Lynn Novick. The chapter entitled "Moth and Rust" was published previously in the journal *Image*. Special thanks to Laura Hart, Joe Gannon, and the editorial team at Bellevue Literary Press, whose sharp eyes miss nothing, and to Molly Mikolowski for her support and tireless work putting books into readers' hands. Finally, I am grateful to my longtime agent, Betsy Lerner, and my always exacting and gracious editor, Erika Goldman.

287

Bellevue Literary Press is devoted to publishing literary fiction and nonfiction at the intersection of the arts and sciences because we believe that science and the humanities are natural companions for understanding the human experience.
We feature exceptional literature that explores the nature of consciousness, embodiment, and the underpinnings of the social contract. With each book we publish, our goal is to foster a rich, interdisciplinary dialogue that will forge new tools for thinking and engaging with the world.

To support our press and its mission, and for our full catalogue of published titles, please visit us at blpress.org.

Bellevue Literary Press
New York